THE ROGUE SHAPESHIFTER

THE ROGUE SHAPESHIFTER

IZZIE BERENS: THE ARCANE ENFORCER™
BOOK ONE

MARTHA CARR
MICHAEL ANDERLE

LMBPN

DISRUPTIVE IMAGINATION®

DON'T MISS OUR NEW RELEASES

Join the LMBPN email list to be notified of new releases and special promotions (which happen often) by following this link:

http://lmbpn.com/email/

LMBPN Publishing
2375 E. Tropicana Avenue, Suite 8-305
Las Vegas, Nevada 89119 USA

Version 1.00, November 2024
eBook ISBN: 979-8-89354-311-7
Print ISBN: 979-8-89354-405-3

THE ROGUE SHAPESHIFTER TEAM

Thanks to the Beta Readers:
Malyssa Brannon, Mary Morris

Thanks to the JIT Readers
Diane L. Smith
Dorothy Lloyd
Peter Manis
Dave Hicks
Jackey Hankard-Brodie
Christopher Gilliard
Wendy L Bonell
Jan Hunnicutt

CHAPTER ONE

The unmarked black sedan made slow progress down the choked city street. People on the sidewalks rushing to work in downtown Austin were moving faster. "Was anyone harmed?" Special Agent Izzie Berens tapped the brakes and tucked a lock of dark hair behind her ear as she looked at her watch and back at the traffic. The beginning of a spell made her lips tingle. She knew better than to try it, even if magic was out in the open. It was against agency rules.

Special Agent Rafe Martinez rubbed the top of his smooth, olive-skinned bald head, which had the beginnings of stubble around the rim. He gently pressed his black earpiece. "One, not yet confirmed. Sounds grisly. Body in parts." Rafe tucked his chin as his forehead wrinkled. "Did they say bite marks?"

"We need to get there." The sedan made it through the next light but came to a slow halt on the other side.

"We are. Have a little patience."

"This is me being patient. The area needs to be secured." She glanced at the packed sidewalks and ran through her options again. "We could get out and make a run for it." A necessity she had learned from her mother, Leira Berens, a respected bounty hunter. Always wear your running shoes.

"And save five minutes. You see a parking space? No siren," he added sharply, watching her hand slide over the dashboard. "They were clear on that point. We are to enter quietly."

The traffic moved as she was about to suggest Rafe take over the wheel and she would run on ahead. "No short-cuts," she muttered. "Not a bounty hunter."

Besides, the world was under no obligation to make Agent Berens' life easier, even when she was rushing to save others. Her early life at the School of Necessary Magic taught her that.

Life didn't start that way. Her first babysitter had been a small troll full of good ideas designed to get them both in trouble. A kid's paradise of mischief and magic.

"Yumfuck," she whispered too low for her PDA partner to hear. The troll had created a world within the small house on Rainey Street full of magic train sets, hidden caches of candy, and secret adventures underground with Willens who became friends. The oversized rodents in worn clothes had a penchant for anything shiny and preferred to stay hidden, even now. Izzie lifted her wrist to let the charm bracelet on her wrist catch the morning light. It was a coming home present from a Willen.

They were also still good for the occasional helping hand or useful intel. That was also outside of agency rules, but sometimes it was necessary. Another lesson from her mother, Leira, whom dark magic users feared. In the end, do what's needed to create the most good in your corner of the world. Her mother called it rule number one.

The gnarly twist her life took when she was a teenager reinforced it. She was unceremoniously dropped off at the boarding school, minus her memories as a forced kind of protection and minus the troll. Her parents had been on the run, being chased by too many enemies, especially among the dark families. Everyone thought it was for the best.

Izzie shook her head, trying to shake the old feeling of being disconnected from everything. Thank goodness that was in the past. She quickly learned to go and get what she wanted once her memory was restored. A story for another time that ironically, she wished to forget.

Morning rush hour Austin traffic only tempted her to bend the rules. Maybe use a portal, just this once. "Nope, no, I promised Dad." Her father, Correk, watched over the magical world as the Fixer. He would know sooner than most and would want an explanation.

Izzie let out an annoyed grunt and leaned closer toward the darkened back seat window. Dad was a rule follower as much as Mom knew how to bend them. "Let's take a side street."

"Eventually we have to use a main road, and they're all like this. Not much farther," Rafe stated in a calm, patient tone.

Cars clogged the street. Nobody on the road cared about the nondescript dark sedan with government plates. The same aesthetic choices intended to give the official Paranormal Defense Agency car a low profile also helped it, and Izzie was making a point of blending in with the rest of the traffic.

The curving, sail-shaped Block 185 office tower loomed outside Izzie's car as she drove down Cesar Chavez Street. She tried to bury her annoyance with stray thoughts. She could do nothing until she arrived at her destination, a crime scene.

She glanced at the building. She'd heard the odd shape was intentional and part of local efforts to balance out the overall flow of local magical energies. She leaned forward to watch the streams of different-colored magic flow in looping curves, leaving traces of magicals who had visited the building. A fading black streak barely sparkling with silver caught Izzie's eye. That was never a good sign. "Probably nothing," she muttered.

Right now, she wished for a grand ritual spell to clear the roads. Her destination lay about eight blocks away.

"We should get out and walk." Izzie shook her head. "It'd be faster. That's how this city is going to be destroyed. A crazy monster will fly through central Austin burning everything, but we'll all be stuck in traffic trying to respond. Meanwhile, the cops will be calling us saying, 'Where the hell is the PDA? We're getting roasted here.'"

Rafe glanced at her. His ever-present coffee cup was in his hand. "You should've grabbed a cup when we had the chance." He took a long sip. "That's how I survived the Borderfield case—running on nothing but caffeine and adrenaline. Nearly got myself burned out. Literally."

Izzie raised an eyebrow. "You never told me about that."

He shrugged. A shadow briefly passed over his face before he covered it with his usual smirk. "Some memories are better left buried. But trust me, no fireballs without coffee."

Izzie didn't push, sensing the weight behind his casual tone. She filed that little bit of his past away for later. "Still prefer fireballs."

"Fair. But maybe try it *with* coffee next time."

"I'd prefer a Mountain Dew with my multi-case bursting fireball."

"Nice twist on the caffeine intake." Rafe twisted in his seat, sloshing his coffee. "Is it easy to get a good fireball going when you're spun up?"

"I didn't expect to be called to a scene right after showing up at the office." Izzie was ready to be in the middle of things. Another Berens trait. "And it's going to take forever to get there."

Rafe gently touched his earpiece again. "Wait, we're good. The locals have already secured the scene. The incident itself is over. There's no imminent threat to the public."

Izzie frowned, not satisfied. "Until we find whoever did this, there's a threat to the public."

Rafe tapped on the console display screen to highlight the message and address. "The higher-ups don't want too much more noise on the way. They're worried it'll get people going again. This is the first big, high-profile public incident in a while."

"Pretending a magical incident isn't a big deal doesn't mean it's not a big deal." Izzie's hands tightened on the wheel. "Bureaucratic rules don't constrain rogue magic. Sometimes I feel like the PDA forgets that."

"But we don't know if it's a big deal." Rafe took another sip.

"They called in the PDA. That sets the baseline."

"That just means it's a bigger deal than the local cops can handle and enough of a clear major paranormal element they don't want to dump it on the FBI. You're catastrophizing because you don't have enough caffeine in you." He shook his head.

"We're not emergency response. We're there to investigate and follow up. You don't have to go in there wands a-blazing and slinging magic this time, Izzie. It's not like that thing with the…whatever we're calling those three-headed dogs."

"Cerberuses?" Izzie suggested.

"I still like the sound of Cerberi."

She glanced at him. "What did you say? 'Wands a-blazing?'"

"It's a figure of a speech." Rafe winked. "I know you don't use a wand. Unless you've been tricking me and using an invisible wand this entire time?"

He shrugged and returned to sipping his coffee. "All I'm getting at is there's no Active Hostile Magical Disturbance. It's like sometimes you see a dark wizard plotting the end of the world behind every tree."

"Unless you know something I don't, they didn't nab a suspect from what the alert said." Izzie frowned. "That means we still have a general threat somewhere in the city. In my mind, that means there is still an AHMD."

"That's not how the PDA and the Austin PD classify things."

"We wait for Earth law to catch up with magic, and this city will end up a crater."

Rafe's expression darkened. He conceded her point with a shallow nod. "We'll get our guy, Izzie. We always do. If the higher-ups thought we needed to move faster, they would have told us. That's all I'm saying."

The Paranormal Defense Agency defined an AHMD as any use of magic by any type of magical that represented a clear and present danger to the public at large. Depending on resources, local police departments and FBI field offices might have access to technological or limited technomagic solutions to contain such threats. At the same time, federal, state, and local agencies had rescinded their restrictions on magical employees in recent years. This led to the better overall ability of the federal government to respond to magical problems using a wide range of resources.

That helped. Beyond that, licensed civilian bounty hunters, magical or otherwise, could hunt criminals after the fact.

All of that wasn't enough to keep peace in a world still in transition. It had been decades since the magical gates between Earth and the magical world of Oriceran began to open. The flow of magic to Earth meant an inevitable increase in dangerous incidents involving magical beings, commonly called magicals.

Politicians continued to dither, surprising no one, but they reorganized the PDA's activities and expanded the agency's budget and scope. This was all part of a general federal change in how they approached magical incidents, which offered a better frontline response and investigation of incidents involving rogue magic. The PDA wasn't the only federal entity handling magic anymore, but they had the most responsibility for the average street incident that the local police couldn't handle.

All of that led to the same basic conclusion. Izzie needed to get to the scene with her partner and figure out what was going on.

A turning semi-truck created a pocket of flow and offered a chance to escape. Izzie took advantage of her brief traffic fortune to change lanes and accelerate toward her destination.

Clusters of red and blue spinning lights marked the presence of the Austin Police Department, as did the larger police drones hovering over and beside the buildings. A handful of news drones lingered farther away from the scene.

Izzie pulled off Cesar Chavez toward two police vans parked on a curb. Tall office buildings and a fancy-looking yet massive hotel surrounded the area on three sides.

A small army of police officers patrolled the area, all in bulletproof vests and tactical helmets. Not everyone had weapons out, but many of the officers prowled the area with shotguns and rifles. One SWAT van featured more heavily armored officers wearing vests filled with rifle magazines.

Curious locals crowded the edges of the area, pushed back by police officers or crime scene tape running between cones. Most people held up their phones, desperate to find their next viral video on social media.

Despite his easy smile, Rafe rested his hand inside his jacket on his gun. "Do you sense anything?"

Izzie concentrated. She shook her head. "I sense a little

background magic, not enough to suggest whoever was responsible is still around or any major lingering spells."

Rafe pulled his hand out of his jacket. "See? No AHMD. I told you."

"You weren't sure yourself." Izzie chuckled. "After all that shit you gave me."

Rafe tapped his forehead. "Certitude comes from evidence, not vibes. I'd hate to be the guy who gives a speech about how safe we are, then steps out of the car and gets blown up by a magic bomb."

"Are you more concerned about dying or dying in an embarrassing way?"

Rafe considered the question for far too long before answering, "Both."

A weary-looking police officer headed toward their car. The rank insignia on his uniform marked him as a lieutenant. Izzie and Rafe reached into their suit jacket pockets to pull out their PDA badges.

"Special Agent Izzie Berens, PDA," she announced with practiced confidence. She nodded at Rafe. "My partner, Special Agent Rafael Martinez."

The lieutenant looked between them. "Lieutenant Lee, Austin PD. Which of you is the human, and which is the hocus-pocus master?"

Rafe chuckled. Izzie gave him a stern look. He shrugged.

"I'm the assigned magical for this agent pairing, Lieutenant," Izzie replied.

"No wand? Or do you have one of those magic guns? I saw this wizard gunslinger in New York take do—"

"I'm the magical on this case, Lieutenant," Izzie

repeated, cutting through his doubt with a sharp glance. "I don't need a wand or a magic gun to do my job." She let the silence stretch, daring him to question her further.

"Jasper Elf, right?"

"Among other things."

Lt. Lee scratched his head. "I've seen elves with wands, though."

"Plenty of magicals don't need them." She ignored the urge to explain every nuance. Now wasn't the time for a lesson in magical diversity.

"Just show me the scene," she added, shifting her attention to the bloodstained sidewalk ahead.

"Hey, I can't even do card tricks, so I'm not here to judge." Lt. Lee stared at her face with the careful, fascinated concentration of someone seeing a wild exotic animal in the zoo for the first time. "Elf, huh? But you don't have the ears. Every elf I've seen has the ears."

"I'm part elf and part human." She was less interested in relating her family heritage than learning about the case.

He shrugged with growing disinterest showing on his face. "This is one time I don't mind the feds crowding our asses and taking our case. No offense. I figure we leave the weird hocus-pocus shit to the specialists."

"That's what we're here for, Lieutenant."

Lt. Lee gestured toward a nearby intersection. "Follow me. It's been about an hour since the incident. The department hasn't spotted anything happening nearby that's similar or anywhere else in the city, including the Magical District. We think this might be one and done, but I'm not here to tell you how to do your job."

Drying blood stained the sidewalks and the intersection

of a road. The blood splatters coated the ground in distinct locations linked by obvious drip paths. A single taped outline of a body delineated the last bloody location of a victim in the middle of a crosswalk. Dark scorches and cracks marred the sidewalk, road, and a nearby wall.

"Okay." Izzie glanced around. "We have a confirmed fatality. Time to earn our pay, Rafe."

CHAPTER TWO

Something in the air felt wrong—not only the general hum of leftover magic but a more sinister, familiar undercurrent.

She couldn't shake it. She'd felt this type of magic before, but it had been years and was buried deep with memories she didn't want to dig up.

"Something's off," she muttered to Rafe as the feeling grew stronger.

"What is it?"

She waved him off. She wasn't ready to go there—not yet.

Izzie surveyed the area with a tight frown. The residual magic she sensed wasn't strong, but it was unmistakable. There was an odd oscillating sensation attached to the residue as if the energies flipped between stronger and weaker.

"One second, Lieutenant," Izzie requested. "Rafe, confirm the magical residue, please."

"Something wrong?" Rafe frowned.

"I want to be sure I'm not seeing a scheming dark wizard behind every tree." Izzie shook her head. "And I sense unusual magical residue."

She chanted a spell to turn the magical sensations into visible magic trails she could see. Weak magic pulsed in front of her.

Izzie knelt beside the glyphs. Her breath caught as she traced a finger over the intricate lines. The residue hummed, faint but dark, pulling her back to a time when she was still in training—still running from the shadows of her parents' enemies.

It's just like that night...

"You okay?" Rafe's voice broke through, pulling her back to the present.

"Yeah," she quickly replied, but her heart pounded. The glyphs were different, but the dark magic pulsing through them wasn't. Someone was using techniques she hadn't encountered since her parents had sent her away for protection.

She forced a steadying breath and locked the memory away. The unease remained. This wasn't random rogue magic. It was personal. It was coming for her again.

Lt. Lee looked around with a nervous expression. "Should I be worried?"

"No," Izzie answered.

Rafe reached into his pocket and retrieved a pair of otherwise unremarkable dark sunglasses. Their straightforward yet stylish design helped conceal that they were a cutting-edge technomagical product usable by humans without any magical ability. He slipped on the glasses and tapped the frame on the right side.

The enchanted glasses allowed a person to see and photograph magical flows and residues, along with a handful of additional useful features. Izzie kept her pair for other purposes, including remote feeds. She didn't put hers on since she didn't need the expensive technomagic gadget to see magical flows, although it meant relying on her partner for easy image recording.

"Confirmed magical residue," Rafe announced. "Nothing heavy, though… Huh." He looked at Izzie. "It's almost like it's flickering. The intensity is changing. That's weird."

"Exactly. That's what I saw." Izzie nodded. "I don't know what it means yet."

"I've never seen something exactly like that."

Lt. Lee grimaced. "That sounds bad. You sure I have nothing to worry about?"

"It's not necessarily bad," Izzie replied.

"You saying it's good?"

"Not necessarily."

Rafe frowned and looked around. "There is overlapping residue. And the trails fade pretty quickly. It's like they disappeared."

"You feds get all the toys. But I don't think I'd like being able to see magic," Lt. Lee remarked. "I figure there's nothing wrong with trying to believe in 'What I can't see, can't hurt me.'"

"All right." Izzie wasn't interested in spinning up a cop with tales of invisible magical means of death. "What else do you have for us, Lieutenant?"

He motioned around the area. "We're still looking to gather local cameras and drone footage for evidence. We had plenty of witnesses since the street and sidewalks were full of people, and a mess of people in their cars saw what happened. We interviewed and cleared most of them out already."

"There was only one fatality despite all the people around?" Rafe asked. "That's a miracle. A normal human could have killed far more people with a weapon, especially in such a crowded area."

"Yeah, I'm not going to complain about only one victim," Lt. Lee replied. "The short version is our victim was crossing the street when a muscular white male in his early twenties, around six-foot-three according to witnesses, and easily 200 pounds, rushed off the sidewalk and charged our victim. There was no warning, no threat, no nothing. The big guy just boom, ran at him and stabbed him."

Izzie nodded. "This was flagged as an AHMD almost right away according to the initial dispatch report. The AHMD was subsequently canceled. Why? I'm not questioning your people or the witnesses, Lieutenant, since we've established residual magical traces. I'm trying to get a sense of what might have happened from start to finish."

"The AHMD was attached by dispatch because the witnesses who called in said our victim got stabbed. Then he yanked out a wand and started blasting away with these little magical fireballs. Now that's proper hocus-pocus." Lt. Lee mimed an explosion.

"Then as you can imagine, once our wizard victim started slinging obvious magic, the shit hit the fan with people freaking out and running. Our big guy suspect shoved people out of the way like they were toys."

"He stabbed a wizard," Rafe noted. "But the wizard didn't go down right away. Is that what you're saying?"

Lt. Lee grimaced. "Yeah. He got stabbed, but our victim ran away, not even really bleeding yet. He then started walking in the air while pounding away with magic at our big guy, who shrugged off getting hit by the little fireballs like he was straight from hell and ate fire for breakfast." He shuddered. "You think he could be?"

"I think it was a fire resistance or shield spell," Izzie replied. "Not too complicated. I doubt our killer is anything like you're thinking."

"Oh, the big guy was wearing a medal. Everybody who got a close look at him said so."

"A medal?" Izzie frowned. "What do you mean?"

"You know, like you get at the Olympics? A medal on a chain."

Izzie shook her head. "That sounds more like a magical amulet."

"Sure, just people said a 'silver medal with weird symbols.'" Lt. Lee shrugged. "I'm sure once we get the camera and drone footage, you can figure it out from that."

"That amulet might explain why he wasn't going down. Along with whatever other defensive spells he had on him."

"The medal guy was also a magical?" Lt. Lee looked surprised. "Yeah. That makes sense. Anyway, our big stabber threw the knife at the wizard when he was walking around and nailed him in the back. Guy falls and hits the road."

He frowned. "The suspect rushed over and yanked out the knife, but the wizard hit him with blue fire, and there was a big flash out of nowhere. It blinded a lot of people, and that was when things got really out of hand. Complete chaos. We're lucky nobody got trampled or run over in that mess."

"The victim was alive and could still concentrate enough to cast a spell," Izzie reiterated. "Even after major stab wounds. Is that correct?"

"Yeah, but our suspect had friends, a hot blonde chick in her mid-thirties. That one was around five-five or five-six and 125-135 pounds. The last assailant was a young female Hispanic teen, not much more than thirteen or fourteen. We got her tagged at around five-one, around 90-100 pounds. Witnesses reported both female suspects attacking the wizard after the flash and roughing people up. Nobody saw the big guy after the flash."

"Did the female suspects have the same amulets?" Izzie asked. "Medals?"

"Yeah. They did, actually."

"Was this tiny little teenage girl pushing people down, too?" Rafe sounded curious.

Lt. Lee frowned. "I don't know what to tell you. It was her, the big guy, and the blonde, and they all pushed and shoved people out of their way like nothing. I figured it was adrenaline or drugs explaining how they were so strong, but we also wondered if it wasn't magical strength. I didn't know their medals might have been magic."

"We know magic was involved, but that's not enough to confirm any individual usage of magic past the obvious offensive spell discharges from the wizard," Izzie replied. "Not yet anyway, but more information always helps. Still, I wouldn't put too much stock in the appearances of the attackers. They could have been using illusion magic."

Rafe nodded. "To be clear about this, they were pushing other people, not attacking them?"

"As far as the witnesses have reported. They only stabbed the wizard." Lt. Lee pointed at a nearby police officer. "Anyway, we got witnesses describing the three people stabbing our victim at different times. First the big guy, but like I said, he disappeared after the flash. Then the blonde chick, but she ran in and got nailed a couple of times. That was enough to make her turn and run off."

"And you're sure the second attacker was hurt by these spells?" Rafe asked.

"The second suspect and the victim both got in good licks, but our victim switched it up again and started tossing these orbs of light that didn't explode, and they hurt the blonde. Witnesses heard her scream in pain before running off." Lt. Lee sounded impressed. "Whatever those were made the blonde run off. The victim didn't go down until the teen showed up to finish him off, and she dodged the light balls like they were nothing."

Izzie processed the details of the whole attack, her mind racing through possibilities. Elemental resistances were common enough, as were protective spells, but something about this felt different—deliberate, almost ritualistic.

She glanced at the blood splatters again as a pattern formed in her mind. "Why did they stagger their attack?" she muttered, more to herself than Rafe. "If they'd hit him all at once, they could've overwhelmed him. But they didn't."

Rafe frowned. "Maybe it's symbolic. A ritual, perhaps. Or maybe they wanted to make him suffer."

Izzie shook her head. "No, it's more than that. It's like they were testing him...or testing *something*."

She knelt by the scorched outline of the final blow, her fingers hovering over the magical residue. Something about this felt familiar—a dark undercurrent of purpose behind the attack. Whoever they were, they weren't killing only for the sake of it.

"There's something here." A chill ran down her spine. "Something bigger than a random murder.

"The attackers and victim weren't targeting anyone else other than pushing them out of the way?" Izzie pressed the lieutenant. "You're absolutely sure about that?"

Lt. Lee nodded at the taped body outline. "The wizard was super-careful from what a couple of witnesses said. The only thing he said during the attack was, 'How dare you attack me here, you coward. Have you no shame? These people have nothing to do with this.'"

"That makes it sound like they knew one another," Izzie observed.

"I thought the same."

"Who did he say that to?" Rafe asked. "Which of the attackers specifically?"

"The blonde, actually." A confused expression took over Lt. Lee's face. "To be clear, none of the suspects were exactly gentle, and the attackers were tossing people around, but like I said, they didn't once try to stab anyone else from what we can tell. The witnesses offered conflicting testimony, but the only person we found stabbed was the single fatality."

"There is a good chance they used an enchanted knife," Rafe noted. "And there could have been a limited enchantment on the weapon. The killers' apparent restraint might have been less about mercy and more about, in a sense, not using up their ammo until they finished off their primary target."

"Maybe." Izzie frowned. "Or they were worried about causing too much collateral damage, meaning they get too much attention. A handful of agents investigating them instead of the entire country."

Lt. Lee continued. "Anyway, right before the teen finished off the wizard, there was this off-duty security guard, big guy. He tried to grab her, and she threw him off like he weighed nothing. Then it was all over for our victim." He pulled a finger across his throat.

"The guy got stabbed before and didn't go down, but you can't chant spells when your throat is slit. No chanting, no magic, right?" He clucked his tongue. "She got close and slit his throat, then nailed him a bunch more times in the chest like she was playing every part of the conspirators in *Julius Caesar*."

"You're a Shakespeare aficionado?" Rafe raised an eyebrow.

"My daughter's drama club is putting the play on at her high school." Lt. Lee shrugged. "I only like the part where they kill Caesar."

"Why's that?"

"Because they say it's a tragedy, and the killers were assholes, but at the same time, he had it coming. I figure it's a lesson about not getting ahead of yourself. That's why it's popular even these days."

"Power corrupts." Rafe rubbed his chin and stared at the

tape outline. "You saying our wizard had it coming? He got ahead of himself?"

"That's not for me to figure out," Lt. Lee answered with a slight smirk. "That's for you two feds to figure out."

"Incidentally, chanting requirements depend on the type of magical and the specific spells," Izzie clarified. "Our victim appears to rely on a more traditional magical style, but even then he could have options. Did the attackers use any other obvious magic that people recalled?"

"I don't know. It depends on how you define that." Lt. Lee motioned toward the crosswalk. "The little girl threw that huge-ass security guard a good ten feet through the air with one arm, and he broke an arm." He whistled. "That has to be magic, right?"

Rafe shrugged. "She might have looked like a teenage girl, but I doubt she was a normal teenage girl. She might have been a non-human race that's naturally strong. There are many different ways to hide a person's appearance."

A flash of fear passed over Lt. Lee's face. "One witness went for a gun in his car, but it was all over before he could get back. So, boom, our victim went down bleeding out and gagging after the girl finished him off, and the suspects all blended in with the fleeing crowd, including her. Nobody mentioned seeing the first two again after they ran, so they might have been halfway up the block already.

"The whole thing was over in a couple of minutes at most, could even be one minute. We're still putting together the exact timeline."

Rafe looked around. "You already collected the body?"

"We're not going to do anything with it. We've already

passed along to our boys that you PDA feds are going to do your thing."

"There were three suspects," Izzie reiterated. "Have you identified any of them?"

"Special Agent Berens, we're still trying to pull the footage." Lt. Lee sounded annoyed. "We have a cordon set up, including drones all over the city, looking for any suspicious individuals who match their descriptions. We'll tag 'em when they show up and let you people do your magic fed thing."

A police officer jogged toward Lt. Lee. He slowed when he spotted the agents and offered his superior a questioning look.

"What is it, Wallis?" Lt. Lee frowned. "I was bringing our PDA pals up to speed on our stabbing family friends."

"All the cameras around here, city and private, were out during the attack," Wallis explained. "It's just static the whole time, then footage of us arriving." He shrugged. "We have guys double-checking, but not much to see. There was one nearby news drone, and the station reports it malfunctioned during the attack, too."

"Huh? All of them were out?" Skepticism filled Lt. Lee's tone. "At the same time?"

"Same thing from people trying to film the incident with their phones. We haven't confirmed it with everyone, but we talked to four different witnesses who tried to film it, and they had the same problem."

Rafe cleared his throat. "If we're assuming the attackers were magicals or had access to magic, either traditional or technomagic, there are many ways to pull off that type of interference."

Lt. Lee grunted in frustration. "I don't know if that makes it easier or better for you two agents. I'm glad we APD cops don't have to solve this."

Izzie surveyed the area again while considering the evidence. A selective attack against a magical by a non-magical wouldn't be surprising. There were plenty of anti-magical groups out there, big and small, with a widely varied range of motivations.

The failure to down the wizard with the first attack suggested he had defenses up. Basic spells would have protected him from simple conventional weapons, yet they'd finished him off despite dealing with a man who could cast offensive spells under stressful conditions. Their success implied magical weapons.

Izzie stared at the blood on the sidewalk, and her heart skipped a beat. The residual magic clinging to the scene felt *familiar*, like something she hadn't sensed in years. Her mind flashed back to when she was younger—before she joined the Paranormal Defense Agency—when dark magic had come too close to her family.

She shook her head, focusing on the task at hand. No room for ghosts today.

"This wasn't random." Her voice was harder than she intended. "This was a targeted attack."

Rafe glanced at her but didn't comment on her shift in tone. "Not anti-magical terrorism then?"

"No. This was personal," Izzie added, glancing at the magical residue again. Too personal. "We need to find out who they were after and why."

"Are you sure about the anti-magic terrorism?" Lt. Lee frowned. "I get that they weren't going after anybody else, but that could mean they knew the guy was a wizard, and they went after the first wizard they ran into."

"If it was just about killing any random magical, it'd make way more sense to go to the Magical District to stir up trouble." Izzie shook her head. "I'm also assuming the victim wasn't wearing a big robe or anything that screamed 'I'm a wizard.'"

"Nah, looked like a normal business asshole until he pulled the wand out of nowhere," Lt. Lee replied.

"Do you have an ID on the victim?"

"Not yet. He wasn't carrying ID. To be honest, we secured the body for you all. We figured you'd handle it."

"There's something else," Wallis interjected. "We were crosschecking the witness reports, and one witness reported something strange."

"Stranger than three people with knives whaling on a wizard in broad daylight downtown?" Lt. Lee raised an eyebrow.

Wallis eyed Izzie and Rafe. "Um, yeah. The witnesses said she saw the blonde attacker run around the corner and change."

"Change? You mean she changed outfits? That might have explained how she slipped out of here. Did the witness say she dropped her other clothes? We might be able to pull DNA, or the PDA can do something with it. *Hocus pocus trackius.*" He snickered and waggled his eyebrows at Izzie, far too proud of his joke.

Wallis shook his head. "It's not exactly changing clothes. Uh, I don't know how to explain it."

"Just tell me what she told you. Don't get cute on me."

Wallis cleared his throat and pulled out a notepad to

read his notes. "'She leaned over like she was panting. I remember that strange medal hanging away from her neck. She stretched and twisted like she was made of Play-Doh. She whimpered like she was in pain. She had burns.

"'When she stopped changing, she looked like a Mexican girl without the burns, even wearing new clothes with holes. I've never seen anything like that before, even on TV with other magicals.'" He cleared his throat. "The witness then went on about werewolves."

"Animal shifters can't shift into other human forms," Rafe noted. "Wolf or otherwise."

Izzie and Rafe exchanged worried looks. Different explanations rushed through Izzie's mind, none of them good.

"But what the hell does the rest of it mean?" Lt. Lee asked.

Izzie replied, "It means, Lieutenant, that we likely don't have three attackers. This also doesn't sound like illusion magic." She took a deep breath. "We have one attacker who can shapeshift."

"How are we supposed to catch a suspect who can change how they look?" Lt. Lee asked. "How do we beat that hocus-pocus?"

"You don't beat it. The PDA does." Izzie frowned at the tape outline. "And we do that by using better hocus-pocus."

CHAPTER THREE

"We'll take it from here," Izzie told Lt. Lee. "Thanks for your assistance, Lieutenant."

He looked hesitant. She widened her smile to let him know his briefing was over.

Izzie valued the input the police passed along. They'd already collected vital evidence that narrowed the type of suspect and the magic used in the crime. She also didn't want to waste too much time explaining everything magical to someone who wouldn't be working on the primary case.

"This isn't one of those things where a sea monster's going to appear in the river and attack, right?" Lt. Lee asked. "Or like that crap that happened in Seattle a while back? Because I don't want to work overtime waiting to get stepped on by a giant monster taller than Tetris Tower. This is Texas, for crying out loud."

"They do say everything's bigger in Texas." Rafe smiled. "And didn't they used to say, 'Keep Austin Weird?'"

"I don't mind weird. I don't like giant weird or dragon weird."

"We can safely rule out a dragon or any type of giant," Izzie replied coolly. She didn't want to remind him of Austin's history of major magical incidents in the previous decades and feed his paranoia. "And unless you forgot to pass along a witness statement, our victim was killed by a shapeshifting suspect with a knife and not crushed by any type of dragon. I also think we can safely rule out sea serpents."

Lt. Lee shrugged. "I also have a cousin who works in the LAPD. You know they give their SWAT cops exoskeletons, railguns, and grenade launchers to fight magicals?"

Technically, instead of SWAT, he was talking about the first major non-magical response to rogue magical criminals, the Anti-Enhanced Threat team concept. Expensive and controversial outside the largest cities, the diffusion of magicals into federal and local law enforcement led to police departments reconsidering their use. Izzie didn't see a point in angering him further by pointing that out.

"You want an AET team?" Rafe asked.

Lt. Lee scoffed. "I'd worry less about crazy magicals if the city gave me an exoskeleton and a railgun to deal with them. Here we keep acting like crazy magic isn't a problem when we have shapeshifting hitmen slitting people's throats in public."

"Don't worry." Rafe offered a tight smile. "The PDA is here to help. Fire with fire. Magic with magic. This is what we specialize in. We'll do everything we can to take care of this magical criminal, Lt. Lee. You won't need to get involved, with or without a railgun."

"Whatever you say, Agent Martinez. It's like I told you, I'm more than happy to hand this case off to you."

Lt. Lee sighed and shook his head. He wandered back toward a group of police gesturing for the burgeoning crowd of gawkers to stay back.

Izzie took a deep breath and whispered an incantation. What she'd sensed before grew visible again in glowing lines and faint floating particles, the residue of magic used.

She walked beside a magical trail until reaching an abrupt end near a corner and frowned at a more intense patch of residue. "Our shapeshifter killer escaped quickly after doing what he needed to do," she called. "There isn't enough magical residue here to support a portal."

"If he was skilled enough to do portal magic, I don't think he'd stab a guy to death." Rafe looked up and around before pointing at the side of a building. "See that?"

Izzie craned her neck to look up and squinted. Faint magical traces showed along the wall and went up. "You thinking our killer climbed the building?"

"If the killer climbed and jumped using magic, they could have gotten away fast."

"There are no reports of people jumping from rooftop to rooftop."

"A good shapeshifter would also know an invisibility spell or two, wouldn't you think?" Rafe asked.

"Any halfway decent magical at my old school would have known an invisibility spell." Izzie frowned.

"So you could sneak out when you weren't supposed to?"

"Exactly. But most magicals don't know one that leaves so little magical residue."

Rafe squatted by the taped outline. "If this was a paid hit against a magical, the killer might not be in the country at this point. There are too many ways to get away quickly."

"If that's true, then at least the killer won't inconvenience Lt. Lee soon, but hitmen aren't going to take advantage of the more public ways of getting around quickly." Izzie strolled to her partner. "Especially hitmen mixing dangerous magic into their techniques."

She squatted alongside Rafe. "I don't think this will be as easy as a tracking spell since we can't locate a halfway decent magical trail. Take it from me. It's easy to hide from the most determined magicals as long as you don't care about having a life."

Rafe stood and lifted his sunglasses. "Not to sound cold, but it's that experience of getting chased around by dark wizards and dangerous magicals for half your life that gives you insight into how they think. I believe it's half the reason we have such a high case clearance rate. Not that I'm complaining."

Izzie offered a shallow nod. Her parents were important figures in the magical community. They played major roles in helping keep the balance during the early years of the return of full magic to Earth as the connections between Earth and Oriceran reopened.

That had made their only child a target. They'd been forced to rely on extreme tactics to keep her alive and away from the dark wizards determined to hunt her down and make use of her power and connections for their twisted rituals.

A few years back, before she joined the PDA, Izzie

ended the most dangerous threats from the dark wizard order targeting her family with the help of her friend, a half-dark elf named Alison Brownstone. Defeating the evil magicals responsible for terrorizing Izzie didn't give her all the years back she'd spent on the run.

Rafe was right. Those years had left an indelible mark.

Izzie let out a pained chuckle. "You think it was inevitable I joined the PDA. That it's like the Seventh Order and their flunkies trained me to be a PDA agent."

"Nobody knows the threat of rogue magic more than a victim of rogue magic," Rafe murmured. He stared at the blood on the road. "In the end, it's all the same garbage when you think about it. Ambition and greed. Magic, drugs, guns. Human, elf, dwarf, whatever. It doesn't matter. Different weapons, same basic crimes."

He snorted. "Somebody wants something somebody else has. They figure out how to take it from them and eliminate them if they get in the way."

"Trust me, it does matter when the fate of a city is in the balance," Izzie replied. "What I'm more worried about right now is why our shapeshifter attacked this guy in public. Our suspect had to know that'd all but guarantee PDA involvement and make it harder for him to get away."

Rafe glanced around the area with a thoughtful look. "How many protective wards do you have at your place?"

"What's that have to do with anything?"

"Just answer the question."

Izzie chuckled. "I have enough that I can sleep at night without having to keep one eye open and assure I won't have new nightmares about my past."

"Imagine if you were a paranoid, old-school wizard,"

Rafe continued, gesturing at the tape outline. "One who knew he had somebody after him. How many more would you have?"

Izzie nodded and squinted at the magical traces floating in the air. "Point taken. You're suggesting our victim knew his attacker? That would track from the way he talked to the attacker."

"His little speech was too general for us to be sure." Rafe shook his head. "That pushes us out ahead of our evidence, but I think our victim had reason to believe he might be attacked." He motioned to her. "You're one of the more paranoid magicals I know, and even you don't walk around with defensive spells and gear all the time."

"It'd be pretty hard. And draining. You'd need a reason to put yourself through that."

Rafe gestured at the dead-ending trail of magical residue. "Somebody jumped him from nowhere and didn't manage to finish him off in one hit with what was likely an enchanted weapon. That means our guy had enough passive defensive spells and enchantments he didn't go straight down."

"From what was described, he was giving as good as he got until the third form appeared," Izzie replied.

Rafe indicated the curious crowd being held back by the police. "The so-called teenage girl threw a fully grown man ten feet away. It's a safe assumption that our shapeshifter was striking with that level of strength regardless of form, if not more. And that's ignoring if our shapeshifter climbed a wall using a normal ability instead of an active spell."

"Why change form two times? That's the part I can't

figure out. Our attacker didn't finish off the target and ran away and came back. So what are we dealing with?"

"He might have needed time to strengthen his defenses between attacks." Rafe shrugged. "Could it be a dark elf?" He held up his hand. "I know you have a dark elf friend, but it wouldn't be the first time shapeshifting dark elf assassins have caused trouble. And it's not like all of them are satisfied with their current governmental situation."

"Dark elf politics has about zero connections to Austin, Texas." Izzie shook her head. "Besides, dark elf shapeshifting isn't an active spell. It's an inherent ability that doesn't stress the body. The witness mentioned the shapeshifter showing signs of pain during the process. That doesn't sound like a normal spell, and the more I think about it, that pain restriction excludes most of the shapeshifting races."

"Maybe he was reacting to other injuries, but I see what you're getting at. It also doesn't sound like an illusion spell. Illusion wouldn't hurt like that either unless they'd really pushed their magic to the limit. If that were the case, they wouldn't have been able to get away so easily."

"The amulet it sounded like they were wearing might be responsible."

Rafe shook his head. "Wouldn't that have been a little obvious? What good is changing your shape if you have to wear a big magic item that will make any magical nearby perk up at your approach?"

"True." Izzie frowned. "Using an illusion spell would have made it easier to sense someone coming anyway if the target wasn't otherwise expecting strong magic nearby."

"What are you thinking then?"

"I'm betting this is a true shapeshifting spell, something that would have registered as magical to a nearby spellcaster, although not as much once the change was finished." Izzie frowned at a bloodstain. "But does it mean the shapeshifter was naturally that strong?" She cupped her chin.

Rafe walked toward the end of the magical trail and looked around. He pointed at the nearest corner. "We should see if we can find anything over there."

They jogged to the corner. Izzie narrowed her eyes as she spotted new, subtle magic residue displaying oscillating brightness.

"Do you see this?" She gestured in that direction.

Rafe lowered his glasses over his eyes. "It's weird. It's disappearing and coming back. Is that what you see?"

"Basically. Kind of."

Izzie frowned and inspected the area, seeking another obvious magical source. What she could see and what she could feel weren't in agreement. She sensed stronger magic nearby.

Izzie's eyes widened as she spotted the symbol etched into the victim's belongings—a spiral design that made her blood run cold.

"What is it?" Rafe asked, seeing her pale.

"This symbol," she whispered and stepped back. It was the same one they'd used back when they came for her family. The ones who had forced her parents to hide her away, leaving her to piece her life together on her own.

"This isn't just about magical trafficking." Her voice was tight. "It's them. They're still out there."

Rafe's expression darkened. "You mean the ones that—"

"Yeah. And if they're involved...we're all in trouble."

Faint trails of magical residue snaked across the ground. She squinted and followed the trails to a trash can.

Rafe gestured at a tree near the trash can and a second tree farther away. "Notice anything?"

Izzie stared at the trees. "They're trees? I don't see any magical residue on them."

"Look at the leaves on the first one, the one closer to the trash can."

Brown and yellow withering leaves on the first tree. The other tree retained its verdant glory.

"That's uneven tree care," Izzie replied.

"Do you think it means anything?"

"It could mean everything from bad spells to the city needing to update their public plant irrigation program." Izzie peered at the garbage can. "I don't like that our dying tree is closer to this garbage can."

She frowned, pulled rubber gloves out of her pocket, and slipped them on her hands before grabbing and flipping the lid over. A complicated series of glowing glyphs covered the lid's interior.

"That's a little suspicious," she muttered.

Rafe tapped the right side of his glasses. "What are we looking at? None of these are standard protection wards. Nor do they look like any standard trap glyphs. The overall style is strange."

"I'm not an expert with these types of glyphs. And you're right. The whole flow..." She shook her head. "There's tons I don't know about these."

"Expert is relative in this situation. Tell me what you do know."

She set the inverted lid on top of the can. "These are inversion glyphs, not protective wards or traps." She grimaced. "I remember doing terrible on a quiz on these types of glyphs back in school. I swore a brief vengeance against whoever invented them."

"Inversion glyphs?" Rafe echoed. "They're for suppressing magical signatures."

Izzie glanced at him with a smile. "Oh? You knew this whole time?"

Rafe laughed. "Why so surprised?"

"They're a little obscure. Were you messing with me?"

"No. I didn't know their patterns. Once you identified them, I knew." Rafe grinned. "Just because my little human self didn't get to go to a fancy hidden School of Necessary Magic doesn't mean I haven't picked up a little working this job. I just haven't memorized every random glyph and ward pattern out there."

"I didn't mean to sound so surprised." Izzie sighed.

"I know, just busting your chops, Izzie." Rafe leaned closer to inspect the lid. "On a serious note, correct me if I'm wrong, but aren't inversion glyphs considered a joke? I learned about them from a book titled *Wastes of Magical Technique and Time: A Disgruntled Gnome's Review of Arcane Dead Ends on Earth and Oriceran.*"

Izzie shook her head. "It's a matter of perspective. It's more they're not that good."

"How is that not the same thing?"

"Because they aren't totally useless."

"Okay."

"They're super-draining for what they do," Izzie explained. "And they can be dangerous to set up. The risk-versus-reward ratio for the spell is way off, and it's not like they completely suppress the magical signature anyway. Not totally useless, but also not a joke."

"The book claimed they can be taken out by touching them."

"Sometimes, not always."

Rafe nodded at the glyphs. "Do you think we can trace that back to the source?"

"No way, not inversion glyphs." Izzie lifted her hand and reached for the glyphs. "It means whoever set this up was gambling that no one would touch these directly."

"Does it have to be something living? Or would a stray drop of cola break the spell?"

Izzie laughed. "No, they aren't that useless. Generally, it needs to be a living creature with magical potential even if they aren't a true magical or have magic. In other words, a rat or pigeon wouldn't disable the glyphs, but the touch of a human might."

Rafe nodded at the glyphs. "I haven't read anything about these blowing up."

"Same. But get pictures first."

He tapped the left side of his sunglasses. An audible click and shutter noise followed.

Izzie pressed her palm against one of the glyphs. They all flared and disappeared, leaving their shapes burned into the lid. "The blowing up part is only when they're being set up."

Eliminating the inversion glyphs also killed the strange oscillating magical flows she'd sensed. Everything looked weaker around her, yet the closest magic felt stronger.

"This is a pretty busy street." Rafe gestured up and

down the street. "And there's a risk every time someone changed the liner in the can that it would disrupt the spell. At the same time, the attacker had to set this up and risk being exposed. They could only mess with the cameras so much without getting noticed."

Izzie yanked the bag out of the can and set it aside. She peered into the receptacle. An elaborate array of interlaced glyphs lay at the bottom. "That explains it." She motioned Rafe over. "I'm guessing our shapeshifter knew the change schedule, or they could have impersonated an employee and handled it themselves before the attack."

Rafe groaned. "Shapeshifters. Lt. Lee was right. It is annoying when your suspect can change their appearance."

"We should check with the city employees and see if anyone had sick days recently."

Rafe nodded at the revealed glyphs. "And these? More inversion glyphs?" He peered inside. "No. Spell amplification and body modification from what I can see."

Izzie shook her head. "I don't recognize the entire glyph array, but you're right. We should get pictures of these, too."

Rafe took more pictures with his glasses. "Spell amplification and body modification, huh? I don't know how I would have done on a School of Necessary Magic pop quiz, but that sounds like something related to shapeshifting to me. I bet the gnome who wrote *Wastes of Magical Technique and Time* wouldn't have put that spell in it."

"I'm sure you would have done fine on the quiz." Izzie reached toward the glyphs. "I'm going to have to disable these directly. I suspect the inversion glyphs were more about hiding this than anything else." She shook her head. "These aren't amateur techniques, and these spells could have made the shapeshifter even more powerful than we realize."

"They were taking attacks like nothing according to the witnesses," Rafe replied. "And they were strong. No wonder our wizard had trouble putting the shapeshifter down."

"Just give me a minute." She pushed the flow of her magic into the glyphs, pulling and tugging at the static strands of magic to disable them. First, she relied on gentle pulling.

Then she probed the different strands, exploring the feel and sense of the magic. The stubbornness of the magical connections between the glyphs forced her to yank the connections between magical flows apart with more effort.

The glyph array's light faded. A new glyph burned itself into the array's center before turning dark.

"What was that?" Rafe frowned. "I don't recognize the last glyph."

"It's trouble." Izzie wiped the sweat off her forehead. "That was more complicated than it needed to be." She looked at Rafe. "Beyond being dangerous for the spell itself, that last glyph…"

She shook her head. "It's a way of passively converting life energy to magic in a subtle, dangerous way. Random drains once in a while rather than constant drains. It makes it harder to detect the spell." She pointed at the withering tree. "Our shapeshifter is highly skilled, very ruthless, and not afraid to use dangerous magic."

Rafe stared at the tree. "And they're careful and still made a major effort to surprise their target despite it being in public and risking getting caught. That meant they figured all this setup and risk was worth it rather than trying to nail their target somewhere more private."

"Or they had no choice but to attack them somewhere they knew they'd be," Izzie countered.

"I was thinking along those same lines."

"We need an ID on the victim. Nobody goes through this much trouble to kill someone without a good reason. Call it in. We'll need the lab to check the entire can and lid. Not that I expect them to find anything else we can use to trace things."

"Then we're going off the victim's trail. That might dead-end before we can get more leads."

Izzie swallowed. "I have a feeling this won't be our last victim. First things first, I want to follow up with forensics on this garbage can, and we need to talk to whoever is responsible for changing the liners in them."

Rafe chuckled. "Ah, the glamorous life of a PDA agent."

CHAPTER FOUR

Three hours, a mess of phone calls, and several visits to different government offices later, Izzie and Rafe sat in front of their boss, Special Agent in Charge Bill Thomson, to report their initial findings. They'd confirmed the delivery of the body to the PDA morgue while double-checking the police evidence.

The camera jamming worried Izzie. Anyone with the forethought to do something like that when already a shapeshifter was more careful than the typical rogue magical. This wouldn't be an easy case.

Bill sat behind his comically huge desk that dwarfed his modest computer monitor. The size was necessary to keep his desk in scale with his huge body. He listened quietly while his agents related their collected evidence. That didn't stop him from displaying his RBF, Resting Boss Face rather than Resting Bitch Face, a look of perpetual annoyance.

Izzie had long since learned not to take the expression

personally. He wasn't married, but she imagined him having the same look on his wedding day.

"That's how we concluded we're dealing with a shapeshifter," Izzie offered at the end of the evidence summary. "I tried a couple of basic tracking spells on site, and they all failed. No big surprise there given the inversion glyphs. We did a follow-up on the local cameras and didn't find any significant magical traces, so whatever spell or technique was used likely centered around the attack site."

"There were interesting initial autopsy results," Rafe added.

Bill's brow lifted. "Interesting in what way? He's not dead?"

Rafe chuckled. "That would be helpful, but no. The neck wound was the only fatal wound. All the other wounds were shallow. That explains why the level of blood on the scene outside where the body fell was low."

Bill nodded. "Our wizard got stabbed by a shapeshifter with enhanced strength, but it was only his exposed neck that cost him?"

"Yes. The lab confirmed his suit was heavily enchanted, including lasting, permanent enchantment and heavy magical residue from recently active spells. The words 'serious combat grade' were tossed around." Rafe glanced at Izzy. "It's been a while since we had a victim who was this prepared for someone coming after him."

"He didn't pull this suit out of his laundry ready and able to survive multiple stab wounds," Bill concluded. "Have you confirmed the use of a magical weapon?"

"There was clear magical residue in all wounds," Rafe reported. "We've asked about field support tracking the magical signature of the knife, but they haven't been able to pick up anything. It's not strong enough, or the shapeshifter has a way to hide it from our sensors."

"From what forensics passed along on their initial examination, the knife likely isn't a product of the suspect's magic."

"If you have enough magical residue to make that determination, why aren't we tracking him directly?" Bill asked.

Izzie shook her head. "We need more detailed magical residue information for the sensors."

"Understood." Bill grunted. "At least we know our shapeshifter needed somebody else to supply an effective weapon. He's not a one-stop shop. That means he'll be easier to handle."

The shapeshifter already had the weapon and skill in an obscure style of glyphs. That supported him being more resourceful than Bill might believe. There wasn't a strong reason to challenge him at that moment, so Izzie let it go.

Rafe nodded toward the door. "Forensics is still looking through evidence, including the garbage can and samples we grabbed from the wall. They haven't discovered anything Izzie and I didn't spot at the scene so far. Inversion glyphs, draining, the works. We figure it was mostly about covering the assassin's trail. Forensics haven't finished their analysis."

"Have you checked with the city yet about any missing employees?" Bill asked.

Izzie nodded. "It turns out a new hire didn't show up to

work today after impressing his new boss with his work ethic. He worked for the city for a few days, and among other things, was responsible for changing the trash bags in that part of the city. Of course, his work form bore no resemblance to any of the three forms used during the attack."

People always underestimated how mundane techniques, such as infiltration, could make magical attacks so much worse. Well-trained magical criminals and assassins understood the less obvious magic they used, the less likely they were to get caught.

Bill scrubbed a hand down his face. "We have a rogue shapeshifter we can't even narrow down to species or gender? And right now you have no real leads."

"That's about the long and short of it, yes. Forensics is prioritizing the investigation, but it'll take time for them to complete their full examination."

"Our suspect didn't screw up at work? Leave any useful traces?"

Rafe shook his head. "Izzie checked his locker at work. No real magical signatures beyond expected background residue.

"We checked his listed home address. It turns out a nice old *abuela* lives there. She let me freely check her house and basement when I explained who I was. I didn't find any magic unless you count the smell of her tamales. She's lived there for thirty years and didn't recognize any descriptions of the shapeshifter's forms."

Bill frowned. "Our shapeshifter had been working in the city for several days?"

"Yes," Izzie answered. "Public trash collection mostly in that part of downtown."

"And who is he?" Bill asked. "Don't tell me we haven't figured that out."

Rafe leaned forward with a concerned look. "A magical employee in the lab recognized and IDed our victim as Thaddeus Blackstone, a local wizard from the Austin magical community. We confirmed it with the vice president of his company. He runs... He ran a magical artifact import-export business out of East Austin. This is where things get interesting."

"Weapons?" Bill asked. "Dangerous artifacts?"

Rafe shook his head. "All low-key simple stuff, mostly convenient little things, and common magical household goods and supplies. Nothing worth killing over. It's not even that huge of a company all things considered. We asked the vice president about family, but Blackstone had no living family. His company vice president came in for the official identification. The guy was shocked."

"Did he claim that Blackstone had no enemies?" Bill rolled his eyes.

"Nope. He was surprised that somebody had managed to stab Blackstone to death in public. Blackstone made a big point of being 'prepared for trouble' according to the vice president. When we pressed him, he said he didn't know why, only that Blackstone had been like that for decades."

"Do we have an alibi for the vice president?" Bill asked.

Izzie cleared her throat. "He agreed to a magical signature and residue inspection while he was here since he wanted to 'Get it out of the way, given natural suspicions' in his own words. There's zero match between anything we found on scene with the vice president."

"I figured it wouldn't be that easy, or you guys this calm. He could have hired the shapeshifter."

Rafe didn't hide his doubt. "He could have. If he did, he's a great actor."

"We find the shapeshifter, then we'll find out if anyone hired him," Bill replied. "There are always different angles to attack a case."

"We haven't had a chance to do many follow-up interviews other than with the vice president, but Blackstone was a big deal," Izzie added. "His company had tons of customers. Blackstone had connections to the mayor and city council and was an influential part of the local magical scene even before the gates reopened, although he always kept a low profile. He wasn't directly involved with any major modern and known magical incidents in this city, at least nothing I can find in the records."

Bill leaned back in his chair, his RBF not subsiding. "A man that involved in the magical scene could have any number of enemies. A man doesn't go out of his way to be ready for trouble for years unless he expects trouble, and assassins don't go out of their way to put that much effort into killing a man who's not involved in trouble. Where, right now, is your investigation heading?"

"We're checking out the database for consultants while forensics finishes their work," Izzie explained. "The glyphs had an unusual design. Knowing more about the techniques involved might help us narrow down what we're dealing with. That's a stronger lead than trying to harass all his customers."

Bill nodded. "That'll be a last-ditch effort. We don't want it to come off like the PDA is trying to suggest doing magical business is inherently dangerous. At the same time, we can't ignore that he might have off-the-books customers."

Rafe nodded. "Although we can't be sure our culprit's still in town. All evidence points to him being a pro who took his time and prepared for the hit. Blackstone's dead. There's no reason to stick around."

Bill took a deep breath and slowly let it out. "I'm about to tell you something confidential, and it goes more to why I don't want this to be a fishing expedition. This is need-to-know information as far as this investigation goes. Is that understood?"

"Of course," Izzie replied.

"My mouth's shut, Bill," Rafe confirmed.

"There have been three other attacks in the last two weeks on influential figures in the magical community, all in the Magical District. This was the first time an attack target died. In the other cases, the victims drove them off. At least one other victim reported a knife. The third attack we're not sure is connected because it involved a robbery, with our victim only getting attacked when he stumbled upon the robbery."

Rafe frowned. "This is the first I've heard of any of this."

Bill ignored him except for a cool look and continued. "The victim was a wizard and magical artifact collector by the name of Xelius, and he claims he's still determining what, if anything, was taken, although he might be stalling. He's made it clear he doesn't want the PDA involved in recovering his items."

"Xelius is a big deal," Rafe remarked. "I'm surprised this is getting swept under the rug."

"I've heard the name Xelius before, too," Izzie added. "I've never had occasion to deal with him."

Despite growing up with magical parents and having an indirect link to Austin from her mother in the past, Izzie's life had taken her away from the city and its local magical community. In many ways, despite having lived there for a few years now, she still felt like an outsider.

Her heart kicked up. "Rafe's right. Why are we hearing about this the first time just now if it involves people that important?"

"Because I only learned about it this morning," Bill growled.

"Why didn't they pass this along?" Izzie scowled. "We could have saved Blackstone's life if we knew he was going to be targeted."

"Don't be naïve, Berens." Bill shook his head. "You said it yourself earlier. The man was involved in the magical community before magicals operated in the open.

"These older, more powerful magicals are still used to handling problems themselves. They don't like the idea of the government prying into their personal business, no matter how much it's supposed to be different these days and we tell them we're here to help them." He scoffed. "Everyone's so used to hiding in the shadows they forget sometimes the best way to escape a monster is to run into the light."

"Who else has been attacked?" Rafe asked. "Other people involved with magical artifacts?"

Bill shook his head. "It's a grab bag beyond Blackstone

and Xelius. All different positions, but all old-timers who've lived in Austin for decades, including before the beginning of the gate openings. With Blackstone and the robbery victim, that's two who might be plausibly tied to magical artifacts. It's damned hard to throw a rock into the magical community without finding someone that far from involvement with magical artifacts."

"You don't think they're going to cooperate?" Izzie asked. "What if we put pressure on them?"

"We'll do no such thing." Bill scowled. "I only got this information from someone passing along a favor with the understanding that the PDA wouldn't have people knocking on their doors the next day asking questions they don't want to answer. We mess up that trust, and we're screwed going forward. Until I have a strong reason to risk those bridges, I won't."

"Even in a murder case?"

"Yes." Bill pinned a steely gaze on her. "Because I need to make sure we don't have problems with future murder cases, and God forbid, terrorism cases."

"With all due respect, Bill, that information means we don't have a lone assassin who's halfway on his way to Spain or hiding in a secret grove on Oriceran. We have a shapeshifting killer who's only managed to take out one of at least three if not four targets. He's not done."

Rafe nodded. "I agree with Izzie. We should set politics aside. We should be pushing these people for more help."

Bill looked between his junior agents as his frown deepened. "There's no point in doing something without it leading to something useful. You can show up and ask all the questions you want. You can try to be clever with your spells if you really want to stir up trouble, but they'll have better, older spells. That's why they were able to fight this guy off."

"But Bill, they'll have big leads," Izzie countered.

"Not necessarily. This is the difference between being a cop and working for the PDA. We need to be more flexible in how we approach things because we're still figuring this all out."

He shook his head. "The last thing we need to do is rile up the local magical community and make them think the PDA will mess with them when they cooperate and pass on back channel information they'd rather have kept to themselves. I won't allow it."

Rafe scoffed. "Then what are we supposed to do? Wait around until our guy knifes somebody else?"

"Follow up the leads you have for now. If your tracking magic is shit, find a way to make it non-shit. Go yell at forensics until they get you something usable. Any magical who needs to set up special and weird glyphs to lower their magical signature can be tracked. It's just a matter of figuring it out."

He nodded toward his computer. "Do what you said you were going to do. Go find a consultant who can help you. Then find the shapeshifter using that information."

"What about the other victims?" Izzie asked. "Aren't they in danger? We could encourage them to come in for protection."

"These are all wealthy, powerful magicals with access to tons of old-school magic. I'm not worried about anyone sitting in their personal magical Fort Knox. We find the shapeshifter and take him down. The rest of this doesn't matter. Am I clear?"

"Understood, Bill." She stood. The politics frustrated her, yet this was far from the first time they'd been an issue. "We'll find somebody useful, and we'll use them to find our shapeshifter."

CHAPTER FIVE

Izzie sat at her desk in her shared office with Rafe and rolled her mouse wheel to bring up another profile. She was poring through summary information in the agency's Expert Contacts Database, the ECD. A new page appeared, featuring a photo of a scowling, tattooed dwarf who looked like he wanted to murder whoever dared take his picture.

For all she knew, he did. The PDA valued pragmatism in its time of transition. Not every contact, magical or mundane, could easily be sorted into a convenient category of good or evil. Sometimes good enough had to do.

Izzie read the name. "Grissom Stonewarden. He's a magical weapons artisan. That's more relevant than the potions witches the system suggested, and I don't understand how a wood elf lute designer is supposed to be helpful."

Searching the database for a solid consultant was the best thing she could do for now without more leads. Forensics had the evidence and were doing what they did best. Izzie's impatience, not their competence, was the issue.

She kept telling herself it hadn't been a full day. The shapeshifter had already passed up an opportunity to rampage downtown and kill dozens of people.

He hadn't done that. He'd gone after a specific target and spent days planning the assassination, including assuming a fake identity to set up specific spells.

The PDA had time to catch him. She clung to that hope.

Rafe looked over from his desk. "Stonewarden would be useful if we had the murder weapon and needed to trace construction. I can even squint on the potions witches. I figure the lute elf is bad metadata."

"I hope forensics gets us what we need soon. I have a lot of questions for this shapeshifter."

"The shapeshifter should have been nice and done us a favor by leaving behind a sample from the weapon." Rafe frowned at the screen. "I don't expect a shapeshifter would make it easy. I'd like it to be a little easier, though. I get what you're feeling, Izzie."

Izzie turned his way. "You do?"

"This is one of those cases that feels a little off."

She chuckled. "Oh, now you're seeing dark wizards behind every tree?"

"Hey, this time we have a shapeshifter who did tons of prep prior to a public assassination. We have reasons to be concerned."

"If you're freaking out, who's going to talk me down?"

"I'm not freaking out." Rafe smiled. "I'm pumped to find this guy and solve the case."

"Forensics is still looking over everything, including

our can, lid and who knows about the body," Izzie replied, as much for her comfort as anything. "Those aren't dead ends. We're not licked yet." She flipped to the next entry in the database, a far-too-jolly wood elf.

"This guy might be useful. He's supposed to be a world-class expert on..." She threw up her hands. "I put humanoid in the keywords. I don't want a guy who's an expert on changing into deer unless witnesses tagged a bunch of leaf munchers at the scene and forgot to tell us."

"At least he's a shapeshifter of sorts. It's better than the lute elf." Rafe flicked his mouse wheel with a chuckle. "If we understood this suspect's magic a little better, this would already be over. We can take advantage of that."

Izzie looked at him. "How do you figure? Right now this shapeshifter is mocking the cops and us. He killed a man. Even catching him doesn't change that."

"His success will make our suspect overconfident and arrogant. He put in a bunch of effort to hide, and it's working for now, which means he'll feel free to try again."

"That's what I'm worried about. We don't have a target profile and don't know where the shapeshifter will appear next. Plus, other targets in the magical community won't play ball. The longer we take to find this guy, the more people might die."

Rafe leaned forward to stare at his screen with a frown. "You're right, though. Metadata will be the downfall of this country. This time, I'll forgive whatever interns they made sit in the basement and enter all these tags since we have what we need."

"What are you talking about? Did you find something?"

Rafe tapped his screen. "You'd think the first hit would

be a specialist in humanoid shapeshifting magic." He grabbed his phone and tapped away. "We're lucky. He's even local. I'll give him a call and set up a meeting."

Rafe pulled the car to the curb outside a nice but otherwise nondescript white two-story home sitting in the center of a large, well-maintained lawn. Two large oak trees stood on opposite sides of a walkway to the front door.

A simple visual inspection didn't reveal a magical lived there. In contrast, Izzie could already sense magic on the sidewalk and the heavy magic radiating from the property. She rolled down her window and chanted a spell. Magical signatures lit up on the sidewalk to reveal warning wards prepared all over the sidewalk and yard.

"You sure he was okay with us meeting him here?" Izzie asked. "Because this guy wanted to make sure nobody surprised him." She squinted at the trees. "I'm pretty sure those trees can come alive and attack us."

Rafe nodded. "He insisted. He was the one who gave the address."

Izzie looked up and down the sidewalk. She didn't see anyone else. "What are we supposed to call him? Mr. Mask?"

Rafe laughed. "Infinite Mask. That's what he said, and that's what the records say."

"Our records don't have any information about his true identity?"

"Oh, well, there's the name associated with the deed to this house, but I doubt that's a real name. I didn't bother to look that deep into it. Too much time for something not relevant to us. He's in the ECD, so we're cleared to talk to him about the case."

Izzie sighed. "It could be worse. He could go by Evil Mask."

Rafe nodded toward the house. "We'll save that name for our suspect."

Izzie opened the door and stepped out of the car. She surveyed the area again for any obvious threats beyond and took into account the intense magic layered all over the property. After a concerned glance at Rafe, who shrugged, they headed up the walkway.

A warm wind moved the leaves on the trees. Something about that bothered her. Izzie slowed after a few steps. She threw up her hand to stop her partner.

Rafe halted and reached into his jacket. "Is there trouble?"

Izzie cocked her head and stared at the leaves. "I see them moving, but I can't hear them."

"You're right." Rafe looked over his shoulder. "It's super-quiet all of a sudden. Sound barrier. If anything happens, nobody will hear it."

"Not everything can be a trap." Izzie faced the door. "Can it?"

"Not everything needs to be. Evil Mask only needs the one time."

"We'll assume our guy likes his peace and quiet." Izzie tried to talk herself out of getting ready to blast a fireball. "Not everyone is like Pearl. Are you purposefully trying to get me going?"

"Pearl?" Rafe groaned. "I always feel like I need an ibuprofen after I visit her."

The front door opened right before they arrived. A small boy wearing a threadbare pair of brown pants and a white long-sleeve shirt stood behind the door with a cool look of disdain. Magic flowed off his body and clothes.

Satisfied there was no tree or other spell ambush, Izzie pulled out her badge. "Special Agent Berens, PDA. My partner Special Agent Martinez called ahead. We're here to speak to Mister… That is, we're here to speak to Infinite Mask about a case consultation matter."

The boy traced a glyph in the air with his finger while whispering. Izzie tensed but didn't lower her badge.

"I wish to see the watermark," the boy chanted. "I invoke my right to see the watermark of the PDA badge before me."

A slight glow surrounded Izzie. A matching glow surrounded her badge. An elaborate glyph-like symbol appeared on the badge and in front of Izzie along with the floating mass of translucent text, a statement written in tiny script in a half-dozen Earth languages and a half-dozen Oriceran languages.

This badge is the official property of the Paranormal Defense Agency, a federal law enforcement agency of the United States Department of Homeland Security. If found, please return this badge to the nearest field office. Illegal possession of this badge is a felony and will be prosecuted to the fullest extent of federal law.

Rafe walked forward and cupped his chin, looking over the warning. "It's been a while since anybody wanted to see the watermark outside of the security guards at our building."

"We live in dangerous times when wizards like Thaddeus Blackstone can be attacked openly," the boy replied. "When dealing with those who can change their form, one should confirm their identities in different ways." He nodded toward the inside. "Come. We'll have more than enough privacy."

The pair stepped into the arching hallway filled with obvious defensive wards and sinister-looking stone statues with glowing red eyes. They didn't move, but Izzie sensed they could at a moment's notice. It was as if Infinite Mask wanted intruders to know how well-defended the house was.

There was nothing else of note other than a large wooden door at the end. The boy opened the door and led them into a living room larger than Izzie's apartment. A narrow spiral staircase in the back of the room led upstairs.

What Izzie lacked in space at her place, she made up for in taste. She couldn't say the same about Infinite Mask. Discordant styles of furniture clashed in the living room. A gaudy crystalline chandelier hung from the tall ceiling. Portraits lined the walls, all picturing different people and painted in a variety of styles.

It was like someone had flipped through the history of furniture and art for the last five hundred years and picked random pieces to stick in the room. Magic infused every piece of furniture.

She froze. A chill ran down her spine. Four people stood rigid in the corners of the living room. The first two were an older white-haired Japanese woman in a flowing floral kimono and a dusty cowboy with a bushy mustache who looked like he needed to shoot somebody in Deadwood.

A stern-looking elven man in a flowing robe covered with mystical symbols filled the third corner while a wide-eyed maniacal-looking gnome in a white top hat, matching suit, and an odd vest made up of opaque frosted glass tubes worn over his jacket stood in the final corner.

None of the four people moved. Izzie looked at Rafe. He was also watching the four, his hand still in his jacket on his gun.

"They are perfect replicas." The boy smiled. "Nothing more. Statues. There's nothing to fear."

Izzie shivered. "Why are they here?"

"They represent my four favorite forms of the last fifty years. To know my future, I must know my past."

"You're Infinite Mask." Izzie nodded, less worried given the clear identification. "I kind of figured, but it's hard to be sure when you're dealing with a shapeshifter."

"I assume you understand no attempt at deception was intended." He bowed over his arm. "It's a pleasure to make your acquaintance, Agents Berens and Martinez. I've had positive dealings with the PDA in the past, and I hope to continue this relationship into the future."

He gestured toward the myriad couches and chairs. "Sit anywhere you find comfortable. I know many people fail to understand my sense of visual taste. I can assure you, however, all of my pieces of furniture are comfortable. My enchantments assure as much."

Izzie and Rafe both sat in high-backed wooden chairs. Infinite Mask wasn't lying. Despite the rigid look, Izzie's body and back received perfect support. The chair was neither too firm nor too soft.

Infinite Mask wandered with a languid detachment to half-lay, half-sit on a chaise longue. He set his elbow down and propped up his head by resting it in his palm.

"As I was saying, I'm always happy to aid the men and women of the PDA in their thankless task of hunting down dangerous rogues," Infinite Mask continued. "I had good dealings with previous versions of American magical control organizations, and I've helped the Silver Griffins, both their original and reconstituted versions. Despite my magical specialty, I prefer stability in magical enforcement."

His smile grew. "Of course, I expect my standard remuneration for my valuable advice."

Izzie snickered. "Is it stability you prefer or people willing to pay you?"

"Aiding others takes valuable time out of my day. There's nothing wrong with being compensated for that. Wouldn't you agree?"

"We'll submit the signed request the second we get back to the office," Rafe replied.

"Assuming you give us something useful," Izzie added.

"Oh, I will. I always do." Infinite Mask gave her a weak nod. "Your presence here already confirms the authorities aren't being completely truthful about what happened to Thaddeus. That's almost useful payment itself. Curious."

"Why do you say that?" Rafe asked.

"Because there's been no open mention of a shapeshifter being involved in the crime." Infinite Mask sat up. "I've only heard that the PDA and police are looking for between one to three assailants." He sneered. "What a tiresome and bothersome way to use such elegant magic. Assassination? What a child."

"That saves us time in the explanation department." Rafe stood with his phone, brought up pictures of the glyphs, and offered his phone to Infinite Mask. "We wondered if you could tell us more about any of these that might relate to the shapeshifting. We need to know exactly what we're dealing with. We've been able to rule out a few categories of magical shapeshifting, but we're still way in the dark here."

Infinite Mask scrolled through the pictures. "Similar fundamental shapeshifting spells to what I prefer to use. Your suspect is almost certainly a wizard or a witch." His scowl deepened with each new picture. "I was already disgusted with the lack of elegance. This is worse. What an arrogant and stupid fool."

"Why do you say that?" Izzie asked. "Because he killed Thaddeus Blackstone?"

Infinite Mask wrinkled his nose. "No. It's far more annoying than that. It's about the techniques he used. I assume you're already familiar with the inversion glyphs?"

"Yes, but they aren't that dangerous." Izzie glanced at Rafe. "I mean, they aren't exactly dark, forbidden magic, just magic only useful in really specific situations when you have tons of time to set up and know exactly where you're going to be."

Rafe nodded. "Which means he was stalking Blackstone before this happened. That's consistent with what else we've learned about him."

Infinite Mask handed the phone back to Rafe. "The

inversion glyphs aren't the issue." He folded his arms. "You need to understand that shapeshifting magic is different than illusion magic. In all ways, the caster is physically assuming the other form, down to the most fundamental physical aspects of being."

He lifted his hand to inspect his nails. "If you were to take a DNA sample from me right now and test it, you would find the DNA is different than that of my other forms. If I got a sample from a person and performed the appropriate ritual, I could copy their DNA when I changed forms. Although simply copying a person without a sample would result in a surface-level representation. My DNA would be different, but it wouldn't match the subject."

Rafe nodded. "That's useful to know. We're hoping to rely on tracing the magical signature this time, so we're not as worried about conventional means of identification."

"You're not understanding the fundamental issue, Agent Martinez." Infinite Mask gestured around the room. "It is the basic nature of the universe for form to limit function. To go against that means to go against the baseline of reality. This means your shapeshifter is forced to add magic for stability."

He gestured at his body. "I'm sure you sense magic on my person, but it's not as if everything from my body radiates magic. The spells and enchantments you sense are independent of my form. My soul and mind are mine, but this form now means I'm experiencing the world as a young boy."

Izzie eyed the statue of the gnome in the corner. "So if a shapeshifter used magic to turn into a smaller-framed teenage girl, you'd naturally expect them, under normal circumstances, to not be able to throw grown men ten feet away."

"Exactly, Agent Berens. I'm glad you're so quick to catch on."

He lay down again on the chaise longue. His form blurred, twisted, and stretched. Izzie could understand how someone could liken it to Play-Doh or clay. Colors faded, and fabric grew until a distinguished-looking man in an outdated black suit lay on the sofa.

"You didn't need an incantation," Izzie noted.

"The initial spell involves an incantation," Infinite Mask replied. His voice was far deeper, but the cadence remained unchanged. "After that, it's a matter of maintenance for a true shapeshifter."

"It didn't take that long either," Rafe noted. "And it didn't look like it hurt."

"Changing so quickly in public while maintaining power and strength is a different matter. If you observed pain in this barbarian, it's because he or she is maintaining too much power between forms." Infinite Mask wagged a finger.

"That isn't someone layering defensive or physical enhancement spells, which can easily be disrupted by the shapeshifting process. It's a far darker, far more dangerous technique. It goes by many names, the most common being life banking." He scoffed and glared up at his chandelier. "Life banking is eschewed by all shapeshifter specialists of any real standing."

"Because it draws on the life force of other living things?" Rafe asked.

"Yes." Infinite Mask rolled onto his side. "It also has

diminishing returns. It's a foolish, self-limited technique that will ultimately lead one to doom. It's an act of short-sighted desperation, not a true, elegant way to maintain power. The more you use it, the more you'll need to use it, and at a certain point, it will inevitably kill you."

"The shapeshifter was life banking at that specific location," Izzie revealed. "That's why we found withered plants near the glyphs."

Infinite Mask nodded. "But it won't only be that place. I also would presume they have a hideout where they're using similar spells, along with remote areas where people won't notice the death and decay. When applied, this life banking will not only enhance their physical capabilities. It also will grant them greater innate magical resistance, regardless of form, and expand their transformation range.

"Normally, there is a rough physical restriction since it's more difficult to change outside of humanoid forms. Life banking compensates for that, but even with this technique, I doubt they could turn into an insect. Small animals are an option."

Rafe frowned. "You're saying we might have to fight a kitten with the strength of ten grown men?"

Infinite Mask chuckled. "I doubt it. Non-human forms have their disadvantages and can be stressful for those who aren't from true animal shifter lines. Life banking makes such forms an option. It doesn't make them a good option. That said, you should understand your enemy can wear a far greater number of skins than you might otherwise suspect."

Rafe looked at Izzie with a concerned expression. "Diminishing returns means the shapeshifter might graduate from withering trees to killing animals or people to maintain power."

"But there was no magical signature on the tree," Izzie recalled. "We can't be sure if it's a missing cat or a missing person feeding the suspect." She shrugged. "We can't guard every animal and person in the city."

Rafe looked at Infinite Mask. "DNA changes with form, but the soul stays, right?"

"Yes. The soul will maintain an imprint of sorts of the shapeshifter's longer-used physical forms. Few shapeshifters appreciate their true range. As such, they have a true form, often their original form."

"To be clear, the magical signature of the shapeshifter remains the same?" Izzie added.

Infinite Mask patted his chest. "As much as I've changed, that has never changed."

"What about the true form? Is there any way we can magically determine it?"

"Force enough suffering on the shapeshifter they can no longer maintain the baseline magic necessary for their spell. If their current form is too far distant from their soul-imprinted form, their body will reject it and snap back, painfully." He smirked. "It also has the benefit for forcefully bleeding off the power gained from life banking."

His smirk turned into a stern look. "Be cautious, though. This is separate from simple anti-magic efforts. Remember, the shapeshifter is a fundamental change of form. There are other methods, but that would be the one most easily available to you."

"Has that ever happened to you?" Rafe asked. "A reversion?"

Infinite Mask shook his head. "I can barely remember my original form." He gestured at the statues. "If it were to happen, I'd revert to one of those or one of my more popular forms from the decades before that."

"Thank you," Izzie replied. "That's useful to know." She nodded at Rafe. "Even if we can't figure who the shapeshifter is, we gave forensics an entire garbage can and lid covered with glyphs. That has to be enough if his soul and magical signature aren't changing. All we need now is his magical signature, and we can track him down."

Rafe stood with an uncertain look. "I guess we'll find out."

Infinite Mask offered a coy smile. "I'm glad I could be of assistance, agents."

CHAPTER SIX

By the time Izzie and Rafe returned to the PDA building, crickets chirped with the coming of night. Every new revelation about their suspect only highlighted the increased risk to innocent people without giving them a definite lead. The assassination targets offered hope they could find a pattern, but the life banking might portend a trail of random bodies used to empower the rogue shapeshifter.

Izzie clenched her fists as she stood in the elevator heading down to the level holding the magical forensics lab. "I don't like this guy running circles around us."

"We're still investigating," Rafe replied. "And we're investigating under restrictions. It's nothing new. It hasn't even been twelve hours."

Izzie slammed her fist into the elevator wall. "People are going to die because other people don't want to tell the truth."

"That was true even before open magic returned," Rafe quietly pointed out. "And it's not your fault or my fault."

The elevator chimed, and the doors opened. Izzie and Rafe stepped out into the hallway. Their footsteps echoed in the empty space. Izzie took slow, even breaths.

"It's not all on you and me, Izzie," Rafe continued. "It's not like..." He looked away. "We'll find this shapeshifter and arrest him, but..." He stopped and turned to face her. "This is something I've been meaning to say for a while."

Izzie frowned. "What?"

"You're a great agent and a powerful magical. Pound for pound, you might be one of the most powerful field agents in the PDA. I know we don't have anyone stronger in Austin."

"Okay." Izzie nodded slowly, her back stiffening and awaiting the negativity sure to follow the praise. "And?"

"The PDA is here to protect the country, and all the agents help with that. But we're part of a vast law enforcement apparatus that stretches across the country. It's not like it was even ten years ago. There are witches in the FBI. Wizards helping the NSA and CIA with technomagic. The Griffins are back."

Rafe shook his head. "Izzie, this isn't like what your parents had to deal with or what you had to deal with before joining the PDA. Everything doesn't have to be about a small group of people turning back the darkness. We have allies everywhere now. The light is winning. The dark is retreating."

She jerked her head the opposite way. "I know that. It's not about that. I just don't like the idea of rogue magicals killing people in my town. Is that so wrong? I'm a PDA agent."

"I'm not saying it's wrong to care. I'm saying you'll burn

yourself out if you treat every case like it's the return of Rhazdon leading a revitalized Seventh Order and only you can stop it."

Izzie sighed. "I can only be who I am."

"I'm only saying, I'd rather have an Izzie at seventy-five percent who lasts a whole career than an Izzie at a hundred percent that burns herself out after a few years." He smiled. "Whatever the case is, even if it involves the most dangerous lackey of an ancient dragon plotting to eat every virgin in West Texas, you're not alone anymore. Just keep that in mind. Make it your daily affirmation."

"I know that."

"Do you?" Rafe pointed at her heart. "Do you know it in there? Magic or not, human or part elf, people are creatures of habit. And I don't know if you've shed all those old, paranoid habits from years of being alone."

Izzie looked down at the floor. "This isn't about me. It's about making sure nobody else has to grow up the way I did. It's about making sure people can know their parents when they're children and not have to live in fear."

Rafe nodded down the hallway. "Forensics will have a lead. I guarantee it. I don't care if this shapeshifter is hiding as my mom down to her DNA. We'll find our suspect."

"When we stopped by forensics before meeting with Bill, Katya didn't seem all that optimistic." Izzie admitted something she'd been trying to ignore the entire day.

"When is Katya ever optimistic?" Rafe raised an eyebrow.

"You have a point." Izzie chuckled.

They continued down the hallway and around the corner to the magical forensics lab and badged in without announcement or knocking. The sprawling lab offered a maze of tables, cabinets, and high-tech instruments atop lab benches. Izzie didn't know what half the devices did. She didn't care as long as they helped her catch rogue magicals.

Forensic-related technomagic was critical to the PDA's mission, especially when technomagic defenses against traditional tracking spells and similar had become more common. Advances in the area in the last few years had allowed the government to reduce its reliance on third-party bounty hunters and supranational organizations like the Silver Griffins to control rogue magic.

Most of the lab's forensic devices and instruments, such as conventional microscopes, looked normal on surface inspection. Other equipment demonstrated the more mixed nature of the lab, such as a tall, mysterious brass tube sitting in the corner and covered with rune-inscribed jewels. A rack of test tubes filled with different-colored liquids stood beside it.

Almost all the forensic techs were gone for the night. One tall woman with a dark ponytail remained. A bulky pair of telescoping bronze goggles inscribed with runes covered her eyes.

"We hope you have something for us, Katya," Izzie announced.

Katya hunched over the garbage can lid from the scene. It sat on a stone slab on a black lab bench. Although a witch, she headed a lab filled with mostly non-magical employees who relied on a combination of their training and her technomagic gadgets. The garbage can from the scene stood beside the lab bench.

"I'm busy," Katya shouted without looking their way. "Go away. You're annoying me. I have a high-priority examination for Izzie and Rafe."

"We're sorry to bother you, Katya." Izzie felt more relaxed despite the earlier conversation with Rafe. "But it's Izzie and Rafe."

Katya spun, and her ponytail whipped around. She lifted her goggles. "Oh, it is Izzie and Rafe." She sounded doubtful. "I thought the voice sounded the same, but too many people sound the same these days."

She sucked in a breath. "Sorry. Another idiot keeps coming by and bothering me. Something about a softball league. He keeps telling me I'd be a natural."

"You don't strike me as a softball type," Izzie commented.

"He seemed surprised when I asked if I could make the ball explode." Katya clucked her tongue. "Boring idiot."

Rafe gestured toward the lid. "We still hoped you could pull enough of a distinct magical signature off that so we could get field support drones out there and maybe pick up a trace. Things are running a little dry for us otherwise."

"What did I tell you this afternoon?" Katya scowled at him.

"That the inversion was messing with it." Rafe clicked his tongue. "Based on what our shapeshifter magic expert told us, this shapeshifter could be anything from a kitten to the mayor. We can best proceed with this with magical tracking. Normally, that much magic on scene would be enough to begin tracking a suspect."

Katya stared him down. "Normally people don't use

inversion glyphs." She scoffed and waved a hand. "Don't worry. I've isolated the magical signature."

"Then what was that all about this afternoon?"

"There was no guarantee I would, even as good as I am." Katya lowered her goggles and turned toward the lid. "This is sophisticated work. Very sophisticated. I can appreciate a proper criminal with standards." She tapped on one part of the burned-in glyphs and gestured at the bottom of the can. "It's also where the shapeshifter's luck ran out."

Izzie approached the table. "Why do you say that?"

"Because this was supposed to burn out the glyphs when they were disabled," Katya explained. "Not just burn them away. The residual inversion would have made it hard to identify the spells."

"I disabled them," Izzie replied.

"Without setting off the self-destruction component?" Katya offered a thumbs-up. "There's that fighting dark wizards experience again. Good job."

Izzie grimaced. "I suppose."

Katya rubbed her gloved hands and walked to a glyph-inscribed dark wooden side table. A metal net suspended with four small poles held an opaque crystal. She grabbed the crystal with her thumb and forefinger and held it out to Rafe. "Here you go. Consider this your birthday present."

"My birthday isn't until November." Rafe eyed the crystal. "Does it have the signature of our shapeshifter?"

Katya pressed the crystal into his palm. "Happy birthday." She gave him a strange look. "It's important to commemorate special events."

"I'm not disagreeing." Rafe chuckled. "It's just not my birthday."

"The world doesn't revolve around you."

"But you're the one saying happy birthday." Rafe let out an exasperated sigh.

Katya scoffed and waved dismissively. "Go find the shapeshifter, Mr. Self-Involved. Save lives."

Rafe stared at Katya before turning to Izzie. She didn't have a clue about Katya's behavior either and shrugged.

He wrapped his fingers around the crystal. "I'm not kicking any puppies or kittens, Izzie. This suspect better be in a two-legged form when we find him."

"We still have to find our shapeshifter first," Izzie replied. "Then we'll worry about who has to beat up the cute little animal."

CHAPTER SEVEN

Izzie screeched around a corner in the PDA car, her hands tight on the wheel. A red and blue light flashed above from a spell. She glanced at the map of Austin marked with faded dots. Larger triangles moved around the map. They marked PDA drones equipped with magical sensors tuned for the suspect's specific magical signature. The first couple hours of the gauntlet revealed nothing. Then three drones detected hits in the last fifteen minutes.

Rafe slipped on his magical detection sunglasses. "This still doesn't technically count as an AHMD. Don't run down a grandma to get the shapeshifter."

Izzie gestured at the map. "Our shapeshifter is in East Austin and already in the Magical District. All the hits are there. The shapeshifter is moving, although these hits are far apart. What's up with that? More inversion glyphs?"

Rafe shook his head. "Probably the result of background interference."

Izzie clenched her jaw. "Because he's in the Magical District."

"That could be part of the shapeshifter's plan," Rafe suggested. "The PDA is publicly known to be involved. The shapeshifter and any accomplices know they must account for that."

Izzie frowned as two self-driving Currus taxis didn't clear out of the way. She honked. They didn't move.

It was ironic. Lasting successful universal all-environment self-driving required the full return of magic and technomagic integration. Currus' work didn't impress Izzie that night.

"I thought they were supposed to respond to emergency lights," Izzie grumbled.

Rafe chuckled. He reached into the glovebox to pull out a conventional magnetic emergency light with an attached siren. He rolled down the window and stuck it on top of their car.

The siren screeched. The Currus taxis slowed and changed lanes, allowing Izzie through. Rafe rolled the window up.

"I'm not sure if they need the noise too or if they don't recognize magical lights." He shook his head. "I just thought of something. If our shapeshifter is in puppy form, it will be hard to cuff him."

"Are you saying we need an anti-magic cardboard box for evil puppies? Evil fake puppies inside. Don't touch or adopt."

Rafe grinned. "See? That's the fun of our job."

"Your theoretical evil puppy killed a man."

"Which is why we're going to catch him and take him to the big pound to lock him up."

Izzie whipped through an intersection and frowned at

the display. "It's hard to say, but it looks like the shapeshifter stopped moving. It's been the same minor readings for the last five minutes."

"We don't know that." Rafe tapped on the console. Bright circles lit everywhere on the map. They were more heavily concentrated in East Austin.

"What's that?"

"That's all the local magic without the background filter." Rafe adjusted the filter again so the console only displayed the drones and target signature.

"The other victims should have approached the PDA," Izzie muttered before sliding past two fancy sports cars. "Or the FBI or the cops. A freaking bounty hunter. Anybody. We should have known before the fourth attack. We could have saved Blackstone's life."

"I'll never blame the magical community for being tightlipped. It's like I told you earlier. It's all about habits, and that's a habit established over thousands of years."

He shook his head. "Even our government used the PDA as a dumping ground until recently because they didn't trust magicals. Non-magicals acted like magicals were inherently dangerous and untrustworthy, so that resentment will linger."

Izzie scoffed. "A man's still dead."

"Most of that goes back to before we were born." Rafe gave her a worried look. "I get why you're upset, but you're more spun up than normal."

"You keep saying that, but I'm not." She narrowed her eyes as a new magical signature hit the display. "The shapeshifter's moving again. Even if I am spun up, why shouldn't I be worried about a dangerous rogue shapeshifter using forbidden magic?"

"You were spun up before we made it to the crime scene," Rafe noted. His brow lifted. "Oh. That's what Katya was going on about. Everything makes sense now."

"What?" Izzie licked her lips. They were close to the target, so close to stopping the rogue magical.

"It's almost your second year at the PDA."

Izzie groaned. "Is it?"

"That's not a bad thing."

"I didn't even remember myself." Izzie slowed the car. "Now that you mention it. I...have been more nostalgic lately, if you can call it that. It's more accurate to say I've been thinking tons about the past."

"And about dark wizards hunting you?" Rafe pressed.

"Sometimes. But you were right earlier. I don't have to run around hiding. These days I get to hunt the rogues with the help of an entire agency on my side." Izzie frowned. "We'll need an ID of the shapeshifter's current form. That means we need the drones to get closer."

Rafe pulled anti-magic cuffs from the glovebox and clipped them to his belt. "The shapeshifter might notice the drones."

"We have no choice. Have field support tighten the cordon first, then drop altitude. We'll take it from there."

Stone-faced, Rafe entered a message into his phone. "We'll need to give them a few minutes." He lowered the window to pull the light and siren back inside. "We can still take him by surprise."

Izzie killed the slight flow of magic she was using to support her emergency light. She slowed and pulled off into an alley. "Okay, field support gets their time if it'll help us get our suspect."

A tense few minutes passed as the drones tightened their recon cordon. Overlapping sensor feeds highlighted the shapeshifter's current location, now a bright dot on the map. The shapeshifter was only a few blocks away.

Izzie pulled the car out of the alley and passed through the brightly lit streets in the Magical District, illuminated by conventional street lights and bright floating magical light orbs. A pair of hooded elves walking down the street glanced at the car.

Old buildings offering decades of character stood alongside newer, more utilitarian construction. There was a heavy concentration of newer apartment buildings. Obvious magical glyphs, runes, and sigils on buildings grew more common the farther Izzie drove into the area.

She snickered at a stereotypical East Austin Magical District site. A hand-painted sign advertising potions for sale hung on a small storefront beside a hand-painted sign offering henna body art.

"We're close to the suspect," Rafe advised.

He grimaced as a bright orb shot into the sky in the distance. It exploded at the top into twisting, spiraling flames that settled into burning letters in the sky.

Welcome to the second hour of the East Austin Night Market.

"It had to be tonight," Izzie muttered.

"What better place to hide magic than in a crowd filled with it?"

Increasing traffic forced Izzie to slow as they approached the edge of a huge crowd. Magical and mundane night market stalls filled a vast old parking lot.

After thirty seconds of stop-and-go traffic, Izzie located a spot along the street to park.

Rafe entered a command into the car's console before adjusting his sunglasses. "I have the drone tracking overlay linked to our glasses."

Izzie grabbed her pair. She dusted them off before slipping them onto her face. A small map of the area floated in the upper right of her vision, including the dots marking their target's magical signature. Their shapeshifter was walking straight into the night market crowd.

"The shapeshifter likely doesn't know our faces." She wiped sweat off her brow and motioned to her suit jacket. "Even if this screams fed." She gave Rafe a pained look. "We're both wearing suits when it has to be like, what, eighty percent humidity right now?"

"We can't take the shapeshifter down directly in such a crowded area without innocent people getting hurt. That's my main worry."

"First, let's get our eyes directly on the target, then we'll drive the suspect somewhere safer and take him down. Easy."

"Yes, there's nothing easier than taking down a magical who can change their form and has enhanced strength and spell resistance." Rafe patted the holster hidden under his jacket. "Another classic Austin weeknight."

CHAPTER EIGHT

Izzie and Rafe joined the throngs of mundane humans and magicals bustling around in the night market. The din of excited conversation filled the air. The entire area thrummed with magic, making simple detection of their suspect impossible. She focused on the readout in her glasses while trying to avoid bumping into too many people or standing out any more than a suited government agent wearing sunglasses at night already did.

Her choice of eyewear wasn't as suspicious as one might have expected. Not all humanoid magicals with inhuman eyes wanted them on display. Many magicals, including those native to Earth and newer arrivals from Oriceran, enjoyed modern fashion even in inappropriate situations. The agents' visit to Infinite Mask served as a reminder that what was stylish in one context was alien in another.

A pair of frowning dwarves stomping away from a stall forced Izzie to spin around them. She didn't call out to them, not wanting unnecessary conflict while they hunted the shapeshifter.

The stall was a wooden affair stuffed with shelves and a single low counter. Its proprietor sold metal bars and ingots ranging from precious metals like gold and silver to rarer magical metals and alloys. The bright-eyed gnome running the place spread his arms and raised his eyebrows at her approach, no hint of concern on his face about the angry customers who'd just left.

"Why were they so upset?" Izzie asked.

"Oh, they operate their own stall across the market." The gnome clucked his tongue. "Always remember, the true magic is the power of free market competition to lower prices for you, the consumer." He gestured around at his wares sitting on shelves behind him. "We have deep summer discounts."

The gnome stared at her after looking between her and Rafe. "An extra five percent off for magical customers. If you join our mailing list, we can give you an additional ten percent off your first purchase. That stacks with the magical discount. I call it our Super Summer Sorcery Sale. The four S' mean four times the savings!"

Izzie forced a smile, waved, and hurried past. "I don't need any ingots right now. I don't really do that type of magic."

"You should still consider joining the mailing list!" the gnome called. "You never know when you'll say, 'I wish I had a little mithril for this ritual,' or 'I'm ready to fold unless I get gold!' Everybody who joins the mailing list gets a virtual coupon for ten percent off their next purchase."

Rafe escaped the high-pressure sales gnome first and

uncovered a path empty of market dwellers. He jogged that way after motioning for Izzie to follow. Judging by the map, their suspect was hanging around the edge of the night market.

"We have honey from Oriceran-sourced bees!" shouted a witch from a stall with a comically stereotypical large purple witch's hat. "It's good for what ails you. It's probiotic and antibacterial. Recent research suggests it might enhance pro-spiritual auras in even normally non-magical people!"

A frowning young woman with her arms folded glared at the witch. "You're implying that these bees are from Oriceran, but isn't it true they're bred locally? There's no way you could charge this little if you were paying for direct importation."

"They are bred from one hundred percent original authentic Oriceran stock," the witch insisted.

"But they're not feeding off Oriceran plants." The frowning customer threw her hands up. "What's the point?"

Another crush of people, including a group of obvious college students judging by their shirts and hats, forced Izzie and Rafe to scale back from jogging to walking. They drew closer to their suspect but couldn't do anything in the massive crowd until they were close enough to correlate the drone sensor network with an individual target.

A large wolf wearing a beanie padded through the crowd. Nobody paid the animal much mind, likely assuming he was a normal shifter. That was a good bet given his hat, casual demeanor, and intelligent gaze.

Izzie watched the wolf. The sight summoned a brief

flash of nostalgic memory from her teen years. The presence of an animal shifter only reinforced that she and Rafe were chasing a more general type of shapeshifter, one proven to be evil. Their suspect was still over a hundred feet away according to the drones.

"This is a nightmare." She twisted again to avoid getting run over by a gaggle of college girls. "About the only advantage we have is that the suspect might not be able to shift without pain. That should at least slow him down."

"We're closing in," Rafe replied. "This crowd works for us as much as against us. Even if the suspect spots a drone, the crowd gives an excuse for the presence of more drones. And it's not like we mark our drones with PDA on them."

Izzie and Rafe advanced. Their movements became a joint pseudo-interpretative dance as they flowed, pivoted, and wove through and around the crowd until they reached the edge of the lot. A series of small permanent shops formed a natural border. Two alleys, one small and one larger, led past the backs of the nearby closed shops.

Izzie spotted a young, plain-looking man wandering down the edge of the crowd with his hands in his jeans pockets. His plain white T-shirt was comfortable attire in the humid air. He wore a small, threadbare hunter green backpack.

Her breath caught. According to the map, the shapeshifter's magical signature was in that young man's direction. It was hard to tell if it was him given a handful of other people lingered in the area. This included two bearded men in robes having a furtive conservation that involved gesturing at a small glass figurine resembling a giant eyeball with tentacles.

Izzie tapped the side of her glasses for active magic detection. Her natural ability was superior, but using the glasses would make it easier for her to correlate with the drone feeds. T-shirt Man's magical signature matched the shapeshifter. Her heart raced.

"You see what I see?" she whispered to Rafe.

"I do," he answered.

The shapeshifter wasn't going to get away. They would prevent any more murders by taking the suspect down right then and there.

Izzie stopped and whispered, "According to the map, you can connect with the big alley from the small alley. Let's box him in."

"I'll be ready," Rafe replied. "Give me one minute, then push the suspect down the main alley."

Izzie patted him on the shoulder and put on her best friendly smile in case anyone was watching them closely. She couldn't allow tension to tip off the suspect.

Rafe strolled away from Izzie with a wave. He didn't run until he entered the first alley and stepped out of sight of the suspect.

T-shirt Man walked forward and looked around the area with his lips pursed. His gaze swept past Izzie without special notice. She held her breath and kept him in the corner of her eye as she watched the night market, hoping he wouldn't focus on her. She reminded herself she was one magical out of many in the night market.

Izzie's heart thumped harder. T-shirt Man strolled closer to the large alley. He was making it almost too easy. It was like he wanted to get caught.

She took a deep breath and turned toward him. There had been enough time for Rafe to get into position.

"Excuse me," she called to T-shirt Man.

He stopped and squinted at her. "What?" he slurred. "You can't arrest me, cop."

"What makes you think I'm a cop?" Izzie let out a nervous chuckle.

"Your whole look screams cop. And you're tense. I can tell. Cops are always tense." He swayed. "I'm not driving, cop."

"Sure. I didn't say you were. And I'm not a cop."

He grinned. "DWI is a crime. And possession of illegal drugs is a crime, but technically, you can't arrest me for being high if I'm not driving." He flipped her off.

"And what I smoked isn't on the list. You cops should know there's a specific list. I looked it up on the Internet. You can't just say every plant from Oriceran is illegal to smoke." He giggled. "Man, I'm so baked right now," he slurred. "And it's still legal! I'm a damned hero!"

Izzie narrowed her eyes. She didn't know if the suspect was high or acting. Her magical signature link between her glasses and the drones confirmed it was the shapeshifter. An assassin who'd prepare inversion glyphs wasn't the type of suspect who'd go and get high at a night market.

She lifted her left palm, ready to throw a battle spell. Years of training and technique had long since freed her from the necessity of incantations for her most common combat spells.

She reached into her jacket with her other hand to pull out her badge. "I'm not a cop. I'm Special Agent Berens of the PDA. I need you to come with me, sir. I have some questions to ask you about a recent incident."

The handful of other people in the area stopped to watch. Izzie's stomach tightened. She needed to get the suspect into the alley and away from the civilians.

The suspect shook his head. He flipped Izzie off with both hands. "Down with fascism! Up with expanded consciousness! I won't give in to your drug war, fascist. You can't fight the truth. The feds just don't want everybody to know there's magic inside all of us. That's what this is about. PDA might as well be the DEA."

Izzie put her badge away without lowering her left palm. She narrowed her eyes. "On the ground, right now, with your hands behind your head. You're under arrest for suspicion of murder, and while we're at it, the use of life-draining magic without appropriate authorization, fraud, and tampering with city property. I'm sure there's identity theft in there, too, because I doubt you used your social security number when you got your temp job. I'll leave it to the prosecutors to sort all that out after I bring you in."

He threw back his head and cackled. "Birds gotta fly. Snakes gotta bite. Fascists gotta fash!"

"That doesn't even make any sense," Izzie said.

"Doesn't it?" He smirked.

"I noticed you stopped slurring your words." Izzie stepped toward him. "Convenient. And I couldn't give a shit whether you're under the influence of anything. I'd love it if college kids getting high was the only problem this city had to worry about."

"Are you going to stand there and let this fed oppress me?" shouted the suspect. "I'm innocent. Freedom ain't free! Rise up with me, my brothers and sisters. Rise up for your right to get baked on weeknights on Oriceran shrooms! The real magic mushrooms, yo!"

"Everyone needs to step away," Izzie called. "This man is a suspect in a violent crime. I'm a federal agent and a member of the Paranormal Defense Agency."

To Izzie's relief, the civilians backed away. A handful pulled out phones. She didn't care if they called it in or recorded the arrest. The PDA would brief the locals as necessary.

"Turn around, put your hands on your head, and get on your knees," Izzie barked. "I'm not going to ask again."

The suspect lowered his hands and put them behind his head. "Sure. Whatever. Fascist. I hope you cry yourself to sleep tonight thinking about all the evil you do. No one's ever going to love you."

Izzie reached for her cuffs. "There you go, nice and easy. Nothing about this needs to be rou—"

He bolted into the alley and reached into his backpack. Izzie sprinted after him, not lowering her arm. She spat out a bright stun bolt that struck him in the leg.

After stumbling into the alley, he spun and grinned. He yanked a rune-covered knife out of the backpack. "Not good enough, Agent Berens."

Izzie struck him with two more stun bolts to the chest. He didn't even flinch. She blasted him with a third stun bolt, surprised when he cried out but didn't fall.

His body twisted, pulled, and reshaped, ending any doubt about his identity. He grunted and hissed in pain. The backpack flowed into his neck and shoulders.

A silver amulet with an intricate design fell and clattered against the ground. So did dark seeds and small glass bottles marked with alchemical symbols and filled with different liquids and powders. One bottle filled with a yellow liquid shattered and spilled on the ground.

The shapeshifter gritted his teeth and groaned as he grew shorter and more lithe. By the end of the seconds-long transformation, he matched Izzie's appearance down to her clothes.

"Izzie Berens," the shapeshifter taunted, using a close facsimile of Izzie's voice, although it wasn't perfect. "That's who you are, aren't you? I doubt there's another Berens so conveniently in the PDA."

She blasted a bolt of piercing light magic into the ground in front of the shapeshifter. The non-stun spell blew a small hole in the asphalt and produced a small cloud of smoke.

"I tried to do this the easy way," Izzie replied. "But you made it hard. You're going to comply, and we'll cuff you and take you in. Or we'll do this the hard way, and you'll end up in cuffs at the hospital."

"You should have let it go, Agent Berens." The shapeshifter held up the knife. "Izzie Berens. You're famous, you know."

"I'll give you an autograph in the hospital."

"You're the one who survived the attention of all those dark families. You brought down an entire dark order." The shapeshifter sneered. "You think you're so special, don't you? Leira Berens' and Correk's daughter. Oh, the powerful ones, the original rogue hunter and the great light elf."

"You think you're special enough to run from somebody with this heritage who's done all that? We tracked you once. We can track you down again."

The shapeshifter frowned. He looked up and narrowed his eyes. "I thought there was too much magic in too many of your little flying toys around, but answer my question. Do you think you're special, Izzie Berens?"

Rafe stepped around the corner in the alley with his gun drawn. He crept forward, his natural stealth worthy of a spell.

Izzie did her best not to turn her head toward Rafe. Her sunglasses hid her eyes, which helped. "I'm an agent of the PDA, and I'm here to bring you in. I have the magical power to pull that off. That's about as special as I need to be."

"An agent of the PDA? You keep saying that." The shapeshifter's tone turned as mocking as the following tongue clicks. "You're a glorified bounty hunter who has been weaponized by inferior beings. You think because you took down the Seventh Order you're strong enough to protect anything? You think because you went to a special magical school, you know power?"

"On your knees," Izzie barked. "I'm not here so you have someone to practice your evil wizard rants on."

"I know all about you." The shapeshifter knelt but didn't drop the knife. "I know how you had to hide, even from yourself and your memories, for all those years because you're weak, just like your mother and your father. You have power, but you wield it for the wrong reasons."

Izzie took a deep breath. "You can psychoanalyze me all you want. That's not going to change me from bringing you in. Drop the knife and put your hands on your head."

Rafe stopped about ten feet away from the shapeshifter. "I have 9mm anti-magic bullets loaded into this gun," he announced. "The gun is pointed right at your head. And don't think I can't shoot you because you look like my partner."

"Well played, Agent Berens." With another scream of pain, the shapeshifter twisted their body into another form, a hulking man. "But this isn't your business."

Izzie took a step toward the shapeshifter and reached again for her cuffs. "Drop the knife."

"I'll drop the knife. Don't shoot."

Izzie stopped. "Okay. Cool. Let's all be cool."

Rafe kept his gun pointed at the shapeshifter. He took shallow breaths and didn't blink.

The shapeshifter dropped the knife. The flat of the blade struck the seeds. They hissed, swelled, and exploded with a loud pop and a blinding flash.

Hissing and seeing nothing but white, Izzie fired another stun bolt and jumped backward. She chanted a shield spell and swung her arm back and forth, trying to feel any concentration of magic heading her way.

"Rafe!" Izzie shouted.

"I can't see well enough to fire!" he yelled.

Izzie's vision started to return as she heard fluttering. A large hawk flapped his wings with the knife and amulet in his beak.

"No, you didn't!" she shouted.

The hawk shot up and divebombed a dark form hovering in the air. Sparks flew, and the dark form plummeted to the ground for a hard impact, sending smoking electronic and mechanical parts everywhere.

"What is that?" Izzie squinted and blinked. "Oh, that was one of our drones."

Rafe lifted his glasses and rubbed his eyes. "Too bad these things can't protect us against that attack."

The shapeshifter flew past another low-flying drone and sent it spiraling to the ground. A quick banking turn sent him higher.

Rafe raised his gun. "Should I take the shot?

"Don't want to freak people out. Let me try."

She flung two stun bolts at the hawk shapeshifter as he divebombed another nearby drone. One spell missed, and the other clipped his wing. The bird squawked, opening his beak enough that the amulet fell.

The shapeshifter clamped down on the knife and came around for another pass. Another stun bolt from Izzie forced him to turn around. He dropped low and disappeared behind a building before the amulet clattered against the alley's hard asphalt behind Izzie.

She pointed at the amulet and bottles. "He got away, but he was sloppy. He left more evidence. We'll have field support keep tracking the suspect with the drones we have left. This isn't over."

CHAPTER NINE

Rafe paced in front of the alley with his phone to his ear. "What do you mean, gone? How? Even if you can't get it in real-time, we should be able to... Okay, just get it figured out. We had him. Damn. We had him." He hung up, shoved his phone in his pocket, and gritted his teeth.

Izzie understood his frustration. She'd replayed the encounter in her mind, questioning if she should have been more aggressive. She'd miscalculated, believing the suspect's initial compliance proved he was afraid.

They had the amulet. They had a new trail.

She finished talking to an APD officer and jogged back to her partner with an evidence bag containing the amulet in hand. "What did field support say? Have they tagged our suspect again? Even if they can give us his last known position, we can check around."

"They've lost the suspect's signature entirely," Rafe replied. "They were having trouble maintaining the net with the loss of the drones as it was. The shapeshifter flew into a vent on a building a few miles from here. A couple of minutes later, the signature died. They're widening the net, but there's not much hope."

Izzie closed her eyes and took a deep breath. "It could be another trick with inversion glyphs. The way he talked and his attack on the drone implied a familiarity with PDA drones and technomagic. This shapeshifter isn't fresh through the gates to Earth."

"He wouldn't have been able to infiltrate the city so easily if he was." Rafe shrugged. "The shapeshifter can't move that freely with us poking around. We've already forced him to use special techniques. He might avoid anywhere too public that's easy for us to get to, but he'll pop up eventually. For whatever reason, he has unfinished business. We proved that tonight."

Izzie frowned. "We still don't know what the shapeshifter looks like, not really."

"In the case of this type of magic, I don't think it matters. Remember what Infinite Mask told us. The shapeshifter might not care or remember."

"But we didn't catch the shapeshifter. Any piece of evidence that helps us with that is valuable." Izzie nodded. "We're not done. He's on the defensive. That's a good thing."

"We slowed him for tonight." Rafe gestured at the bagged amulet. "We made him give up evidence. We're still ahead in the game, and right now, we don't have any bodies to worry about. For all we know, he was here to assassinate another target."

"Somehow I doubt the biggest, most influential local magicals hang out in the Austin Night Market." Izzie chuckled. "Can you imagine Thaddeus Blackstone caring about honey and the four S' being for savings?"

Rafe chuckled. "You never know."

Izzie nodded toward the crowd being held back by police officers and frowned at the increasing number of news drones. "You think he had a target here tonight?"

"I don't know. The same aspects that made it hard for us to track him make it a good place to make deals without people noticing too much. If he did have a target, we stopped him. That's all I care about."

He motioned at a police officer. "We can have APD canvass a little and ask for witness statements, but I don't want to put anybody through a bunch of work that won't lead to anything. I doubt our suspect was stupid enough to shapeshift in front of anybody in the market crowd."

Izzie surveyed the crowd, looking for copies of herself or Rafe. "You're right. He chose the Stoner Boy persona, but our suspect could have been anyone tonight." She held up the evidence bag. "This time he got too cocky. He should have run. Katya pointed us at him last time. She can point us at him again."

Izzie didn't skip her coffee the next morning before heading to the office. After a quick discussion with Bill and checking her messages from the Austin PD, she and Rafe stood behind Katya, waiting for her results.

By the time Izzie and Rafe dropped off the amulet the night before, Katya was gone, and only a handful of night shift assistants were present. Bill had authorized overtime to ensure the lab didn't get behind on all the major cases. That didn't mean everyone was working twenty-four-seven.

Katya had already put in a twelve-hour shift the night before. Izzie didn't doubt she would again, but she also didn't want her important evidence being handled by an assistant. She instructed the night shift employees to flag it for their boss. That left Izzie with nothing to do but toss and turn through another night of restless sleep.

Unlike Izzie's and Rafe's last couple of visits, assistants filled the lab. Every machine in the lab looked like it was in use. Techs kept pushing past Izzie and Rafe as they waited for Katya to finish typing and give them a new lead.

Katya stood in front of a laptop resting on the lab bench next to her workstation and beside a plastic tray holding the silver amulet. The intricate designs didn't correlate with any ward- or glyph-work Izzie knew. Even more surprising, she couldn't detect any magical residue on the amulet.

"I came in early, you know," Katya grumbled. "You've all been working me relentlessly lately. Even witches need their sleep." She peered at Izzie. "Most living things do."

"We appreciate the effort, Katya," Izzie replied. "We know you're swamped and always busy. We wouldn't have flagged it for you if it weren't so important. We were so damned close to nailing the shifter last night at the night market."

"So I heard. Did you figure out what he was doing there?"

"We told APD to ask around but not to push them-selves," Rafe explained. "They passed on a couple of odd encounters to us. Not much useful, although there was someone who matched our initial stoner version of the shapeshifter and bought alchemical reagents. That matched what we found on scene. None of them were all that special or impressive."

Katya's gaze flicked to a shelf holding jars filled with reagents, everything from modern chemical powders to strange glowing liquids emanating magic. "That means your suspect will hit somewhere else to get what he needs. He obviously intends to make something."

Rafe yawned. "He already has hit somewhere else."

"Right after almost getting caught?"

"A touch of desperation," Rafe suggested. "A potion shop in the Magical District was robbed a few hours after our contact with the suspect. The APD passed it on to us this morning. Somebody went in hard and fast, bypassing door and window wards by bashing in through a wall. Talk about smash and grab."

"That's why I ward the lab." Katya motioned to the amulet. "I know you're short on time and patience yet long on eagerness, so I'll give you the bottom line. This amulet has no magical power. Absolutely none."

Rafe nodded. "Izzie said the same thing, and I couldn't see anything with my glasses, but it has importance to the suspect. Maybe we could use it as the basis of a tracking spell, something to help field support or Izzie." He snapped his fingers. "The more personal an item is, the easier it is to use it to track someone despite their defenses, right? We can find him with a spell now."

Katya snickered. "You go ahead and do that. That ought to be entertaining."

Izzie waited a few seconds for Katya to elaborate on the reason for her sudden amusement before asking, "What's so funny? That's not a bad idea. This killer has powerful shapeshifting magic. It doesn't mean he's the ultimate master of all spells. If this amulet isn't magical, Rafe could be right."

"It's not a bad idea," Katya agreed. "It simply won't work. I mean, it's your time to waste if you want to. I just assume you want to catch this shapeshifter as soon as possible."

"If a normal tracking spell won't work, maybe my clairvoyance would," Izzie suggested. "It's less of a spell than an inherent magical ability," she mused out loud. "Although wards and the like can still block it." She frowned. "Damn. The only problem is that personal attachment doesn't play into it as much."

Katya sighed. "So many great ideas. None that would work. More's the pity. I applaud your creative thinking."

Rafe frowned. "We might be short on patience and time, but what are you getting at? You're supposed to be giving us the important bottom line."

"The amulet itself..." Katya shook her head. "It's all about definitions, you see. I was imprecise earlier when I spoke."

"How?"

"By one measure it could be called a magic item. By another, it's the ultimate non-magical item. That's the source of your dilemma and why your clever plans will fail."

Izzie didn't want to risk derailing Katya's train of thought and forcing a restart of the conversation from the beginning, so she didn't reply. She nodded and folded her arms, waiting and praying for greater clarification to come naturally.

Katya whipped her arm up like a snake to point at an anti-magic grenade missing its detonator on a shelf. "All things new are old. Time is a circle. Such is such."

"The amulet is anti-magic?" Izzie glanced at the grenade. "Is that what you're saying?"

"On a fundamental level, it's more anti-magic than that grenade. Very specialized magical metallurgy, combined with the right spells, right alloys, and poof, you get a so-called hungry or void amulet. I've never actually seen a working one before."

Katya grabbed the amulet with a gloved hand and held it up. "It's not true anti-magic like an emitter or my souvenir over there. It's closer to something like anti-magic cuffs ramped up exponentially, although you could wear this and still cast a spell as long as it wasn't touching your skin. That's how this was designed to work."

Izzy pointed at her chest. "So I put it on a chain, lean over, and I still cast a shapeshifting spell."

"As an example, yes."

Rafe peered at the amulet. "What if someone hit that amulet with a spell?"

Katya waved. "Bye-bye, Mr. Magic."

"Then it's protective equipment," Izzie concluded. "That's why my spells weren't that effective, despite him not having any shield spells up."

Katya laughed. "Of course not. The life banking is more than enough to explain that."

"You just said it's an anti-magic amulet," Izzie reiterated, trying to keep the frustration out of her voice.

Katya held up the amulet. "If I was wearing this, and someone hit me in the arm with a spell, I'd still be affected."

"Then what's the point?" Rafe asked. "Is it supposed to be melted down to make a breastplate?"

"No." Katya shook her head. "That would almost certainly destroy the anti-magic properties. In addition, that would be extremely difficult. The same process that makes it hungry for magic also makes it resistant to most physical damage."

"Oh, I get it." Rafe stepped out of the way of an assistant scurrying by carrying a rack of test tubes. "The point of making these the way they are isn't to protect somebody. It's to protect the amulet."

Katya jabbed a finger in front of Rafe's face. "Correct! Now you're getting it! Good for you, Rafe. You always were a clever one."

"But who cares about preserving this specific amulet?" Izzie asked. "Unless these patterns mean something special, this is just murderer bling."

Katya set the amulet in the tray and leaned over her computer. She typed with furious keystrokes followed by a series of aggressive mouse clicks before a black-and-white image of the amulet appeared on the screen.

"So you can take pictures of it." Izzie shrugged. "It's anti-magic, not anti-camera. So what?"

Rafe shook his head. He pointed at the picture. "Read the caption. That's a digitized version of a historical magical image from Oriceran. The Glorious Foundation. Okay, now things are getting interesting."

"Again, correct," Katya replied. "This specific design is associated with the Glorious Foundation. At least that's what the agency's image search database tells me, and I have no reason to question the database. Unfortunately, I'm not an expert on extinct ancient magical organizations."

"The Glorious Foundation?" Izzie shook her head. "I've never heard of them."

Rafe gestured at the screen. "I'm not surprised. I only heard of them during a cross-agency seminar a few years back. The FBI brought in Terrevik the Wise to talk about the history of dark magical organizations and societies. The idea was to draw parallels in motivations and tactics as a seed for interagency cooperation and planning."

"Terrevik the Wise?" Izzie frowned. "As in the light elf historian? I haven't heard that name since school. Man, is that guy a painful writer. His motto seems to be, 'Why use five words when you can use one hundred?' I thought it was a bad translation at first, but one of my light elf classmates complained to me about the same thing."

"He was doing a limited world seminar tour deal on Earth." Rafe shrugged. "It was an interesting lecture. I've liked the books of his I read."

"Okay, so you did the extra credit. What's the deal with the Glorious Foundation?"

"They weren't a dark family-type organization exactly." Rafe looked down. "They were also an exclusively Oriceran organization. That is, the original organization wasn't about supporting dark wizard families above anyone else.

"Their original idea was that it was important to ensure they understood the weaknesses of dangerous and powerful magical creatures and beings, so they could control them if they got out of hand. They come off more like the original Silver Griffins in early legends, but more focused on the Oriceran than the Earth side of rogue magic."

Izzie frowned. "I'm guessing they got corrupted along the way? They became anti-Griffins?"

"What started as defensive research turned into an obsession with controlling magical beings for its own sake." Rafe shrugged. "That ended up pissing off a bunch of different powerful magical beings. A little shy of fifteen hundred years ago, an alliance led by an ancient dragon got fed up with the Glorious Foundation.

"The dragon led an army to attack them. According to the most commonly told legend, it 'Used such powerful and devastating magics as to render the members of the Foundation and all they claimed dominion over into ash and vapor. So thorough was the destruction that nary even a chip of bone remained and the land wasn't reclaimed until weeping dryads came centuries later to cleanse the tainted lands.'"

"That's hardcore." Izzie grimaced.

Katya gave a knowing nod and folded her arms. "Oopsie."

Izzie shook her head. "Are we saying this ancient order that got tac nuked by an army led by a dragon over fifteen hundred years ago is back?"

Rafe shrugged. "I don't know much else other than what I told you. I read up a little after the seminar, and the only thing I learned is there was a debate about how influential and important the Glorious Foundation was as an organization.

"There are scholars out there who suggest they were only destroyed to set an example and that much of their alleged power and deeds were after-the-fact justifications. Kind of like King Philip of France made up stories about the Templars worshipping demons over here. The Glorious Foundation wasn't known to have operated on Earth, and that was during a period where the gates were firmly closed and travel was way harder."

"I'll keep examining the amulet," Katya offered. "I can't speak to the history any better than Rafe, but I can tell you, without a doubt, that any attempts to use powers on this thing to trace it back to your suspect are doomed to failure. There's a reason why it's called a void or hungry amulet."

"Then we need to figure out why this is important to the suspect, which might help us with their motives." Izzie eyed the amulet. "I finally feel like we're a step ahead of this killer."

CHAPTER TEN

Izzie sat at her desk in her office. Her eyes glazed over as she read what felt like her thousandth page of annotated notes on shapeshifting magic and ancient magical organizations. She sighed and leaned her head back to stare at the ceiling tiles.

This type of pain came with being a PDA agent. Magical criminals often had strange, ancient links. Maybe investigations would be different in a hundred years with the help of advanced technomagical AIs to do all the hard parts. As it stood, the analysis support division had pre-collated useful sources and sent them to Izzie and Rafe for review.

"What's wrong?" Rafe asked. "You find something?"

He'd been reviewing background database records as much as her, but he kept making happy little noises or murmuring, "That's fascinating." It somehow made Izzie's experience more excruciating. She was never sure if Rafe found magical history more interesting because he didn't grow up in a magical family or if it was more a reflection of her idiosyncrasies.

The current case played to his strengths. Their next clue might be hidden in an obscure historical reference nobody else had cared about for centuries. She'd do whatever it took to find the shapeshifter and end the threat.

"What's wrong is that our suspect got away, and we don't know where said suspect is," Izzie replied. "And all the drones and technomagic sensors available to the PDA aren't finding that suspect." She frowned. "Katya's right. I tried tracking spells and my clairvoyance on the amulet and everything else. Nothing worked."

"Did you expect it to?"

"No, but a girl can hope, can't she?"

Rafe shook his head. "You told me once that one of the ways you used to avoid tracking was using a magic ring."

"Sure, what about it?"

"It wasn't that the ring was a unique artifact, right?" Rafe squinted at his screen and brought up a new record. "For every technique, there is a counter, magical and mundane. Our job would be boring and easy if that weren't true."

"This is one time where I want everything to be boring and easy. I care more about taking down rogues than being entertained." Izzie glared at her screen and an article discussing the history of dragon hunting that had only surfaced because of a brief mention of the Glorious Foundation near the end.

"I worry there's something more here. And, no, this isn't me being paranoid. This is me wondering why a shapeshifter with dangerous magic and ancient amulets has shown up in town and is killing people."

"I don't disagree with you being worried," Rafe replied. "Everything we've found points to something deeper and more dangerous. We still need to be careful not to jump to too many conclusions. We don't want to end up following the wrong path."

"If jumping to conclusions will help me find this shapeshifter, I'm all for it. This is an annoying and dangerous case."

"This isn't the first time we've had an annoying case." Rafe leaned forward. His eyes widened, screaming that he found something useful. "Remember that case I told you about with the gnome and the birds?"

"That was before we were partners. Wasn't it?"

"Exactly. It was one of my earliest. I was two hundred percent committed to solving it, and I didn't have an active magical partner at the time."

Izzie laughed. "Oh, yeah, the serial pet store robber. How did it go? The gnome kept breaking into pet stores with careful magic that helped him avoid the alarms, yet never stole anything.

"Despite all that careful preparation, you had tons of surveillance camera footage filled with the masked gnome rousting birds at night. And you were going nuts because you couldn't figure out why he was doing it."

Rafe nodded. "Yes. Then we caught him, and he claimed he lost a magical bird construct and was trying to find it." He laughed and hit his leg.

"Everyone thought he was full of it and making up an

excuse until the mayor asked the PDA to explain why his new parrot was ranting at him in a language he didn't understand that didn't sound human. The mayor tried to bring in a priest for a bird exorcism, and the local bishop tried to explain the church didn't do bird exorcisms and pointed him back at the PDA."

Izzie snickered at the mental image of two priests splashing holy water on a foul-mouthed parrot turning its head around a hundred eighty degrees. "What's that sneaky gnome have to do with this case?"

"It's about understanding the nature of crime. Magic's nothing more than a tool, and all crimes are the same because they come back to motive in the end. Motive, more than anything, rules all."

Izzie swiveled her chair to face her partner. "He knew who I was. He taunted me about it."

"I heard most of that. I know what you might be thinking. I don't believe it means much."

"You don't?"

Izzie didn't want to believe it either. She also couldn't shake the fear that she'd brought trouble to Austin because of her background.

"Nope. I think he was trying to get under your skin and work your nerves because he knew he was outclassed. If he thought he could win the fight, he would have gone at you instead of blinding us and running."

Izzie frowned. "I want to believe that, but I'm not so sure."

"At the end of the day, you are special and well-known among certain people in the magical community. You and most people don't want to stress it for obvious reasons, but we shouldn't be surprised that an assassin would have heard of you and tried to take advantage of it before a fight."

"Then you really don't think it has anything to do with me?" Izzie asked. "You're not just telling me that to make me feel better? In my defense, it's not like I believe every case has to do with me. Most cases don't involve the suspect taunting me about my parents."

"I don't think a new anti-Berens dark wizard plot would start by attacking victims in the magical community you don't personally know. On top of that, we're not the only PDA agents in Austin. There was no way to ensure you got assigned to this case. Your presence is pure chance and coincidence, as is mine.

"If this was about you, they've gone about it in the clumsiest way possible. The way I see it, our shapeshifter had the bad luck of you getting assigned to this case. He doesn't know what an insane bulldog you are when it comes to rogue magic."

Izzie stood. She folded her arms and paced, hoping it would stir her subconscious mind into better action. "We need the other victims to come forward. We should go talk to Xelius." She grabbed her phone out of her pocket and held up a picture she'd found of the wizard. His weathered face and salt-and-pepper hair still belied how old he likely was from what she'd read. "I couldn't find exactly where he lives, but we could ask around."

"You heard what Bill said." Rafe frowned. "Xelius won't cooperate, and there's no guarantee they'd have anything useful even if he or anyone else did. They might lack the big picture, and without Bill backing us on that, it will make things harder for the PDA." He took a deep breath. "I'm not ready to piss off Bill unless I think it'll pay off."

Izzie walked to a dry-erase board in the back of the office. She picked up a marker from the bottom tray and started writing. "Then we need to figure out the big picture. One, a shapeshifter is using dangerous magic to enhance himself or herself and assassinate magicals who have influence in the local magical community.

"Two, the shapeshifter was carrying an amulet of an ancient order that supposedly was destroyed almost fifteen hundred years ago. Three, said shapeshifter is not done with his overall mission. I think we can be sure about that."

"Because they haven't left the city?" Rafe asked.

Izzie nodded. "It makes no sense to stick around town and wait for the PDA to come after them. The longer they mess around, the more we pull in the local cops, the FBI, and even bounty hunters. That means they must have a good reason if they're sticking around. The problem is we have no idea how many targets remain or who might be targeted."

"But we can isolate targets only to magicals." Rafe pointed at the board. "The APD would be beating down our door if mysterious people with knives were appearing and killing random non-magical citizens.

"If there'd been a rash of unexplained stabbings, the FBI would have noticed and likely passed it on to us given their minimal magical staffing in this area." He smiled. "The upshot is there are far fewer magicals in this city than non-magical people. That reduces the target pool exponentially."

"But there aren't so few we can guard them all and wait for our suspect to show up." Izzie wrote WHY? in large letters at the top of the board. "I still get the feeling the suspect is a professional or someone who doesn't have a strong emotional attachment to the victims. This doesn't feel personal. I could be wrong."

Rafe folded his arm with a thoughtful look. "I'm not disagreeing. I still want to hear your thought process."

"When the suspect had a chance to talk to me, he messed with me by changing into my form and taunting me about my life and parents. A suspect who killed Blackstone or attacked Xelius for personal reasons would have been far more likely to rant about why they deserved it. There would be more emotion there."

Izzie shook her head. "You're right. He only said what he said about me to put me off my game. He didn't care about justifying his crime."

"Agreed, and that's my logic, too," Rafe replied. "The Blackstone attack was about prepping and bringing prey down, not necessarily making him suffer, and you're right. Our shapeshifter didn't try to imply that our investigation was unjust."

"A pro implies a client," Izzie noted.

Rafe sucked in a breath. "That's what I'm worried about, too. A puppet master can get a new puppet if we cut the strings of the first one."

Izzie penned a couple of other additions to the board. Talking the case out with Rafe improved her mood.

Killer is shapeshifter and is a pawn? Who is pushing pawns around the board?

"Killing people of influence means diminishing the magical community's ability to act in concert," Rafe added. "It's not like everybody knows who they should contact when threats show up, especially these days. The proof's there with the previous victims trying to keep things quiet. This might be about spreading chaos."

"Weaken the defenses." Izzie wrote it down. "Then push in for the final attack?"

"It could be a coincidence, but presuming it's not, that would make sense." Rafe stared at the board. "They don't have to do serious damage for that plan to work. All they need to do is convince people that if they get involved, it'll be dangerous.

"You and I both know how this goes. Whether it's mundane humans or magicals, people will look the other way if they think they'll get swept up in other people's trouble."

Izzie capped her marker and set it on the bottom tray. "You keep circling to the same idea. The magical community in general doesn't trust the PDA and police enough to cooperate fully and directly with us. That means there are people out there who could know what's going on and can help crack this case if they choose to cooperate."

Rafe nodded. "That's true for most cases, except in non-magical cases. People don't have to worry about their killer being able to change forms to surprise them."

Izzie thought through the implications. "There are magicals out there, not in the government, who are our friends and trust the PDA. Their lack of direct government connection means they might have heard things we haven't."

"That's also true." Rafe tapped the side of his head. "But we can't expect them to always understand what we need or when we need it."

"They will if we tell them what we need."

CHAPTER ELEVEN

"Stay close," Izzie told Rafe as they walked down a sidewalk. "I don't know if Pearl's technically keyed the maze to you, and you know sometimes she can be finicky about disabling it."

Rafe scoffed. "Finicky? She thinks it's funny to mess with me. She told me she thinks it's funny."

Izzie wanted to deny that. She would have preferred if her witch friend Pearl Storm didn't take pleasure in petty pranks. Unfortunately, she could only deny reality for so long.

"It's not like she has anything against you. She's done the same thing to other people, too. It's a Pearl problem, not a you problem."

Rafe scrubbed a hand down his face. "That doesn't make me feel much better."

"Think of it this way. She's never done anything to you that's hurt you."

"You're setting the bar real low, Izzie."

"All the easier to jump over."

Rafe scoffed. "Let's hope this doesn't turn into a limbo contest."

They arrived at a locked wrought iron gate featuring a thin mail slot. The gate divided the fence and the tall hedges lining the front lawn of the cute southside bungalow. The entire property radiated strong magic, although Rafe wouldn't be able to tell without his glasses.

"I'll make sure she behaves," Izzie offered.

"We'll see." Rafe snorted.

Izzie grabbed the handle and whispered an incantation. The gate clicked open. She held it and motioned Rafe through. He eyed the gate with open skepticism.

"Nothing really bad ever happens here," Izzie insisted.

"That's a matter of perspective." Rafe shook his head. "She better be helpful."

"She almost always is."

Once Izzie and Rafe stepped past the gate, the simple lawn and path disappeared. A solid wall of hedges shimmered into existence, far higher than the ones outside. It blocked their way, offering two paths, one to the left and one to the right. The ground rumbled, and the hedge wall slid into the ground, followed by other hedge walls until there was a straight path to the home. The agents started down the path.

"I think the same thing every time we come here." Rafe sighed. "This is overkill. I mean, who does all this? It's not like she lets random salespeople through the gate. From what you told me, she doesn't have a bunch of enemies. Who is she trying to trap? The guys who sell those expensive water filters?"

"Think of it more like a hobby, and it'll make more

sense. You like reading. She likes overelaborate magical hedge mazes."

"It's still overkill," Rafe grumbled.

"You say that, but we're working a case where a rogue shapeshifter is targeting powerful magicals. Extra defenses can make the difference between being alive and having your throat slit downtown." She sighed. "Pearl's helped me tons with cases since I joined the PDA. She might mess with you, but she's stuck her neck out there for both of us."

Rafe waved it off. "I'm not questioning a powerful witch helping us, and I get she's your friend. I'm just saying the whole creepy hedge maze thing is a little too witchy. She might as well live in a candy house and hang a sign saying 'Lost children welcome. Oven-sized preferred, but will accept all comers.'"

Izzie laughed and stopped at the front door. "Don't tell her that. She might think it's a fun idea until the first angry parent shows up and asks who's been fattening up their kid with free candy."

Rafe stared at the door and back at the hedge maze. "Does she let trick-or-treaters come?"

The door swung open, and a short, dark-haired woman in glasses popped her head out. "Yes. I've heard they like my house because I give out full-sized bars. It used to be they avoided my house because they were afraid, but Halloween is one of the few times I lower my defenses, and the children have learned bravery is rewarded." She smiled. "They call me Pearl the Candy Storm. I rather like that."

"Of course they do," Izzie replied.

"As for the other concern, I'd consider the sign, but I'd

have to get rid of the hedge maze for anybody to see it. Where's the fun in that?"

Rafe snickered. "And the candy house?"

"That's not really my aesthetic." Pearl stared at him. "I am a witch, Rafe. How can my yard be too witchy? That's the real question. Can you be too agenty?"

"With the appropriate styling and speech patterns, yes."

Izzie chuckled when Pearl moved clear of the door. Her friend's sense of fashion was on full display. A black gothic dress with a long skirt fell to her ankles. Pearl didn't wear a pointy hat over her long, straight black hair, but the beautiful, tiny, dark-eyed woman embodied a certain stereotype of magic-using women. A thin black wand rested in a wand holster connected to a black belt holding small pouches on the sides.

Rafe folded his arms. "Even if I was too agenty, that wouldn't end with somebody's arm stuck halfway down a giant carnivorous plant."

"Are you still mad about the plant trying to eat you that one time? That was a year ago. Come on. You need to learn to let go of things." Pearl put a hand to her mouth and snickered. "You pushed right out of the plant, you big baby."

"The past is the past." Izzie stepped inside at Pearl's gesture. "Aren't you always telling me to focus on the future, Rafe?"

Rafe followed Izzie into the living room. "I'm not going to die on the job. I'm going to die in Pearl's yard. Then I'll have no future other than my skeleton being a Halloween decoration for the neighborhood kids."

Pearl's living room's aesthetic was half old roadside

museum. Magical knickknacks of different shapes and cultural traditions, Earth-based and otherwise, filled the shelves. Her furniture choices included hints of stability and rationality as color-coordinated dark pieces from the same set. That established a favorable contrast with Infinite Mask.

She lacked a television, computer, and stereo. An old-fashioned record player stood on a desk in the corner. As far as Izzie knew, cell phones were one of Pearl's few concessions to twenty-first-century technology.

Izzie dropped into a comfortable chair. "Sorry to pop up with so little notice. We're working a case and need a fresh perspective from somebody deeper in the magical community with no government connections."

"Don't you count as a government connection?" Pearl smiled.

"You know what I mean."

"You're lucky I'm in town." Pearl sat on the couch and crossed her ankles. She smirked when Rafe sat in the chair farthest from the couch. "It just so happens I was over in Russia collecting rusalka tears until last night."

"I vaguely remember you mentioning something about going out of town," Izzie admitted, not remembering Pearl mentioning anything about Slavic water spirits. "Do I want to know what you do with rusalka tears?"

"They're great for certain potions. Nothing's illegal about it if that's what you're worrying about. I have a fancy official importation license and everything for them." She rolled her eyes. "It's amazing how annoying and tedious things have gotten when it comes to magical sourcing."

"It's about safety," Rafe replied.

"Safety is boring," Pearl countered. "Earth will keep on carrying on, and if something bad's going to happen, it won't be little ol' Pearl Storm who blows it up with a rusalka-tear potion. It'll be a crazy dark wizard plot or a crazy regular human with a nuclear bomb."

She waved it off. "Anyway, my old tear supplier suddenly dried up a few weeks ago, so it took me a while to get everything else set up." She wrinkled her nose. "I don't mean that drying up part literally, but at the same time, I kind of do. Sourcing's annoying even without the bureaucracy."

"Who was your old supplier?" Rafe asked.

Pearl gave him a suspicious look. "Izzie, I'm not being investigated for anything, am I?"

"Nope. We came to you for help. By the way, if you have any potions that can take down a shapeshifter, I'd love to have one."

"Not as such, but I'll have to do some research. As for the other matter, I had a standing deal with Blackstone Imports. Thaddeus' company was reliable up until a few weeks ago. Then next thing I know, he's suddenly saying he can't complete my orders."

Rafe frowned. "You had an importation deal with Thaddeus Blackstone."

"His company, although I preferred to deal with him directly. They're reliable and handle most of the annoying paperwork, so I don't have people like you in exoskeletons trying to blow up my hedge maze with railguns."

Izzie sucked in a breath. "Then you probably don't know."

"Know about what?" Pearl looked between the two of them. "Something bad's happened, hasn't it? Oh dear."

"We have a rogue shapeshifter going around trying to stab people," Izzie began. "Thaddeus is dead."

"And the shapeshifter got away after that." Izzie shrugged. "Drones, cameras, the works. Yes, I tried a tracking spell and my clairvoyance. They didn't work." She shook her head. "That killer is hiding somewhere and mocking us."

Pearl folded her arms. "As I told you, I was in Russia until yesterday night, but your mention of the Glorious Foundation is...concerning." She shivered and rubbed her elbows. "That's got me worried, and now it makes me wonder about Thaddeus. I wasn't the only customer annoyed by sudden supply disruptions. I didn't understand why it was happening, considering it wasn't as if he was the only employee at this business. At the same time, many of his other customers were completely unaffected. He must have been more proactive in handling the VIP customers, so his troubles showed up as an erratic relationship with the overall customer base."

Rafe frowned. "Are you worried that the Glorious Foundation is back?"

"Not that I know of, but there are always rumors floating out there among the magical community, worrisome rumors. It's hard to keep track of what's true and what's BS that somebody bored is pushing out there."

Pearl tucked a stray strand of hair behind her ear. "None of these rumors are concrete enough to call the FBI or PDA and tell them, 'There's going to be trouble.' Because if we did that, you would be working twenty-four-seven and still not have enough time to investigate real threats." She gave Izzie a sympathetic look. "That's before you get into prophecies and other evidence people still have trouble believing."

Rafe patted his chest. "I understand that prophecies are a legitimate and real magical phenomenon."

"Not everybody else does, Rafe."

"Have you heard any concerning prophecies lately, Pearl?" Izzie asked.

Pearl shook her head. "Not prophecies, but regular rumors. I've heard bits, here and there, about factions on the move, dark families in certain cases, non-dark yet ambitious types in others, and newer groups that see it as a chance for them to seize control or gain influence. Many dangerous organizations have been taken down in recent years."

"You're saying taking down rogue magicals is causing problems?" Izzie asked.

"No, no." Pearl put a finger to her bottom lip. "I'm only saying that nature and the underworld abhor a vacuum." She gestured at Izzie. "Consider your and Alison's work on the Seventh Order or that dragon incident on Oriceran with Alison's father. Add aggressive moves by all the various governmental organizations both here and abroad taking advantage of the fact they now have access to boring and honest magicals to take down the rogue ones."

She snickered. "It means dark and evil organizations face concentrated justice in a way they might not be used to when they had more opportunities to hide in the background. They never know what elves or witches might be hunting them. While other groups think they can get ahead of those good little magicals."

Pearl snapped her fingers. Her record player turned itself on, and the needle descended to a waiting record. Despite all her pretensions toward being a traditional, old-fashioned witch, the high BPM heavy metal guitar solo erupting from her tinny speakers proved she was a more modern witch than one might believe. She snapped her fingers again, and the music came from all directions.

She closed her eyes, took a deep breath, and smiled. "Nothing like a little power metal to relax you when your nerves are going. Yes. That's the stuff mommy needs."

The head-pounding music played for thirty seconds before another snap lowered the volume. Rafe shook his head in disbelief. Izzie didn't say anything. Her friend needed to be free to think the situation through.

"What does any of this have to do with the Glorious Foundation?" Rafe pressed. "Are you saying they're back?"

"There's a rumor the fourteen hundred and forty-fifth anniversary of the destruction of the Glorious Foundation is coming up," Pearl explained. "I have no idea how anybody figured out the exact day and year they were supposed to have been destroyed. I hadn't heard of them before these rumors started popping up.

"When I looked into them, it confused me because nobody could tell where the rumors were coming from, only that many different factions were suddenly inter-ested in the anniversary. What you just told me also explains why certain magicals were pulling back and hiding. I didn't realize people had been attacked before

Blackstone. They kept that quiet, and not just from the PDA."

"Do you know Xelius?" Rafe asked. "He got robbed, but he's not willing to cooperate with us. We're not sure if he thinks he can get this property back without help or doesn't trust us to make it worse."

Pearl shook her head. "I only know him in passing. I don't know if I've spoken a full sentence to the man in years. He was an insufferable snob with no sense of humor."

Rafe pulled out his phone and entered notes. "Somebody else could be trying to pick up where the Glorious Foundation left off. That goes to their motivations, although we still don't understand why they're going after their particular targets."

"You'd think a story that ends with a group getting annihilated by a dragon-led army would be a good object lesson for people to steer clear of messing around with it in the future." Pearl's smile twitched into a deep frown. "You two should be careful. There are always rumors flowing around the magical community, but these are more strident and immediate this time."

She rubbed her shoulders. "These feel different. I'm not claiming prophecy or special insight, but there's something in the air. Your shapeshifter proves there's someone out there willing to risk PDA attention to get what they want."

Rafe observed, "From what you've told us, if Blackstone knew he was being targeted, it might have been from weeks back. He might have been distancing his activities from other magicals because of the threat of the shapeshifter. You mentioned not every customer was having trouble."

Pearl shrugged. "All I know is I didn't get my rusalka tears."

"He might have worried about the shapeshifter coming after you."

Pearl scoffed. "He's welcome to try."

"This is serious, Pearl," Izzie reminded her.

"So am I." Pearl frowned. "My rusalka tears required additional paperwork. Now that I think of it, the other customers, at least the ones I heard about, had more complicated requirements. We all shared Thaddeus' personal attention in our efforts."

She snapped her fingers to lower the volume of her music again. "I'll leave the mystery-solving to you, but I'd suggest it was less that we were being targeted as much as Thaddeus was distracted by his own threats."

Even with the volume down, the music distracted Izzie. Every time a new thought came, pounding drums or high BPM guitar licks threw off her thought. She never could reconcile Pearl's taste in music with the rest of her lifestyle.

"Thank you for telling us all that," Izzie replied. "We need more concrete leads, although your shipping problem and theory align with the other earlier attacks." She nodded. "Once we grab the shapeshifter, we can find out If there's anybody else behind these attacks. It might just be these other factions are on the move because the shapeshifter is stirring up trouble and they think it'll give them an opportunity."

"Anything I can do to help, Izzie, let me know."

Rafe's phone buzzed. His brow lifted. He swiped on his screen and snorted. "Speaking of fortune, fate, and luck."

"What is it?" Izzie asked.

"Finnegan must be aching for money." Rafe shook his phone. "I sent messages to a few of my informants earlier to see if they'd heard anything. He claims he has info for me. He wants to meet around 7:00 PM."

"Finnegan?" Pearl shuddered. "You're still working with that snake? You can't trust a man like that. He's selling information about you to the magical underworld at the same time he's selling their information to you. You do understand that, don't you?"

"Then it'll be a race to see who can take advantage of the info first." He checked his watch. "I'm glad he gave us plenty of time to change. This is one time we don't want people to pick us out of a crowd." He stood. "Thanks for not getting me eaten this time, Pearl."

She smirked. "Anytime, Rafe. Too bad you're heading right into the snake's mouth. Enjoy being eaten."

CHAPTER TWELVE

A large neon outline of a horse surrounded the glowing words Bucking Bronco on the huge sign standing next to a dingy bar. Cars and motorcycles almost filled the entire parking lot despite it only being early evening. The thin walls could only do so much to muffle the loud rock music pounding inside.

Izzie kept thinking back to what Pearl had told her. Rumors of dark forces on the move were common. Even if the rumor mill overstated the problem, that didn't mean the rumors lacked any basis.

Rafe groaned and rubbed his temples. "It's not a good day for me and music."

"I could use a spell to filter sound for you," Izzie offered.

"Nah. I don't want anything that draws extra attention to me. I need to react like I'm getting blasted with loud, hearing-shredding music."

"Your ears, your choice."

Izzie didn't care about Pearl's or the bar's musical

choices. She cared about the heavy levels of magic pouring out of the place. Nothing about the muscle cars, choppers, and cowboy hat-favoring crowd screamed magicals hangout from the outside.

The PDA had identified the bar as a location frequented by magicals, but not necessarily the most law-abiding ones. She'd never been to the place before, although she had read about it in reports.

"You ready?" Izzie asked.

"This is where he told me to meet him." Rafe frowned. "The question is are you ready?"

"I always wanted to throw somebody through a window of a biker bar." Izzie rubbed her palm with her fist. "I'll need a good wind spell to do it. Ah. Memories."

Rafe laughed. "We'll try to avoid that tonight." He walked toward the door and stopped after a few steps. "Just a question. Have you thrown somebody through a bar window before? Just not a biker bar?"

"Do taverns count? I didn't technically throw them. It's more I shoved them through with a spell. Trust me. The guy had it coming. Dark wizard assassin."

"Gotcha."

Rafe put on an exaggerated smile as he opened the door to the bar. He'd slicked back his hair and put on a nice pair of slacks and a shirt that showed off his toned arms. Izzie had thrown on a pair of jeans and a faded T-shirt. Neither would win a fashion competition, but their clothes no longer screamed federal agents.

Izzie entered the bar first. The blaring music assaulted her ears. She put on her best winsome smile for Rafe. Anybody watching them needed to be convinced the couple were there on a date and not two federal agents looking for an informant.

Rowdy men and women laughed, drank, and ate at their tables. Nobody paid attention to the new arrivals. A small group of people danced in a corner. A busty waitress in a tied-off shirt presenting the ultimate in plunging necklines navigated the packed room with grace and an easy smile.

A drunken man's elbow shoved a glass off the table. The waitress caught it with her foot and kicked it back onto the tabletop, where it landed with a click. Nearby patrons cheered and clapped.

"You better not have done that on purpose," the waitress scolded. She winked at the customer. "The boss won't stand for too much trouble."

Izzie whispered a chant under her breath. The magical flows of the room shifted from mere sensations to visible trails and active flows. Nobody reacted to the spell. Enchantments covered a good chunk of the people in the room, including the waitress. A strong, clear wall-sized enchantment separated the bar's main space from a far corner in the back.

She took Rafe's arm and leaned in to whisper, "Far left corner. They're hiding something there."

Rafe stared that way. "A misdirection spell for non-magicals, I'm betting," he whispered.

"How do you know? I'd have to examine the spell flows to figure that out."

Rafe grinned. "Effect is more important than cause this time. It's hard for me to concentrate and look that way. I can only do it because I expect it and you told me. That screams misdirection spell."

"Oh. Good observations." Izzie eyed the boring-looking corner. "Misdirection and illusion make for a good combo."

When a stern-looking cowboy eyed them with a frown, Izzie giggled and spoke above a whisper. "Oh, babe! Sometimes you're too much."

Rafe smirked and whispered, "Don't try so hard. It ends up obvious."

"I'm many things, but I never claimed to be a good actress."

Rafe led Izzie by the arm to the back corner. They passed through the wall-sized enchantment. A couple of patrons watched with interest.

The music died down, muffled, and the rest of the building grew blurry and indistinct. Magical flows marked an invisible door written in something resembling a dwarven script. The letters glowed and reshaped themselves into English.

Bring no trouble here, and you may rest your bones for a short while. Bring trouble here, and your bones will rest here forever.

"I wonder how long places like this will last." Izzie stared at the text.

"You mean secret magical gathering spots?" Rafe asked.

"They already feel like a throwback."

"Aren't you the woman who went to a hidden magic school?"

"That's different. That's about safety for kids." Izzie shrugged. "Not that my school was entirely safe when I think about everything that happened there." She shook her head. "But that was…"

"Don't say your fault," Rafe interrupted.

"It was Alison's too." Izzie grinned.

"Too bad she's always so busy. I'd love to meet her someday." Rafe motioned to the door. "Aren't these about safety, too?"

"I'm not sure anymore. The magical community being clannish and inward is why we have to rely on scum like Finnegan for help finding a magical killer. Keeping secrets means being less safe."

Izzie reached toward the door. A handle appeared. She tugged it open, revealing a whole new bar, but one far more dimly lit by oil lamps floating in the air. Cowboy hats and boots maintained their fashion domination in the new area, but the music changed.

The vibe and overall style were similar to the conventional rock outside, but the instrumentation was more exotic, and the singer's guttural voice was inhuman. There were more pointed ears and obvious non-human bodies, including a cowboy dwarf demonstrating his mastery of a hovering bucking bull statue made of pure bronze.

Other patrons included obvious old-school magicals such as a pale wizard in a robe. His staff rested behind him to mesh with the new. A silver-haired, dark-skinned drow sat at the end of the bar wearing a cowboy hat and drinking beer. He chatted quietly with a furry humanoid that vaguely resembled a bipedal koala. Izzie didn't recognize his conversation partner's species.

Rafe tugged on her arm and led her across the room to a hooded man sitting in front of a pitcher of a dark purple liquid with a strong, acrid scent. He sipped from his glass. Two other empty glasses sat on the table.

Nobody paid Izzie and Rafe much attention. Rafe pulled out a chair for Izzie. She sat and faked another smile after he joined her and the hooded man. Izzie sensed an uptick in magic. The music and background chatter faded until it wasn't much louder than a whisper.

"That saved me the trouble," she commented.

The figure lowered his hood, revealing a bald, sharp-featured man with wide-set eyes. His grin at Rafe highlighted his long, eerie, fang-like incisors. Izzie stared at him before realizing he was looking back with yellow eyes with vertical pupils.

The last time they'd talked, the man had been far less obvious about his true nature as a snake shifter. It wasn't a surprise. They'd met in a non-magical bar and tolerance didn't always extend as easily to all types of magicals. Many mundane humans could still tolerate the beauty of a light elf far easier than tolerating animal shifters, even ones whose features didn't bleed over to their human forms.

It didn't help that many magicals still associated and blamed shifters for their dark magic origins from centuries ago. Someone like Finnegan, who straddled the line between the worlds of dark and light magic, didn't do much to offset the suspicion and stereotypes.

"It's been a while, Finnegan," Rafe greeted. He poured Izzie and himself a cup of the strange purple liquor. "Your information was helpful with that other case. You helped the city more than you know."

Finnegan took another sip of his drink. "You say all

that, but you're looking right through me." He grinned. "What's wrong? You don't trust me anymore, Martinez?"

"I trust you'll give me good information when paid." Rafe swirled the liquid without taking a drink. "Otherwise, no, I don't trust you. That what you want to hear?"

"It's good to know you're not an idiot. I don't like working with idiots. But I've got premium goods for you tonight. You're going to love this shit." He licked his lips. "I'll even give you a discount. Five percent off my normal asking price for high-priority tips. Aren't I a generous man?"

Izzie frowned. "Since when are you so generous?"

Finnegan gulped down his liquid and let out a long, satisfied sigh. "I don't like shapeshifters. They creep me out. I'm cutting you a break to help catch a creeper."

Izzie scoffed. "You don't like shapeshifters. Isn't that hypocritical?"

"We aren't the same, Berens." Finnegan leaned forward, blinking first his nictating membranes, then his eyelids. "I'm an animal shifter, not a shapeshifter. Don't get it confused. I've been blessed with a permanent superiority, a fusion of two creatures. I don't have to use magic to twist myself."

He sneered. "Or is the PDA following the old ways? You don't trust shifters? You think we're waiting around for dark wizards to say, 'Come help us take over.'"

Izzie rolled her eyes. "I had a…" She took a deep breath and chose her words carefully. "I have a good friend who is a shifter. We went to school together, and I'd trust him with my life."

She scoffed. "You're a big pile of garbage because that's

your nature. It's got nothing to do with you being a shifter, Finnegan. You'd be a scumbag as a wizard, a non-magical human, or a dwarf, a troll, or a ferret."

Rafe gave her a look of warning. "We're here for information, not to relitigate the past."

Finnegan laughed and gestured at Izzie. "Same old, same old, ten, twenty, thirty years later. Everywhere there's trouble, a Berens woman is stirring it up. It was inevitable becoming what you are, considering how important your mom and d—"

"We're not here to talk about my family," Izzie interrupted in a tight voice. "We're here because you said you have a tip for us."

Rafe set his glass down. "You want your money. We need your tip. Don't waste our time, Finnegan. You want to mess with my partner? Do it on a night we're not hunting one of your hated shapeshifters."

Finnegan hissed. "I have my pride, Martinez. Don't push me."

"You have your bank account." Rafe inclined his head toward the door. "Should we leave? We have a killer out there. We don't have time to sit around drinking whatever this purple crap is."

"Your shapeshifter's brought nasty attention to this town and the underworld." Finnegan glanced around the room. "Nasty attention that not everyone wants to hear, even those of us in the shadows. A name keeps popping up, a name I've only heard whispered in the dark corners where you precious little good boys and girls don't like to play. Dead bodies and trouble come with the name. Too many dead bodies mean not as much money to be had."

"What's the name that's worrying you?" Izzie demanded.

"The Arcane Syndicate," Finnegan whispered. He smiled and spoke louder. "Now here's the weird part. Rumors and whispers are all over out there. I have people saying this Arcane Syndicate is hunting the shapeshifter. Other people say the shapeshifter works for them.

"One thing's clear. Nobody was talking about the Arcane Syndicate until that shapeshifter showed up, and now these last couple of days, the noise is loud, almost like people are yelling. The Syndicate is in town, they're causing trouble, and the shapeshifter is at the heart of it all."

Izzie almost asked Finnegan about the Glorious Foundation. She averted her eyes instead. She didn't want to give Finnegan useful intel to pass along to his more criminally inclined customers.

"What is it, Berens?" Finnegan asked.

"Nothing."

Rafe frowned. "I haven't heard of the Arcane Syndicate. You haven't mentioned them before."

"I didn't have a reason to." Finnegan shrugged. "I give you information relevant to your cases, no more, no less. We're not friends, Martinez. We're business associates. If it makes you feel better, the Syndicate hasn't sniffed around Austin before."

"Tell us more about the Arcane Syndicate," Izzie requested.

"No."

Izzie glared at him. "Excuse me?"

Finnegan shook his head. "I don't know much more

and don't want to be involved in this case more than that. I like your money. I like my life more."

Izzie scoffed. "We could make you talk."

"No, you can't." Finnegan laughed. "You agents have your rules. And you're a Berens. Everybody knows you Berens are good girls, no matter how tough you talk."

"Tell that to all the dark wizards I've killed." Izzie glared at him. "Tell it to the Seventh Order that I wiped out. I'm not letting rogue magicals hurt other innocent people. If I have to bend the rules to do it, I will. You understand me, snake?"

Finnegan's nostrils flared, and he laughed. "Keep that fire, Berens. You'll need it." He stood and shook his head. "I've told you what I know and what I'm willing to pass along. Whispers, rumors, suggestions. These are my currency in my world. Truth and justice, that's for your world." He leaned over with a mocking wave at Rafe and Izzie. "Have a good night. Try not to die. I'm saving for a new car, and I need more money from you." He stared at Rafe expectantly.

Rafe snorted and pulled out his phone. He poked around on it for a half-minute before looking up. "It's in your standard account."

"A pleasure, Martinez. Berens, I wish I could say the same." Finnegan waved one last time and wandered away from the table. "Have fun, you two."

Izzie clenched her fists under the table. "You know that guy's going to go and sell the fact the PDA is looking into the Arcane Syndicate to every piece of crap he can."

"It doesn't matter," Rafe replied. "Whoever this Arcane Syndicate is, they'd already know the investigation into the murder of Thaddeus Blackstone is a PDA matter. Finnegan wouldn't be giving up anything that matters."

"That makes you think." Izzie watched Finnegan until he left the room. "What if he's only giving us information about the Arcane Syndicate because he doesn't think it'll matter that we know?"

"We have a name now. A name that's not from a dead organization from fourteen hundred and forty-five years ago. That's better than we had before we came in here." He picked up his glass and sipped. He gagged. "This tastes like somebody squeezed out the sweat from my socks after a long work day." He set the glass down. "We should get out of here and see what we can find in the database. I'll also pass it along to analysis support. Maybe the infomancers can find something we can't."

Izzie glared at her office computer. "We don't have sufficient clearance? What the hell is this?"

Rafe frowned. "This happened before, remember? That smuggling case? Something about NSA nonsense. 'Compartmentalization of national security-related intelligence.' It's not analysis support's fault. They're passing along what they found."

She yanked out her phone and dialed Bill. "To hell with that. If the NSA wants to come and hunt the shapeshifter, they should get their asses down here with their people."

"Has something happened, Berens?" Bill sounded as annoyed as Izzie felt.

"We have the name of an organization that might be

related to the shapeshifter. The Arcane Syndicate. Analysis support claims we don't have access to info about them. Do you know this Arcane Syndicate?"

"Nope, but obviously somebody in the government does. I'll have to make a few calls and send a few messages. I guarantee I'll have you approved for info about them by the morning."

CHAPTER THIRTEEN

Izzie munched on a donut and sipped from a cup of coffee as she waited at a long table in the briefing room. Bill had sent a notice to Katya, Izzie, Rafe, and a handful of other staff including some from field support that he'd be hosting an early morning meeting on the Arcane Syndicate. The PDA had a lead that didn't require Xelius or anyone else to cooperate. They couldn't let it go now.

Izzie yawned and tried not to stretch. She had more trouble sleeping the night before, worried that she was passing over an opportunity or missing a clue that would help her and Rafe track the shapeshifter before the next attack. Being frustrated over investigation restraints didn't serve any useful purpose. She needed to figure out ways around the roadblocks.

"It'll be fine, Izzie," Rafe murmured behind her. He had bags under his eyes. "Bill will get us the access we need, and we can move forward. We're closing in, and the shapeshifter doesn't know it."

"He's out there," Izzie muttered. "He's still laughing at us and planning to hurt someone. I won't let bureaucracy get in the way."

Katya flicked her thumb and fingers one by one in a line while staring into the distance. Her face was a perfect mask of boredom. "I have evidence to examine. This is inefficient."

Beside her, a thin, bespectacled man named Allan looked up from his phone. He was the senior drone support technician in the field support division. "We've been trying to see if we can adjust the drone sensor sensitivity. I can't promise anything, but we're doing our best. We're installing the sensors into replacement drones, but we need time for finetuning."

Izzie shook her head. "We appreciate everything you're doing in field support, but I think we've lost our chance at finding our shapeshifter by trying to detect his magical signature. That's not your fault. I let him slip through our fingers." She clenched her jaw. "Sorry about that."

"We both let him slip through, Izzie," Rafe countered. "We'll get him. Coming that close to getting caught means he'll be more cautious, but you and I both believe he still has a mission to accomplish."

"He's going to drain a park of life to strengthen himself."

Rafe grimaced. "I meant to tell you about that." He reached for his phone and brought up an article.

Police are transferring park defoliation investigation to PDA, claim no general risk to public.

"A bunch of dead trees and other plants in two different parks across town from one another," Rafe added. "It likely happened yesterday or the day before."

"At least we know he's still in town. This means big trouble."

Rafe shook his head. "His techniques make him more dangerous than normal. They don't make him immortal. Now we know what to expect. It won't go down like last time."

Bill burst through the door with his RBF in full effect. He slammed the door closed behind him and dropped into a seat. "I'll make this quick, people. Everyone in the room has been granted limited access to information about the Arcane Syndicate in the main research database, and I'm working on getting Luisa from analysis support approved. I've reviewed the relevant information and liaised with other agencies to ensure we get priority access to anything useful that might be helpful."

Rafe frowned. "We're still in charge of the investigation, aren't we?"

"Yes. The relevant agencies only cared about keeping their sources and relationships with relevant overseas agencies quiet. We'll pass along our investigative notes to them once this is all over. Basic references to the Arcane Syndicate are now officially declassified, so you can ask your informants more about them if you think it'll be helpful."

Izzie folded her arms. "I love how we have to tell them everything, but we have to beg for information from them."

"Inefficient," Katya murmured, still playing games with her thumb and forefinger.

"Welcome to the US government." Bill looked around the table with a deep scowl before clearing his throat. "The quicker we catch this guy, the better for this case and other investigations. The long and short is the Arcane Syndicate is suspected to have, but has not yet conclusively been proven, to have been involved in multiple incidents of magical terrorism in recent years."

"Who are the Arcane Syndicate?" Izzie asked. "I've never heard of them before, even when I was swimming in dark wizard muck full-time. And what do they have to do with our shapeshifter?"

"They're a shadowy organization. Their history and membership remain unclear. While they've only come to the recent attention of US authorities, there is evidence they've been around for centuries, if not longer. They appear to be an Earth-founded organization focused on recruiting and controlling rogue magical beings for their own ends."

"Like the dark families crossed with the Glorious Foundation."

Bill shook his head. "This isn't about certain bloodlines, not according to our available intelligence. We don't have clear information on the goals of the Arcane Syndicate, only that they are ruthless and will use whatever tools they can."

"Are they a continuation of the Glorious Foundation?" Rafe asked. "It's like Izzie said. They seem to share similar goals, and we found that Foundation void amulet."

"Hell if I know. Hell if anybody knows. That's for you all to figure out." Bill scoffed.

"From what your research uncovered, that Glorious Foundation was more an Oriceran thing, but the Syndicate started here on Earth. Convergent goals. It might be a coincidence, or maybe they think of themselves as the Foundation's successors. I don't know how that helps us find them, but it might help us better understand them in the future."

Izzie thought through everything they'd uncovered during the investigation. "Or it might be the Glorious Foundation knew or had something the Syndicate wants, and the amulet is the first step or a tool to figuring that out? Or it's a tool they need for something else, a ritual. It wouldn't be the first time I've run into a mysterious artifact that was important to something far more terrible than you'd suspect."

Rafe looked her way. "You think the amulet is a clue or a tool?" He nodded. "You could be right. The Glorious Foundation was known for its sophisticated keys and locks. There are many recovered references to their so-called locks of truth and locks of fate. There's a big debate about what that meant in practice and how much of it might be a metaphor."

"A key to another artifact? A hidden map to an important magical spot? It could be either." Izzie shook her head. "I'm throwing things out there. I'm not sure. All we know right now is the amulet doesn't do much to help individual magicals."

Katya still looked bored. "If the amulet is that important, won't they come looking for it?"

Bill scoffed. "There's no way they'd be arrogant enough

to try raiding the PDA. I'll assign additional security to secure storage until the case is over, just in case."

"From what you told us about that amulet, they can't track it using magic," Rafe reminded Katya. "But you also said it's not magical in itself."

"It's anti-magical," Katya corrected. "That's the whole point of its construction."

"Maybe we could consult Dax," Izzie suggested. She'd thought about checking with her gnome artisan friend the same day she and Rafe visited Pearl. Finnegan's call and the subsequent meeting with the informant preempted that.

Katya shook her head. "That gnome is clever enough, but his specialty is more modern-style technomagic. The void amulet is a product of techniques from over a millennium ago."

Bill cleared his throat. "We're going to want to limit access to the evidence unless you can convince me your contact will offer us actionable leads."

"Setting Dax or any other consultants aside, it's the object itself, the physical object, that's needed," Rafe concluded. "That's what I've taken away from everything I've read. Either that amulet or something with the same physical characteristics."

"That would be accurate to the best of my understanding," Katya confirmed.

Allan sighed. "Does this void amulet emit any non-magical energy signals? We could put additional conventional sensors on the drones."

"No." Katya shook her head.

Allan frowned. "There's not much we can do about

adjusting the sensors if we're supposed to look for more of these amulets."

Rafe looked sympathetic. "If I had to gamble, I'd bet the only void amulet in this entire state is the one locked up in our secure evidence storage. I'm talking about the shapeshifter coming up with a substitute."

Izzie's brow lifted. "I doubt our shapeshifter can turn himself into an amulet even with life banking that consumes every tree and bush in the city."

"That's also not what I'm getting at." Rafe looked at Bill with a pleading expression. "You mentioned in a previous discussion…" He cleared his throat and paused for a few seconds. "You mentioned the suspect might be associated with a robbery attempt but said the victim wasn't cooperating."

Izzie wasn't sure if Rafe asking that way violated Bill's prohibition about keeping the previous victims a secret. The farther the case moved along, the more untenable that position grew. She appreciated and understood the difficult politics of balancing the magical and non-magical communities. That didn't free the previous victims of their duty to help the PDA stop a dangerous rogue magical criminal.

Bill nodded. "The victim never passed along any other information about the robbery. This is not a situation where we can push."

"What if it was the amulet?" Rafe asked.

"It could be. We don't have that information at this time. They aren't going to tell us if we ask. Trust me. I already did twice, including after the Blackstone incident."

"What if we've been going about this the wrong way?"

Izzie asked. "If the amulet is important, somebody has to know about it. Before, we were trying to find the link between the Glorious Foundation and the suspect, but that could be starting at the end of the path. We're missing all the candy a nice witch sprinkled along the way."

Katya turned her way. "The object itself is more important than the organization with this theory?"

"Exactly." Izzie gestured at Rafe. "I don't know what the point of the amulet is, other than it might be a symbol, map, or a key, and even coming to that conclusion involves tons of guesswork. We need more information from somebody who would know. We need to consult an expert on ancient Oriceran artifacts specializing in that era."

Bill frowned. "That's no guarantee your theoretical expert can help. Are you claiming Dax is that type of expert?"

Izzie shook her head. "No, Katya's right. Dax wouldn't be the right fit. I meant someone else. I was thinking more of a historian."

She brought up the browser on her phone. She entered search keywords with all the excitement of someone on a dating app on a Saturday night and let out a satisfied hum when a webpage for Central Magical Academy came up. She clicked through the webpage onto a staff profile.

"There just so happens to be a local expert on Oriceran artifacts from that period who lives in town, a professor of magical history named Gareth Roth. He's a wizard and instructor at Central Magical Academy."

"Aren't they supposed to be pretty prestigious?" Rafe asked.

"They're a newer magical academy. They have a good

reputation and made a big deal about being open and interested in new techniques and magical ideas, with instruction for everything from younger magicals up to advanced graduate-level specialists. They're closer to a prep school feeding directly into an on-campus college than a high school like the School of Necessary Magic." She shrugged. "That's what I've read. I've never been there."

Bill's RBF relaxed with such subtlety only Izzie and others who'd known him for a while could tell. "Okay, we have a magical egghead who knows history. What's that get us? Now that we almost cornered the suspect, I need you and your partner to be more focused, not running around questioning every egghead in town with half-formed theories."

"Understood, Bill." Izzie skimmed his list of publications. "But listen to this. Among other things, Roth recently published a paper called 'On the Complexities of Anti-magic-Magic Artifact Interfaces in Ancient and Modern Artifact Design: Looking Backward to Find Pathways Forward in Traditional and Modern Magic.' It was published only three weeks ago." She looked up from her phone. "That sounds like he'd be right up our alley."

"That's interesting timing," Rafe noted. "He published this paper three weeks ago, and our shapeshifter showed up not long after."

"The suspect's a shapeshifter," Bill countered. "For all we know, he's been sitting around for six months in town working at Whataburger."

Izzie clicked through to load the paper on her phone. She searched for "Glorious Foundation" and let out a knowing scoff when the search returned multiple hits.

"Yes. This is definitely our guy. The paper's full of references to the Foundation."

Bill stood. "If you're so sure, go talk to him." He nodded at Allan. "Field support should continue trying to refine the sensors. It'd be easier if we could track this shapeshifter down and throw the cuffs on. Katya, is there anything else you think forensics can pull off the existing evidence?"

"Talking to the scholar could help direct our examinations," Katya replied. "More evidence is always welcome."

"In addition to more armed guards, we'll keep the amulet secure in an anti-magic vault when you're not working on it," Bill ordered. "We can never be too careful with shapeshifters running around." He looked at Izzie and Rafe. "Berens, Martinez, get something useful out of your egghead. We need the shapeshifter under more pressure. The more we squeeze, the more mistakes he'll make."

"We'll set up a meeting," Rafe replied. "We should probably read his papers first. This will be interesting."

Izzie groaned. "Why do you sound so excited?"

Izzie had always considered herself pretty smart, but slogging through dense paragraph after paragraph of magical academic work challenged her, including Professor Roth's obsession with using jargony replacement words like hypomagic instead of anti-magic.

"Oh," Rafe commented. "This is it. Are you on Section 3.1 yet?"

"One second."

Her gaze slid to the relevant paragraph. She grinned at

the header, not needing specialist knowledge to understand.

"The Ancient Use of Hypomagic Artifacts as Keys in Complicated Magical Systems: A Glorious Foundation Void Amulet Example," Izzie read aloud. "Yes. I think we're on the right track."

CHAPTER FOURTEEN

Luscious lawns gave Central Magical Academy's campus a lively feel. Happy, well-adjusted-looking young teens in color-blocked school uniforms mixed with young adults in robes, a small concession to the traditionalists. Covered arched pathways led between the buildings. The mundane flavor of the campus aesthetics struck Izzie as they walked past the bubbling fountains and modern buildings covered with walls of windows.

"This place is a little different than my school," Izzie admitted.

Rafe chuckled. "Sure, we didn't have so many younger kids at my college, but otherwise this reminds me of that."

"My school was more obviously magical. I got used to it when I was there, but at the same time, you would never forget you were in a magic school."

"A magic school hidden from the general public," Rafe reminded her. "If a big place went full magical in Austin, people would be uncomfortable."

"That's true."

Izzie spotted a teen girl, around fourteen or fifteen, holding a remote control with two D-pads and watching the sky. Other students surrounded her. A jeweled bird automaton circled overhead, turning and flapping its wings in response to her careful control. After a couple of passes, the jeweled bird plummeted to the ground.

The girl put her palm to her forehead. "I knew it wouldn't be able to maintain a magical charge for that long. I told him so! That idiot!"

Rafe nodded toward the girl. "Do you miss that kind of thing?"

"We had our good times in school. And our dark times. It's hard to separate them, you know? I have so many happy memories, but I dealt with awful things at the school thanks to the dark wizard hunters."

"That's the advantage of a place like this," Rafe observed. "It's out in the open, which means security can be open. Sunlight is the best disinfectant. Any dark wizards show up, the PDA, FBI, and cops can all come. Heck, the National Guard can pop in for fun."

"I don't know. Sunshine as a disinfectant? Sometimes it's about tossing the monsters somewhere so cold and dark they freeze to death." She pointed at a tall office building across the lawn. "Roth's office is in the main administration building. We should hurry before we need disinfectant."

Izzie and Rafe stepped up to a reception desk. The main administration building's interior offered the same modern office building banality of most of the campus except for a magical self-moving model of the solar system floating in the main lobby. The concentration of obvious non-humans was higher, including an overweight pixie in cat-eye glasses, a beehive hairdo, and a dress straight out of 1952. She sat in a tiny chair on top of the front desk. A nameplate on the desk read Madge, Senior Receptionist.

Madge held a tiny physical magazine written in a swirling language Izzie didn't recognize. Judging by the cover, it was a pixie-centered fashion magazine.

"Excuse me." Izzie reached into her pocket to pull out her badge. "Special Agent Berens, PDA. We're here to consult with Professor Roth."

Madge looked up from her magazine with all the disinterest of someone who should have retired two hundred years prior. Her voice was deep and gravelly. "I'll beep him and let him know you're coming, hon. Third door on the left." She nodded toward the hallway and lifted her magazine again.

Izzie and Rafe made their way to the hallway. Her partner's chuckle stopped her before they reached Roth's door.

"What is it?"

"I was thinking a pixie receptionist is more what people expect at a magic school." Rafe grinned. "I swear with a voice like that, she must chain-smoke at home. Did you have a pixie receptionist at your school?"

"We had all kinds of different types of people." Izzie shrugged. "We didn't have to worry about scaring anyone who was quote-unquote normal, so... You can imagine."

They arrived at Gareth Roth's already open door. The man sat in a black robe inside a cramped office filled to the brim with bookshelves, scrolls, and ancient engraved tablets of varying materials. Stacks of books lay on the floor and the desk. He looked up with weary yet kindly brown eyes.

"You are the agents from the PDA?" His voice held a hesitant quality. He forced a smile, although it trembled.

Izzie walked over and offered her hand. "Special Agent Berens and this is my partner, Special Agent Martinez. We appreciate you taking the time to speak with us, Professor."

Gareth leaned forward to give her hand a weak shake and offered the same to Rafe before sighing. "Sorry, I didn't think to bring any chairs in. I can get some if you think this will take long. I've never dealt with the PDA before."

"It's okay." Izzie closed the door. "We can stand."

"Berens," Gareth repeated. Comprehension dawned on his face. "I didn't think of it before when you contacted me before. Berens as in Leira Berens?"

Izzie nodded with a tight smile. "She's my mother."

"I met her in passing, only briefly, years ago." Gareth shook his head. "All that derring-do isn't my calling. But you're in the PDA now. You're protecting people. That's good. Like parents, like daughter, protecting the magical and non-magical worlds."

Rafe smiled. "That's right."

"Now, what can I do for you fine agents of the PDA?" Gareth leaned back in his chair. He put his trembling hands together. "I can't imagine any of my work would be relevant to your jobs. I'm a dusty old historian. Even most academics find what I do too niche to be of interest."

"Is everything all right, Professor?" Rafe asked. "You seem nervous."

"Who wouldn't be nervous talking to the PDA? Especially when you haven't done anything wrong and can't figure out how you would be relevant to their concerns."

"The PDA exists only to contain rogue magic that hurts innocent people," Rafe replied.

Gareth swallowed. "Of course. I don't intend to insult you. I only want you to understand that I've lived my life in a way to avoid danger. The presence of PDA agents implies danger."

"Your recent paper caught our attention," Izzie explained.

Gareth blinked and stopped shaking. Wonder filled his voice as he spoke. "It did? My paper 'On the Complexities of Anti-magic-Magic Interfaces in Ancient and Modern Artifact Design: Pathways Forward in Traditional and Modern Magic?'"

"That's the one," Izzie confirmed with a flourish of her hand for emphasis. "That's the exact one. Once we read that paper, we knew you were the man we needed to consult."

"May I ask why?" Obvious disbelief colored Gareth's voice.

"You've done previous research on inherent anti-magic artifacts," Rafe answered.

"Yes, that was in my paper." Gareth pursed his lips. "If this is about that importation matter concerning the Ogelian artifacts, I can assure you that all my permits were in order. I can get the documentation right now if you don't believe me. We have specialists in administration for that sort of matter. CMA prides itself on obeying the relevant laws and regulations concerning the importation of magical items."

Izzie tried her best attempt at a soothing smile. "No one's accusing you of anything, Professor. We have questions for you as an expert. This specifically concerns void amulets of the Glorious Foundation era."

Gareth's eyes widened. "The amulet I examined and referenced in my paper was lent to me by a local collector after considerable cajoling and the aid of a third party. The collector was helpful but also adamant that I not publicly advertise their name since they didn't want to be harassed about the amulet by more unsavory types."

"These amulets are rare, right?" Izzie asked.

Gareth looked at her like she'd said the silliest thing he'd ever heard. "Exceedingly so. I was blessed to have the opportunity to examine one. I've wanted to examine one for decades."

Izzie glanced at Rafe. "Our robbery victim."

Rafe nodded. "I can't imagine it wasn't."

"Robbery?" Gareth gasped and put a hand over his mouth. "Somebody stole the void amulet?"

"It's all right, Professor," Izzie replied. "We recovered it. It's now safe and secure in our custody."

Gareth sighed in relief. "That's wonderful news, but if you've already recovered it, why are you here?"

"Because we wondered if you could give us more insight into the void amulets. There was a whole section in your paper about using them as keys. That may relate to a case we're working. We had a theory that the amulet might be wanted as a key or map, something of that nature."

"A key. Yes. I see." He nodded and relaxed enough for a

smile. "Yes, it's a difficult and convoluted process to make mechanisms that worked with such artifacts, but they could prove useful when dealing with powerful magical beings. You could protect people, items, whatever from said beings through a combination of such artifacts in conjunction with appropriate spellcraft."

"What about alternatives? If you lose a void amulet you needed, is it possible to do the equivalent of sticking a token in for a quarter?"

"Harmonic oscillation interference," Rafe quoted.

Izzie remembered the statement from the paper, but she didn't understand much of the paragraph around it.

"Exactly!" Gareth shook a finger. "We discuss void amulets as if they are pure anti-magic, but they aren't. That's why I was trying to coin and promote the term hypomagic in the paper. In a sense, their immunity to magic gives them a unique role in magical artifacts and systems, almost like resistors or capacitors in modern electronics systems. Not fully analogous, but you get the idea."

"That sounds like with enough knowledge of how those systems work, someone might be able to come up with a solution," Izzie countered. "Hypomagic lockpicking. Every attack has a defense. Every spell has a counter. Every lock has a way to open it."

Gareth's smile faded. He trembled again. "Oh. Yes. Of course. With sufficient understanding of anything, that's theoretically true. But you have to understand this is all theoretical anyway.

"It was accomplished in the past, but that's not the same thing as us understanding how to do it anymore. The greatest experts in this type of system, the Glorious Foundation, were annihilated. And only..." He gasped. "That is, i-it's only recently that researchers such as myself are starting to revisit these t-techniques. It could take d-decades or c-centuries for us to fully understand them again."

Izzie narrowed her eyes. "Is there a problem, Professor?"

"No, of course not."

"Are you sure?"

"Y-yes. Why wouldn't I be?"

"Because there's something about using the amulet to unlock stuff that you're holding back. You seemed really nervous when we came in, then you relaxed for a bit and got nervous again. I don't think this is about you being uncomfortable with the PDA. It's like you remembered something you didn't want us to know."

Gareth's eyes widened. "I can assure you, Agent Berens, that's not the truth."

Rafe's brow lifted. "You have anything else you want to share, Professor?"

He swallowed. "I'm not involved with any forbidden magic. I explained why I was nervous. I'm not a criminal, and I resent being t-treated like one."

Izzie frowned at him. "That's not the same thing as saying you've done nothing wrong."

"I...I've done nothing wrong. I thought I was being helpful."

"Then you have nothing to be afraid of by cooperating with us. We're trying to find a killer. Why don't you want to help us? Why are you holding out on us?"

Rafe put his hand on Izzie's shoulder and stepped

forward. "If there's anything you want to tell us, Professor Roth, now is the time. We can't help you if you're not honest with us. Sometimes people can get caught up in things beyond their control. We understand that."

Gareth started hyperventilating. "I didn't know. You have to understand that."

"Know what?"

"That this would lead to anything."

"What are you saying?"

Gareth closed his eyes and took a deep breath. "A few months ago, I received an enchanted disappearing letter that claimed to be from a wizard who insisted on using a pseudonymous title, the Patron. The sender set up a spell system so I could send letters back to him. He was interested in my research. He said he could help me uncover rare and expensive materials I needed to move it along.

"I was ecstatic. It's been hard to source the materials needed, and although my department head supports my research, my resources are limited at CMA. My progress has been glacial."

Izzie rolled her eyes. "Yes, none of that sounds suspicious at all."

"I spent years having to be careful," Gareth snapped. "Until recently, many completely non-dangerous magical reagents and other materials were illegal for direct import because of the silly overreaction to magic by Earth governments." He scoffed. "Yes, we had our ways and places to source them, but we've had to balance living openly with ignorant rules and regulations that made our lives unnecessarily difficult."

"I get it. You have a sob story." Izzie circled her finger in the air. "I want to know how your sob story ends up with Thaddeus Blackstone stabbed downtown. Because he can't have a sob story now that he's dead."

Gareth averted his eyes and lowered his voice. "My new source was very helpful. The Patron made me aware of local members of the magical community who had things I needed and were less interested in obeying mundane regulatory constraints.

"It was at the Patron's direction that I was able to contact Xelius to borrow the amulet for my research. Xelius insisted on many restrictions and his people were always there at home when I was doing my experiments, breathing down my neck. Still, it was enough that I was able to achieve proof-of-concept for my paper."

Rafe smiled at Izzie. "Xelius."

"It feels good to be right." Izzie refocused on Gareth. "Now I get why he didn't want to talk to the PDA."

Rafe nodded toward the door. "You performed your experiments at home?"

"My ward and ritual arrays are already there," Gareth replied. "I was doing this research before I joined the CMA faculty. It's easier to do it at home than to spend months setting them up here and wasting space. My department head doesn't care where I work as long as I get results."

"Where does Thaddeus Blackstone fit into all of this?" Izzie narrowed her eyes. "Because he wasn't robbed. That was an assassination by a shapeshifter who didn't bother to take anything off his body."

"A shapeshifter?" Gareth's eyes widened. "I heard he'd died. I didn't realize a shapeshifter was involved."

"The suspect is a shapeshifter using dangerous

enhancement magic," Izzie added. "Since we don't know what their true appearance is, the shapeshifter could be the Patron or work for him. We have…evidence that points to this shapeshifter being interested in void amulets, but we don't understand why the shapeshifter would murder Thaddeus Blackstone. What about you?"

"I-I don't know!" Gareth shouted. His shoulders slumped. "Thaddeus helped me avoid the aforementioned unnecessarily cumbersome import restrictions. The Patron recommended I speak with him about getting things I had been too afraid to ask for. You have to understand none of it was dangerous. It just was taking too much time and money to obey all the rules."

"Alchemy ingredients, low-level artifacts, that kind of thing?" Rafe clarified.

Gareth groaned. "Yes. Without his help, I wouldn't have been able to gather everything I needed to get my experiments done so quickly. It was never anything dangerous. I assure you."

Rafe frowned. "Why didn't you contact the authorities when you'd heard he'd been killed?"

"B-because…" Gareth sighed. He looked down at his hands.

"Holding back information that will help us catch the shapeshifter means you might be charged as an accessory," Izzie warned.

"He was late with certain reagent requests, nothing special, just things I needed. It delayed my research." Gareth shrugged. "He wasn't returning my messages. I was doing everything through him directly because of the extralegal nature of my requests."

"Then he got stabbed to death in public?"

"I tried to convince myself it was a coincidence. Yes, our activities were technically illegal, but we weren't hardened criminals or dark wizards plotting to undermine the world. I've been publishing my research results. They aren't secrets. I had no reason to assume they were linked."

Izzie frowned. "Or you didn't want to get questioned by the authorities because you were breaking the law. And maybe breaking the law in worse ways than you've admitted."

Gareth averted his eyes. "I believe, or at least I convinced myself, that Thaddeus had involved himself in something far darker than sourcing reagents and artifacts for me. I didn't see the point in coming forward and ruining my career over something that had nothing to do with me. I didn't want to believe that anything I was studying could lead to death. It's not dangerous magic. It's the opposite. It's hypomagic."

Izzie held up two fingers. "Xelius and Blackstone. That's two targets linked directly to you. Professor, you're living in a fantasy world if you think this doesn't have anything to do with you, and I'm not talking about Oriceran."

"You have to believe me," Gareth pleaded. "I didn't ever think any of this would lead to anyone getting killed. I still don't understand why it's happening." He sniffled and wiped tears from the corners of his eyes. "Am I going to prison?"

"Not today and not yet," Izzie replied. "You're lucky the PDA is handling this and not the FBI. Our agency has more flexibility in how we approach these things." She took a deep breath. "Whether you're charged with anything won't be our final call." She glanced at Rafe.

"Somebody's been using you, and I believe they're not done with you. We need you to figure out what they're up to before somebody else gets hurt. You help us right now, and we can help you stay out of prison."

Izzie needed to take control. Xelius' cooperation after the robbery might have saved Thaddeus Blackstone's life. Gareth could disappear into the magical underground or end up dead if she cut him loose. He was naïve but also a victim in his own way.

"We need you, right now, to help us to the best of your ability," Izzie urged. "No preconceptions. No bias. No worry. The more you help us now, the more you can make up for everything else that's happened. You're the subject matter expert. Only you can help us figure out what this is all about."

"This isn't the best place to do it," Gareth replied.

Rafe's brow lifted. "A magical academy isn't the best place for a magical researcher to help us find out what we need?"

"He has a point," Izzie added. "The School of Necessary Magic had one of the greatest arcane libraries I've ever seen."

"The School of Necessary Magic." Gareth harumphed. "This is a newer facility." He shook his head. "I have everything we need at home, including the most relevant books. It'd be best to go there."

"Then it's time for a magical book club at your place."

CHAPTER FIFTEEN

Real estate was the true magic. From what Izzie could see, Gareth's mid-century modern home in central Austin was less than eight hundred square feet but was worth millions given the location. She checked on her phone out of idle curiosity after stepping into the dusty living room and winced at the prices for the neighborhood. It would be a long time before she could afford that on a government salary.

Izzie looked around with a frown. She could sense almost no magic in Gareth's living room, although there was a strong source down the hallway. While she didn't expect a defensive hedge maze like Pearl or whatever tree-army magic Infinite Mask had going on at his house, it was rare to enter a magical's home and encounter so few enchantments.

She tilted her head, peered down the hallway, then walked down it. She threw open doors to a bathroom, bedroom, and a room with a table filled with flasks and beakers in racks. That room also had boxes containing different metals in various forms—bars, thin leaves, ingots, and shavings.

A rune-covered silver and gold brazier sat in the center of the table. Complicated glyphs and other arcane sigils written in chalk filled the walls, all covered floor-to-ceiling by blackboards. Soot-covered tongs hung from a rack on the wall.

Izzie chanted a spell to visualize the magical flows. The residual flows coated the entire room. A brief cold sensation ran down her back, although she didn't sense or see any spikes in magic. She rubbed her eyes, and the unsettling sensation vanished. She backed out of the room with a frown.

"Is something wrong?" Rafe asked from farther down the hallway.

"I...don't think so." Izzie yawned. "I haven't slept well since this case started, and it's messing with me. I found his lab. It's more twelfth-century than twenty-first century."

Gareth folded his arms and frowned at her. "What were you expecting?"

"I don't know. Your paper mentioned both the ancient and the modern. I expected more of the modern."

"I need to understand the past fully in a practical sense before I can merge it with the future." Gareth nibbled on his lip. "But please, we're not here to worry about my lab."

Izzie looked around one last time and headed back to the living room. "Lead on then, Professor."

"Follow me." Gareth waved Izzie and Rafe into a den stuffed with thick, desiccated ancient tomes, scrolls, and tablets. The environment and vibe were similar to his office. The dingy den was a little larger than his office, yet easily held double the academic materials. There was only one narrow path to his small desk and no open spots on the floor.

"These are more relevant than the materials in my office." Gareth crept between towers of books to make it to his desk without knocking them over. "The books in my office on campus are mostly for general background consultation. I've brought everything relevant to my current research here since I have no assistants. I converted one of the bedrooms into a lab, as you saw, but I don't keep background materials in there."

Rafe chuckled. "I wonder what the zoning committee has to say about magical labs in central Austin single-family residences."

"Those are the type of outdated regulations and restrictions I was talking about earlier. How can the city make laws restricting magical labs when they don't understand magic? What utter foolishness."

"Isn't that more of a reason to restrict things?" Izzie asked.

"My research isn't inherently dangerous." Gareth scoffed. "I've nothing against non-magicals. At the same time, I question how we magicals have been forced to adapt so much to their rules."

"I'll let the politicians iron all that out," Izzie replied. "I'm way more interested in finding out the reason the Arcane Syndicate and the shapeshifter want that void amulet."

"Answers don't always come easy, Agent Berens. I've had to learn this the hard way as a scholar."

"I know that. It doesn't mean we don't go looking for

them. There's one dead wizard because of this shapeshifter. I don't want anyone else to die. Think of it this way, Professor. Your research could help save a life."

"I..." Gareth blinked. "Of course. I...understand that. I'm only trying to prepare you for the possibility this won't end as easily as you'd like."

"We passed that point a long time ago, Professor." Izzie frowned. "I'd suggest getting analysis support involved, but it would take weeks and months just to get everything sorted and digitized to make their help worthwhile."

"We have the dream team here." Rafe reached down and picked up a book. He blew dust off the leather cover and revealed an intricate embossed image of a robed elf holding a glowing vine-covered staff. "I'm guessing most of these research materials aren't in English or Spanish?"

"There are a variety of languages used," Gareth answered. "Although English is more common than you think in modern reviews and articles. It is the current *lingua franca* of scholarship research on this planet, after all." He pointed at different stacks of manila folders filled with printed articles. "I prefer a more traditionalist approach when thinking through a problem."

Izzie blanched. "This isn't going to be fun."

"Speak for yourself." Rafe grinned.

Gareth pulled open his desk and retrieved a heavy-looking pair of crystal spectacles. "You might find these useful, Agent Martinez." He looked between the two agents with an uneasy expression before handing the spectacles to Rafe. "These will help with translation. In addition, a portion of the materials are self-translating. I know a translation spell that should work for everything else in that it'll allow me to share my linguistic knowledge, but it requires personal magic to maintain."

Izzie nodded. "Go ahead and hit me."

Gareth reached into his pocket and pulled out an engraved wooden fountain pen. After a series of elaborate movements and flares of magic, Izzie realized the pen served as his wand. He offered the world's most monotone incantation before a pair of spectral black glasses appeared on Izzie's face.

"You need to feed it your magic now," Gareth prompted.

"That's easy." Izzie reached out and poured her magic into the spectral glasses. They flared before calming down, turning a light blue, and settling on her face with a tickle.

She picked up a book featuring an unknown language on the front. The symbols didn't change, but she could read the title.

"*A Treatise on Glyph Combination: An Ogelian Applied Approach,*" she read. "Nice spell."

"They say the next model of our sunglasses will have translation technomagic," Rafe told Izzie.

"I can understand it. Yet it's the same. It's a little weird." Izzie's brow lifted. "I wonder if our glasses will work the same way. I also hope and pray that our next case doesn't require us to read through stacks of ancient documents."

"Not all languages, especially the ancient Oriceran languages, are so easily translated by technomagic solutions." Annoyance slipped into Gareth's voice. "Keep that in mind. You can't replace dedicated researchers with convenient spells and contraptions."

"No one wants to, and thanks for your help, Professor."

He lifted his chin with a haughty look in his eye. "We all have to do our part."

Rafe picked up a book. "If you could give us any hints, Professor, that would be helpful. Right now, we're mostly interested in figuring out any links between the Glorious Foundation's void amulet, the shapeshifter, and a group called the Arcane Syndicate. Such as if the void amulet could serve as a key for anything else they'd want. To be clear, we doubt the Arcane Syndicate is mentioned in there, but anything that seems like dark magics a rogue group might use or want would be relevant."

Gareth gasped. He reached toward a pad of paper with a badly shaking hand, all the pride and contempt glimpsed a moment earlier gone. "I…"

"Is something wrong, Professor?" Izzie asked.

He shook his head, grabbed his wrist to steady it, and swallowed. "The severity of the situation is beginning to become clear to me. I hope you don't think too poorly of me if I admit I'm frightened."

"Of course not. With your help, we'll find the shapeshifter, and we'll put an end to all of this."

"And I really won't have to go to prison?"

Izzie nodded. "Help us find this guy, and we can get you a slap on the wrist for whatever low-level import laws you've broken."

Rafe nodded his agreement. "The important thing now is the murder and stopping the shapeshifter."

Gareth surveyed the room with a careful nod. "Of course. Give me a moment to gather the most useful materials, and I'll write down a list of phrases and concepts you'll want to pay special attention to. Fortune might yet smile on this investigation."

Izzie rubbed her eyes. She'd been sitting on the floor surrounded by books for far too long, at least a couple of hours. She hadn't suffered through this level of dry, old, magical academic pain since her school days. Even the more modern journal articles overflowed with painful jargon and annoying references to texts and people far older than half the countries on Earth. She was beginning to appreciate Gareth's academic style compared to many of his field's contemporaries.

Her combined Jasper and light elven heritages always made magic a far more instinctive matter for her. The complicated theories and techniques her wizard and witch friends relied on never weighed her down as much. An incantation and wave of her hand there, and she could get what she needed, even if she didn't always have the finest low-level understanding of all the magical principles involved. She controlled the magical energy. That was enough.

Magical scholarship had grown into a foreign world to her. When she was on the run from the Seventh Order, she valued straightforward, pragmatic magic that protected her and destroyed her enemies. She hadn't worried about the esoteric concerns of scholarly magicals who devoted their lives to broadening the scope of what people believed was possible with magic.

On a certain level, Izzie wondered if that had made her

abilities stagnate. Her baseline power was higher than many other magicals when she truly let loose. Her current job let her employ spells she'd mastered over the years for battle.

Her magic wasn't as strong as her mother's, but it served her well. It had kept her alive long enough to sit on the floor reading the most boring books of two worlds with a frightened academic and her partner.

Gareth hummed under his breath. He'd long since stopped trembling. He no longer cast nervous glances at Izzie and Rafe. He pored through the texts, taking notes, and occasionally offered cheerful advice to the two as if they were graduate student assistants and not agents investigating a dangerous shapeshifter's links to the mysterious Arcane Syndicate.

The dark thoughts about magical stagnation fed another more immediate worry. They didn't have infinite time to find the shapeshifter before another attack occurred.

"There has to be something we've missed." Izzie shook her head. "Something obvious. I doubt this shapeshifter and the Arcane Syndicate have a bunch of professors working for them doing low-level research."

Rafe looked incredulous. "You don't believe an ancient group of evil magicals doesn't have somebody who'll take the time to look for power?"

"You know what I mean."

"True scholarship rarely is obvious, Agent Berens." Gareth was still perusing his latest book. "That said, I don't know if we'll be able to accomplish what you want here. Combining threads of lost history and knowledge can be a difficult, unrewarding task that requires significant levels of careful, applied effort. It could take months or years to yield something useful, if I'm being honest."

He set his book down. "I only agreed to this because I was terrified out of my mind earlier. Now that I've had more time to think, I question this approach."

"We don't have months or years to track down this shapeshifter. And you should consider, Professor, if he came after Blackstone, he might come after you," Izzie pointed out. "That should terrify you into finding something."

Gareth started trembling again. "B-but he has no reason to come after me. I don't have what he wants."

"You don't know what he wants. You can't be sure because we can't be sure." Izzie stared at him. He needed to understand he couldn't brush them off with cries of inconvenience. "You were dealing with Blackstone and involved in void amulet research. Did Blackstone know what you were studying?"

"He knew about the research, yes. He didn't know where I got the amulet from. Xelius was very clear that I should not pass that information on."

Izzie frowned. "Maybe Blackstone ghosted you to keep you safe. We've heard from somebody else who had a similar experience."

"But I don't have the void amulet," Gareth protested. He wiped the sweat off his brow. "You said you had it. Doesn't that mean the shapeshifter knows I don't have it?"

"It's in PDA custody." Izzie set her book down, stood, and stretched. "That doesn't mean the shapeshifter doesn't think there's an alternative to the amulet. If this amulet is important as a key to something else, whoever wants that something else will either need a new amulet or an alternative, and you're the local expert on these amulets and their alternatives."

Gareth reached into his pocket with a weary sigh. "As I told you in my office, I don't go in for all this derring-do. A proper wizard shouldn't be risking his life in pointlessly violent situations." He lifted his phone and tapped on it. His eyes widened, and he gasped. "No, no, no. That can't be right."

Rafe looked up from his book with a concerned expression. "Is there a problem, Professor?"

Gareth swallowed and tried to set his phone down. His hand shook so hard that he dropped the device on the desk. "I had my phone muted. I don't like to be disturbed when I'm reading and lose my train of thought. Madge, our receptionist, sent me a message to let me know that Special Agent Berens of the PDA stopped by *again* about an hour ago and left a message about wanting to talk to me about a recent patron. She told *that* Agent Berens I might not answer my phone, but I was at home."

Rafe frowned. "When you left the academy, did you tell them you were going home with PDA agents?"

Gareth shook his head. "I left a message with reception that I was going home to take care of a few matters. Considering I left shortly after the original Agent Berens and you arrived, Agent Martinez, she might have understood the implication. Whether she passed it on or not, I don't know."

"That shapeshifter asshole is seriously using my form in public *again*?" Izzie ground her teeth. "Text your receptionist right now and let her know that if I or my partner show up again, she should demand to see the magical watermark on our badges. If our fakes refuse to show her, she should call the police and explain there's a shapeshifter pretending to be a federal agent."

"That was an hour ago," Rafe noted. "We've been at it for way longer than that, let alone the time it took to drive here."

"The shapeshifter's on his way, or he will be soon." Izzie snapped her book shut. "We need to be ready."

"Shouldn't we call someone to help?" Gareth asked.

"The PDA is already here. We'll protect you, and we'll catch our suspect at the same time."

CHAPTER SIXTEEN

"Go grab extra anti-magic magazines," Izzie told Rafe. She stood and dusted off her pants. "His life banking can only do so much if I'm nailing him with spells and you're shooting him."

"No, no, no." Gareth shook his head. "We need help. We need more than two people. He killed Thaddeus. This shapeshifter is too powerful for just the two of you to handle."

"What we need to do is lock this place down as much as we can." Izzie gestured at a wall. "That'll allow us to buy time for help to arrive. If we're lucky, the shapeshifter is hiding somewhere waiting for you to be alone. In that case, he won't come after you as long as we're here."

"And if we're unlucky?" Gareth's voice shook.

"Then he's outside in a van sharpening his knife and licking his lips."

"He ran from us before," Rafe added. "And that was when we didn't have wards to help protect our location."

"This is insane," Gareth protested.

Rafe put on his sunglasses, jogged to the living room, and opened the door. "If it makes you feel any better, there are no other cars on the road but ours and a white Toyota down the street."

"I know that car," Gareth replied. "It's a neighbor's. Lovely woman. Terrible baker, though. Her food is so bland it should be a crime."

"That's good," Izzie countered. "it means there aren't tons of people around right now. We can guard this house with the two of us, but we can't guard the entire neighborhood if things get out of hand."

"A shapeshifter coming to kill me is already out of hand!" Gareth shouted.

Rafe hesitated and pulled off his jacket, revealing his shoulder holster. He tossed his jacket on the couch. After a return to the front door and a quick survey of the front yard, he darted to the car to open the trunk.

Grim-faced, he slipped on his enchanted bulletproof tactical vest and tactical belt. The enchantments provided additional protection but not as much as a well-cast shield spell, one of the reasons Izzie didn't tend to wear a vest. After clipping anti-magic grenades to his belt, he loaded pistol magazines and shotgun shells into his vest and belt pockets.

"I'm not sensing that much magic off your home," Izzie told Gareth. "The lab's the only place I felt any real magic. Where are your defensive and warning wards? Did you somehow suppress them with inversion glyphs?"

"No, I have almost none beyond the lab." Gareth cast a nervous glance behind him. "I'm a magical academic. I don't need to live in fear of assassins, and I've never been all that good at those types of spells anyway. Wasting time putting them up might even draw attention I don't want by making it easier to pick out my place from far away."

Izzie groaned and scrubbed a hand down her face. "A shapeshifting assassin is on his way, well, her way, since the shapeshifter might look like me to come after you. We could have used more wards."

Gareth shuddered. "But w-we can tell this person the PDA has the amulet. He'll leave. He has no reason to want to kill me."

"I doubt that'll help." Izzie rushed to the front window and raised her hands. "I don't care if you're good at defensive techniques or that fast at setting up wards. Just do your best. Start in the back and put up what you can. Anything we can do to slow this guy down will help keep you alive until more help can arrive."

Gareth froze, staring at Izzie. His knees buckled, and he trembled.

"It's not the time to shut down, Professor. I need you to stay with me until this is over. It's your life that's most on the line."

"Yes, of course." He shook his head and ran down the hallway.

Izzie chanted and pushed through careful movements with her hands to layer a basic blocking defensive ward over the front window. Rafe jogged back into the house with a shotgun over his shoulder.

"If I knew we would have to fight, I would have signed out an anti-magic emitter." He sat on the couch and loaded shells into the shotgun. "Do we want to call it in? We technically don't know he's coming."

Izzie finished her chant. An intricate arcane pattern flashed on the front window and disappeared.

"We need at least field support in the area looking for the magical signature," Izzie replied. "I don't want the APD here. The shapeshifter's too dangerous for them to handle with the gear they have available. We need PDA tactical support."

Rafe let out a dark chuckle. "Lt. Lee was right. Austin needs an AET team. This town's not quiet enough to rely only on the PDA."

"It'll have to for now."

She moved over to the front door to set a ward there. "Go ahead and call the PDA to ask for tactical backup. Tell them the truth. We suspect the shapeshifter has been using my shape, and make sure they double-check our badges if they encounter you or me outside the house."

Rafe pulled out his phone. He made the call and spoke in hushed tones. Izzie concentrated on casting a ward on the front door, confident in leaving the gathering of reinforcements up to her partner.

They could be wrong about the shapeshifter coming for Gareth. Depending on how the conversation with the receptionist had unfolded, the shapeshifter might have realized the PDA agents already made contact. Attacking now meant confronting two highly trained agents with experience fighting rogue magicals.

The shapeshifter also knew Izzie's past and family history. That meant the shapeshifter knew what a terror she could be when fighting rogue magicals. That thought lingered in her mind during the layering of her latest ward until Rafe's sharp tone and scowl shoved it into oblivion.

"Any deaths?" Ralf scowled. "Here? No, we're securing the location. We only know that the suspect was spotted at CMA imitating Agent Berens. We haven't confirmed the suspect's coming here, only that there's a chance. But it's a solid chance that the shapeshifter... Yes. Yes. I understand, Bill. No, it makes sense."

He sighed. "We'll call again if the suspect shows up." He cursed under his breath and slipped his phone into a pocket on his vest. "I let myself believe we were a step ahead this time."

"That didn't sound good," Izzie replied. "Lay it on me."

"There have been three separate magical bombing attacks in the Magical District in the last twenty minutes. They have separate eyewitness reports of unidentified individuals blinding groups of people with a magical seed, then setting off explosive magical seeds."

Izzie frowned. "If they're blinded, how do they know about the explosive seeds?"

"Other people farther away or those who managed to shield their eyes. Quick actions on the part of civilian magicals present stopped anyone from dying." He grunted in frustration.

"The APD, FBI, and PDA are mobilizing tactical teams to sweep the area for the reported suspects. An AHMD has been declared for the entire Magical District and the surrounding neighborhoods. Law enforcement resources are stretched thin. They're forced to play the numbers game. Bill says it doesn't make sense to send more people to guard one professor when the PDA already has one of its strongest field agents there to protect him."

"I'm a secret weapon," Izzie replied. "On any other day,

that'd make me happy. And any other day, we wouldn't be guarding a high-value target in a place with almost no wards. I'll continue setting up what I can."

"We can't play around with this shapeshifter. He shrugged off your stun bolts like they were nothing. When he shows up, I'll try the grenades if I can get a position that doesn't risk affecting you. If those don't work, we'll need to take him down with lethal force."

"Agreed. The shapeshifter surrenders or the shapeshifter goes down." Izzie cut through the air with her hand. "Simple as that."

Gareth stepped back into the living room. "I'm really not interested in this type of violence." He clasped his hands together. "Might I offer an alternative? Shouldn't we be fleeing? Doesn't that make more sense than waiting for a killer?"

"It's better to hunker down in a defensible location than drive across town when we can be attacked at any moment by someone who can look like anybody," Rafe explained. "We've seen this suspect turn into a bird and fly away."

Izzie pushed into the kitchen and located a side door and a window in need of wards. "Our suspect had the flash seeds at the market, but he didn't use any explosive seeds. Why the change in tactics? Why the sudden terrorism?"

"Because he can become that damned bird," Rafe replied. "I looked into it the other day. Average hawks can fly between twenty to forty miles per hour, and with life banking, who knows how fast he can fly to get here? I doubt we'll be lucky enough to have a drone tag him in a vehicle. Why would we now when we haven't before?"

Izzie spun to face him. Her stomach tightened. "The attacks were a distraction."

"He probably figured out from the conversation with the pixie that we're with the professor." Rafe picked up his shotgun. "The timeline matches up. He's coming, but Bill won't send backup until we confirm arrival."

Izzie shook her head. "Because he can't risk a bunch of kids on the east side getting blown up by the shapeshifter."

Gareth fell to his knees. "This can't be happening. Not only three weeks after I published that paper. You have to understand. It's been very well received in magical history and historical magical engineering circles. All my years of work are finally paying off, and now I'm going to die because of it?"

"Not if we have anything to say about it. We need more wards." Izzie walked over and frowned at Gareth. "No offense, Professor, but we don't have time for your self-pity. I understand why you didn't want your place strengthened, but we need to do everything we can to slow this guy down.

"You don't have to be an expert in combat magic to cast a half-decent ward. Now keep going. We might not have much time left before he arrives, and we have no idea when we might be able to get backup."

Gareth stood and rubbed his wrist. "Yes, yes, of course."

"I'll go keep an eye out in the front." Rafe opened the door and put on his sunglasses. "We could get lucky."

Gareth took a deep breath and let it out slowly. "Thank you both for protecting me."

"No thanks needed, Professor," Izzie replied. "It's our job."

CHAPTER SEVENTEEN

I zzie backed away from a window at the end of the hall overlooking a thin side yard with a tiny flower bed. The new defensive ward flared with activation. Properly securing even a small location took time and patience. She lacked both at that moment.

Weeks of detailed warding followed by constant maintenance helped secure her apartment from standard surprise attacks. Even then, that only allowed her to sleep at night. She didn't trust her wards to protect her from every threat. Having only minutes to get ready in her present location meant the most she could hope for was to slow down the shapeshifter.

Something else nagged at her. It was like she'd missed a vital clue that went beyond not understanding the shapeshifter's or the Arcane Syndicate's end goals. Ancient tomes about lost history shouldn't have been this important. Still, all lines of the investigation pointed to the shapeshifter and Arcane Syndicate wanting something and the amulet being the key.

"Izzie!" Rafe shouted from the living room.

She ran to him. Rafe stood in the living room with his shotgun pointed toward the front door.

Gareth held his wand pen up in front of him with shaking hands. "What's going on?"

"I spotted a ton of magic on a bird that flew overhead," Rafe explained. "The bird circled a few times, then flew off."

Izzie motioned at the door, then the curtains. "Coming in by air made it easier to spot him."

"It also made it easier for him to get to us." Rafe slammed the front door and locked it. He pulled the curtains open. "He can't be that tough. There are two of us here."

"We don't know what he's been feeding into his life banking spell," Izzie reminded him. She lifted her hands and pushed them through intricate movements while murmuring the incantation for shield spells for her, Gareth, and Rafe, covering them all with a slight glow. "And we have no idea what else that knife could be doing for him."

"W-what should I do?" Gareth asked.

"I didn't see any windows in your den, Professor," Izzie replied. "Go hide in there. If you can pull off any shield spells, layer them over the one I added."

"My lab would be better," he protested. "There are no windows there, either, and it has protective spells."

"Then go there." Izzie gestured down the hallway. "Now! Don't come out until I yell 'Yumfuck.'"

"Yumfuck?" Gareth blinked.

"He's kind of a family friend, and it's something only I would say."

"I…understand."

In theory, any well-trained magical was a powerful threat. In practice, winning in fights came down to discipline, bravery, and training more than absolute ability. A wizard who could barely string together defensive wards wasn't going to be fast-casting fireballs regardless of his age and experience in other areas.

Gareth tore away with enough speed that one might have mistaken him for enhancing his speed using a life banking spell. The den door slammed loudly.

"Did the shapeshifter see you?" Izzie asked.

Rafe frowned and peered out the front window. "Most likely. Assuming he also gains the visual abilities of the bird form, it's almost certain."

"Call it in." Izzie took a slow, deep breath, looked across the street at the unassuming blue house, and hoped no civilians were inside. "Now Bill has an excuse." She shook her head. "This is why you don't do dangerous magical research at your house in the middle of a residential neighborhood."

"He didn't think his research was dangerous."

"All magic can be dangerous when misused. Otherwise, they wouldn't need people like us. I can—"

She jerked her head up. "I feel something."

Rafe lifted his shotgun. "Roof? Did you get enough array linkage for your wards to extend to the roof?"

"I didn't exactly have tons of time." Izzie swallowed and lifted her palm. "Better warning than blockage, but it's still enough to keep him out. Hurry, and it i—"

A deafening explosion tore off half the roof and shot the material into a billowing cloud of flaming debris. The blast threw Rafe and Izzie to the floor. Their shields protected them from serious injury but left Izzie's side stinging. Scorched chunks of roof shingles rained down, striking the floor and bouncing off Izzie's and Rafe's shields to weaken them further.

Rafe reacted before Izzie did. He jumped to his feet and jerked his shotgun back and forth as he sought a target. "Without the wards, he might have taken down the entire house!"

"That couldn't have been the plan. I hope." Izzie stood and waved smoke out of her face, allowing a little pride into her voice. She raised her hands and strengthened their shields.

Heavy footsteps sounded above from the other end of the surviving roof. She spun toward the source, a muscular dark-haired man in a tracksuit wielding the same rune-covered knife they encountered in the night market alley. There was something familiar about the shapeshifter's appearance, but Izzie didn't have time to figure it out before he leapt through the gaping hole.

Izzie nailed him with a stun bolt. He didn't grunt or blink before landing with a *thud* and slashing at her chest with the knife. The blade met the shield and didn't penetrate.

She jumped backward and held her wrist, concentrating on pouring her magic into a destructive and penetrating light bolt. The shapeshifter ducked before she fired her spell. Her bolt tore into the wall as she leapt behind the couch.

Rafe reached for an anti-magic grenade, his hand hovering. He glanced between the shapeshifter and Izzie with a frown. The momentary hesitation allowed the shapeshifter to charge Rafe across the room and bring back his knife.

The shotgun roared with a quick trigger pull from Rafe. The shapeshifter jerked backward, clutching his chest. He growled. His blood dripped from a mess of pellet wounds.

"Surrender," Rafe ordered. "Or I will be forced to shoot—"

The shapeshifter leapt toward and pushed off the wall to escape Rafe's next shotgun blast. He flew through the air and shoved the knife hard toward Rafe's throat.

Again, the shield spell deflected the first attack. Rafe tried to line up another shot. The shapeshifter snapped a kick into his chest that launched him into a wall. He grunted, the shield still active, but the next slice tore the spell down with a flash.

"Not going to happen." Izzie launched two light bolts into the shapeshifter's back. He staggered, allowing Rafe to shove the shotgun against his chest and pull the trigger again.

The shapeshifter flew backward and hit the floor, growling and bleeding from his half-shredded chest. He jumped to his feet, the quick movement shaking a portion of the shotgun pellets out of his chest.

"You're a tough one, aren't you?" Izzie remarked. "All that life banking."

She nailed him in the leg with a light bolt, leaving a blackened wound. He hissed, dropped to his knees, and raised his arms above his head. He still held the knife.

"Now you're understanding," Izzie growled.

The shapeshifter let out a pained laugh. "The gun hurt rather badly. Unexpected." He nodded toward his oozing chest. "You hurt me far more than Blackstone. Impressive."

Rafe kept the shotgun trained on the shapeshifter. "Anti-magic shells. What's wrong? The Arcane Syndicate didn't brief you about how well-equipped the PDA is these days?"

The shapeshifter narrowed his eyes. "If you know about my Syndicate masters, you should step aside before you die, Agent Martinez."

Izzie scoffed. "I thought so. There was a question about whether you were running from the Syndicate or working for them. Once we drag you in, we'll get you to give up everything on the Arcane Syndicate."

"You two know nothing."

"We know enough that you're the one bleeding right now and surrendering. You're only not dead because Rafe didn't shove that gun against your face."

The shapeshifter winced. His gaze darted between Rafe and Izzie. "I underestimated you. It looks like you win."

"All the bluster's gone that quick?" Izzie narrowed her eyes. "Drop the knife and put your hands behind your head. I don't see any magical seeds for a trick like last time."

"You want me to get rid of my knife?" The shapeshifter's faux credulity was agitating.

"You want to survive this, you better start cooperating."

"Very well, then, Agent Berens. I'll get rid of the knife."

The shapeshifter dropped to his knees and flung the knife toward Izzie at the same time. The knife tore through her weakened shield and struck her shoulder. Her knees buckled with the pain spiking through her arm and chest.

Rafe fired again. His expensive rounds ended up in the wall. The shapeshifter grabbed the edge of the couch and flung the piece of furniture into the air one-armed to absorb the next shotgun blast.

Izzie's arm was on fire. She gritted her teeth and launched another light bolt at the shapeshifter. The falling couch took the hit.

The shapeshifter spun around the couch and darted past Izzie. He backhanded her with a stunning and powerful blow. He might as well have hit her with a car. Her nose spurted blood as she flew across the room and crashed into the wall.

The shapeshifter's laughter echoed through the space as it circled Izzie, shifting between forms like a twisted mirror of her nightmares.

"You should've known they'd come for you eventually," it hissed, its voice warping as it took on yet another face. "Your parents might have escaped, but you...you were always unfinished business."

Izzie's hands clenched into fists as her magic pulsed at her fingertips. "I won't let you finish it," she growled, forcing herself to stay calm. She couldn't lose control, not now.

The shapeshifter grinned. "It's too late. This is only the beginning."

Izzie summoned all her strength as the memories of her family fueled her resolve. "No." Her voice was steady. "This is where it ends."

The shapeshifter jumped toward the knife. He grabbed it and rolled back to his feet.

Rafe tossed his empty shotgun to the floor and yanked out his pistol. He emptied half the magazine, trying to clip the weaving and bobbing suspect. The shapeshifter reached the edge of the kitchen, grabbed a knife block, and launched the knives with a wide, arcing swing at Rafe before taking a round in the leg.

A half-dazed Izzie chanted her quickest gust spell ever before falling to one knee. The powerful wind shoved the knives off-course. They all thudded into the wall beside Rafe.

The shapeshifter slammed the kitchen door shut. Rafe fired through the door until he ran out of ammo. He ejected the magazine and reloaded a new one.

"Izzie, you okay?" he asked.

"I'm fine." Her heart pounded, and adrenaline suppressed the pain from her shoulder and face. Izzie wiped blood out of her eyes and ran toward the door. "Three, two, one," she counted and kicked it open, ready with her palm out for another light bolt.

A trail of blood led to the open door. She rushed outside and found more blood. They'd hurt him way more than he'd hurt them.

"Stay with the professor!" Izzie shouted, jogging away and following the trail of blood. "It could be another misdirection play."

The blood ended at a brick wall. She jumped and pulled herself to the top, finding more spatters of blood and a little in the following yard before the trail ended. Izzie squinted and looked up at birds flying in the distance.

"You weren't ready for the shotgun, were you?" she whispered.

Izzie's shoulder and face throbbed. Running after the shapeshifter had only made the pain worse. She placed a hand on her shoulder and chanted a healing spell, hoping the knife didn't contain a deadly curse or strange poison. Her wound closed, and her pain faded. After healing her face too, she jumped back into Gareth's backyard.

She lingered outside for a minute more, seeking any sign of a magical feel for the suspect, then headed into the house and the living room. Rafe swung his reloaded shotgun at her.

Izzie frowned. "What's going on?"

"What did you get me for my birthday last year?" he asked.

"A book about the history of louper. Because I overheard you going on and on about being interested in magical sports."

Rafe lowered his gun. "We can't be too careful with a shapeshifter. You were gone for longer than I thought you'd be. I thought he might have grabbed your badge, too."

Izzie shook her head. "I prefer suspects who keep one form." She frowned. "You okay? Do you need me to heal you, or did you use your emergency potion?"

"He knocked me around a little, but I'm not the one he knocked across the room and stabbed," Rafe eyed her with concern.

"I've had much, much worse." Izzie waved it off. "Something about the guy's form was familiar. That might be a clue."

Rafe chuckled and shook his head. "He looked exactly like the main hitman from *An Elf Marries a Mobster.*"

"I don't think I ever saw it, only the commercials." Izzie rolled her eyes. "Now he's trolling us. Is the professor okay?"

"I told him to stay in the room while we secured the scene."

"I'll go check." Izzie headed toward the lab and knocked on the door. "Yumfuck."

Gareth edged the door open. He peeked out with one eye. "Is the shapeshifter dead?"

"No." Izzie frowned. "He got away. We wounded him pretty badly, but he's using powerful magic to enhance his abilities."

She rubbed her nose, although the pain was gone. "He implied he could regenerate under normal circumstances, and his knife cut through my shield spell like a layer of paper." She patted her shoulder. "The important thing is he didn't get to you."

Gareth groaned. He opened the door and staggered to a table to brace himself. "He's not dead. That means he'll come back. You're going to get more people here, right?"

"Yes. Although we will need to take you into protective custody until we catch this guy or put him down. We only stayed here because it was our best play at the time."

"But you hurt him."

"My partner nailed him in the chest with anti-magic shotgun rounds." Izzie shrugged. "It should have killed him. It only slowed him down. And it didn't slow him down enough to stop him from changing forms and getting away. We should assume he'll be back, which is why we'll have to take you into protective custody."

"I can't leave my home for an extended period."

"You have to." Izzie pointed at the gaping hole in the roof. "He blew up half your roof. It's not exactly livable."

"I can't account for that," Gareth protested. "There are spells. My research is important."

"The PDA will protect you. That doesn't mean we'll let you put yourself in unnecessary danger."

Gareth put a hand to his chest and took slow, deep breaths. "He won't stop until I'm dead or he is, will he?"

"Probably." Izzie sighed at the bloodstains all over her jacket. "For whatever reason, he's convinced you have what he wants, and he's willing to go through two PDA agents to get it. Understand?" She gave him a pleading look. "If you know anything else, a small clue that might help, now is the time to tell us. We can't protect you if you don't protect yourself."

Gareth stared at a glyph on the wall and sighed. "There's something I didn't tell you before. This wasn't a surprise. I was worried somebody would come after me."

CHAPTER EIGHTEEN

Izzie ground her teeth. Gareth's reluctance to be honest must have been what she'd sensed earlier. Getting stabbed and backhanded across the room fed into her frustration at not catching the suspect.

The professor kept holding back information. She wanted to ensure he was a man worth defending and not a dark wizard manipulating her for his own purposes.

Rafe walked into the lab. "Field support will have drone coverage of the neighborhood in five minutes. Bill asked if the APD should send units. I told him no."

"Good call," Izzie replied. "If that guy's surviving battle spells and anti-magic rounds, regular weapons aren't going to do much. And PDA backup?"

"The best they can do is a half-hour. There are still strong worries about the AHMD in the Magical District."

"But he was here."

"Bill knows. He also gave me a rare 'I'm sorry.'" Rafe shook his head. "He figures we drove the guy off for now, but we can't guarantee he won't attack the Magical District again or go after another target there. We need to figure out how to handle everything going forward."

Izzie nodded at Gareth. "Before that, it's time for a little truth game. He was about to admit he's been lying to us."

"That's not true!" Gareth shouted. He took a deep breath. "I didn't lie to you. I simply didn't make certain information available to you."

Izzie stomped to Gareth and grabbed his shirt. "My partner and I almost got killed by a super-charged shapeshifter assassin who works for a dangerous underworld organization. Thaddeus Blackstone is lying in a morgue, dead."

She glared at him. "We don't have time for games, Professor. If you're as innocent as you claim, you don't know how rogue and dark magicals think. These people are ruthless killers who won't stop at anything to get what they want. No matter how safe or secure you think you are, they'll keep coming and coming and coming and killing and killing and killing until somebody stops them or they've gotten what they wanted."

She let go of his shirt. "Convince me why we shouldn't let them get what they want."

Gareth stared at her wide-eyed. He swallowed. "I-I-I…"

Izzie stepped away. "You're not safe until we catch this guy. If you're the victim, we'll protect you. If you're helping them, for whatever reason, then confess now. We'll still protect you, and you can at least clear your conscience."

"She's right," Rafe offered quietly. "Tell us what you know."

"Thaddeus didn't ghost me as you called it." Gareth

looked away. "Although your initial suppositions were correct."

"Keep going," Izzie growled.

Gareth stared forward and refused to make eye contact with Izzie or Rafe. "He sent me a warning via letter a couple of days before he was murdered. He said I needed to stop my research until he could confirm matters since he'd become aware of unexpected dangers."

Izzie frowned. "I see. What did you do in response to this warning?"

"I told him, via a letter, I would not stop. I said these aren't the days of fearing the return of dark wizards hiding in the shadows and Rhazdon's forces plotting against everyone." Gareth let out a strangled mix of a whimper and laughter. "It was nothing but paranoia leftover from a darker time, I argued, and I couldn't see what it had to do with my research."

"Then he ended up dead," Rafe finished.

"And you realized it wasn't paranoia left over from a darker time," Izzie added. "What I don't get is if you got a warning like that, why didn't you go to the authorities? Even if you didn't want to talk to the police, you could have talked to the PDA. Instead, you knew that Blackstone had been murdered, and you withheld evidence that would help us better understand the background of that murder. Why?"

"I didn't have anything to do with his murder," Gareth protested. "I'm not a killer."

"I'm not saying you are." Izzie struggled to keep the anger out of her voice. "But you had reason to suspect it was going to happen."

"So did he." Gareth stared at the floor and licked his lips. He jerked his head up and blinked as if remembering something. "Yet he didn't go to the authorities either."

Rafe gave him a pitying look. "That justification stopped working when we showed up at your office, Professor. You knew we were looking into this matter at that point."

Gareth clenched his fists. "You have to understand how close I am to making breakthroughs. I'm so close to learning truths hidden in history for centuries. I'm supposed to stop that research because of common thuggery from underworld criminals? It's not fair."

"Not-so-common thuggery," Izzie countered. "And how fair is it that Blackstone is dead?"

"I never told him to deal with disreputable people." Gareth's gaze flicked down. "I only told him I needed certain materials. That was his choice to deal with such people."

"But you never thought it would affect you?" Izzie pressed. "There's a big difference between being naïve and being a willful idiot, Professor."

He flung his hands up. His voice grew louder and shrill. "I couldn't be sure. How could he be sure he wasn't being targeted by someone else over something unrelated to my research or requests? You still can't be sure."

Izzie pinned him with a glare. Sweat rolled down the side of his face. He hadn't been able to make eye contact for the entire conversation. He looked everywhere but at Izzie and Rafe. More than once, he stared at the floor in a different part of the lab. She waited until his eyes moved again and shifted her attention to the floor.

"Forget protective custody." Izzie narrowed her eyes. "Forget about smuggling. This is obstruction, accessory to murder, and conspiracy."

"What?" Gareth shouted. "That's absurd. Have you gone insane? I'm the victim here. You came here to protect me. I'm not the killer. You already know that."

"You lied to us. You're still lying to us. I can see it in your face. I can see how there's something you don't want us to know."

Rafe stepped forward with a smile. "Let me try, Izzie."

"Please, you need to talk sense into her," Gareth pleaded. "I assume you know about her childhood. I'm not a psychologist, but it's obvious to me she can't set her personal feelings aside. It's affecting her judgment."

"It's because she can't set her personal feelings aside that she's such a good agent. She empathizes with victims of rogue and dark magic. She knows what it's like to suffer at the hands of magical conspiracies."

Rafe's smile turned cold. "Sometimes she might see too much in the shadows. In this case, she sees the same thing I do, a man lying to protect himself. This is your last chance, Professor. Tell us what you know, or you'll end up in prison, assuming you survive all this."

Gareth gasped. "I…" He lowered his chin to his chest. "It wasn't supposed to be like this."

Izzie scoffed. "'It wasn't supposed to be like this' is right up there with 'I didn't mean to do it' in the big list of annoying and pointless confession statements." She shut up and harumphed when Rafe gave a warning look.

"All I've ever been interested in is advancing my research," Gareth continued. "Research that would help the magical world. People mocked it, said it was old-fashioned and pointless. It's only grown worse in recent years. Everyone claims technomagic is the future. They say Oriceran is dying anyway, so why should we care about its history?"

"But you care," Rafe replied. "And you've made big discoveries."

"You know what one of my favorite sayings is?" Gareth asked. "'When you have a hammer, everything is a nail.' That's mainstream magic, even the so-called traditionalists. They think they've learned to control the great forces of the universe, yet they have gaping holes in their knowledge. There are ancient, powerful ways of doing impressive things that they've been ignoring because they couldn't figure out a way to do it within the limits of their preferred techniques."

Izzie scoffed. "You figured out something big they didn't?"

Gareth's tone grew mocking. "There are things out there, Izzie Berens, that all those professors at your School of Necessary Magic would claim are nothing more than fables because they don't fit into how they believe magic is supposed to work, things that powered entire lost civilizations or ancient, powerful groups."

"Like the Glorious Foundation," Rafe suggested.

"Exactly." Gareth wagged a finger. All the fear melted off his face, replaced by wide-eyed manic pride. "About sixty years ago, freelance salvage divers recovered a metal and crystal box of unknown provenance from a sixteenth-century sunken ship. Other than a few pictures, which were subsequently lost in a questionable fire, no one had been able to study it because it was stolen not long after recovery."

He took slow, deep breaths and locked gazes with Izzie. "When the gates began to open between the worlds, and magic started to return to Earth, the person who'd stolen that box realized it was something special. It resonated in a way it never had before when probed with magic, but no matter what he did, he couldn't figure out a way to open it."

"That was you?" Izzie asked.

Gareth chuckled. "I'm older than I look, but that wasn't me. It was another collector of ancient artifacts, but he relied on my research to identify the box as belonging to the Glorious Foundation following the beginning of the gate opening. He didn't know much about what to do with the box either. Unfortunately for him, his preferred long-term residence was in Seattle's more secret magical area, if you catch my drift."

Izzie grimaced. Not long after the gate opened and before Izzie was born, a dark wizard faction, the Galbrathians, executed a horrific terrorist attack. They annihilated the Seattle kemana, one of the old hidden magical areas required for magical recharge when Oriceran and Earth were separate. The attack still held the record for worst modern magical terrorist attack and resulted in thousands of deaths, almost all magicals.

"Yes." Gareth sighed. "The box was believed lost by the few in the ancient artifact community who had any knowledge of it. Then it resurfaced about ten years ago."

"This is where you come in?" Rafe asked.

"It was pure chance, pure fate. Or perhaps it was destiny." Gareth sounded almost rhapsodic. "A rather elderly collector had gotten his hands on it, and he was also interested in my theories about hypomagic. They weren't as refined then.

"Despite that, he made the box available for my research. To my surprise, he willed the box to me when he passed away." He smiled. "He appreciated my efforts and my work to understand what had been lost because of a paranoid dragon. Of course, having such a valuable artifact can make one a target. I understood that, especially when I realized how I could open it."

"With a void amulet," Rafe concluded.

"Correct." Gareth smiled. "But it was more complicated than that. The box is a special type of artifact attuned to the passage of time. You can think of it as akin to having a time-lock on a safe." He frowned. "The problem was the box was created on Oriceran, not Earth, which caused odd interactions. I had to spend years learning to understand the box and how it interfaced with Earth."

Izzie folded her arms. "You had a super-special artifact box this entire time and never told anybody, never wrote any papers?"

"Of course I wrote papers on it," Gareth replied. "I simply wrote from a theoretical perspective informed by what I knew was true from my experiments without letting anyone know I had the box. I suggested new theories based on what I learned, but I couldn't risk losing the artifact. It was too valuable."

He sighed. "Then these last few months, everything clicked into place. I figured out how to account for the differing effects of the flow of time between the worlds and how to adjust the opening rituals accordingly. After that, I needed the final key, a Foundation void amulet. Thaddeus had been trying to find one for me for years, if only to borrow for research purposes."

He shook his head. "Then it turned out that Xelius, of all people, got his hands on one." He scoffed.

"What's wrong with Xelius?" Izzie asked.

"I've never gotten along well with Xelius. He's one of the small-minded traditionalist wizards I've been complaining about, a man disdainful of the true past while claiming he's defending it. Despite that, Thaddeus acted as a go-between, and Xelius agreed to lend me the amulet for research purposes. I borrowed it for two weeks."

Rafe frowned. "Only two weeks?"

"That's all it took. All my years of preparation made it almost trivial." Gareth's smile turned annoyingly smug. "I had everything else set up and ready."

He tapped the side of his head. "All the theory, all the adjustments were prepared. All I needed was an object of certain exact composition and construction that no one left alive knew how to build, a hypomagical amulet designed to interface with a combination of hypomagical locks."

Izzie gasped. "You opened the box?"

"I opened the box." Gareth rubbed his hands together. "You're too young to understand, Agent Berens. My entire life had led to that point, to me pulling something ancient and powerful out of that box, something only I could. Don't you see? The time-lock would only open in the fourteen hundred and forty-fifth or later years following the destruction of the Glorious Foundation."

"What's so special about this year?"

"One year for each martyred member of the Foundation destroyed by the dragon's army." Gareth slapped the table. "Don't you see? I was meant to find the box. I was meant to open the box right here in this city in this time."

Rafe gestured around the lab. "From what we've heard, tons of people think there's something special happening for the anniversary of the Glorious Foundation's destruction, even if they didn't know about the box and its lock. Didn't you worry about anybody else coming after you for whatever was in that box?"

"Nobody knew I had the box," Gareth insisted. "That's the important part. The old collector and I were the only two who knew about it outside of the executor of his estate, a gnome working with a prestigious firm. It's not as if that gnome understood what the box was. He dismissed it as an ugly ancient piece of sculpture."

Izzie pointed at the floor. "You were looking there earlier."

Gareth gasped. "You noticed?"

"That's where it is, isn't it? The box?"

He nodded. "The box and its contents."

"What was inside? Don't tell me it was empty or only had a message saying, 'Peace is all we need.'"

Gareth scoffed. "Of course not. My decades of work wouldn't have been rewarded with finding something so insignificant."

"Yes, yes." Izzie rolled her eyes. "Fate chose you. But what did fate choose for you? What's in the box? Keep in mind there's a shapeshifter who's determined to get whatever you have. You might have tried to hide all this, but they know or at least suspect."

Gareth frowned. "Which is the part I still don't understand. Thaddeus wasn't specific enough about why he thought I was in danger. Could someone have been reading my papers and realized I had samples I'd only theorized about before?"

"Other people have studied the relevant history," Rafe interjected. "They could have inferred your possession of the box indirectly."

Izzie wanted to strangle the professor. He kept missing the point. "What was in the damned box, Professor?"

"Power," he intoned.

"Power? Okay. Show us."

CHAPTER NINETEEN

Gareth knelt on the floor right where he'd been sneaking glances. He pulled out his pen wand and murmured a spell. Bright sigils appeared on the wooden floor. An entire square panel retracted with a hiss. A wooden ladder led to a small, stone-lined chamber beneath. Various magical symbols covered the walls.

"I really didn't mean for anyone to get killed." Gareth headed down the ladder. "If you don't believe anything else, believe that."

Izzie watched him to confirm he wasn't going for anything before jumping the small distance and landing in a crouch. She waved her hand over her body and chanted to conjure another shield spell. Rafe began his descent. Before he could arrive, a cold wave passed over Izzie, leaving her shivering.

She leapt to her feet and lifted her arm, ready to blast Gareth with a stun bolt. Almost every spot on the wall contained a ward, glyph, or other magical symbol of some type, including a series of even more complicated inversion glyphs. He stood beside a striped metal flat-topped rod. Additional glyphs and illuminated wards covered the base. A small bracelet covered in filigreed runes floated above the top of the rod.

Izzie scooted to the side to allow Rafe to step off the ladder. Unsettling chilling waves kept passing through her. Goosebumps broke out all over her arms, and every instinct told her to get away from the floating artifact. The bracelet pulsed with dark *and* light magic. That same power faded away every few seconds before returning.

"This ancient, powerful magical item could easily tip the balance of power in the magical world," Gareth murmured reverently. "I never cared about that. I only cared about the historical implications."

Izzie dropped her shield spell and rubbed her arms, trying to drive out the chill determined to settle into her body. She looked at Rafe. "Can you feel that? The cold? The ominousness?"

"It feels unsettling for me," Rafe admitted. "There's something not right about it, but I can't explain what."

Izzie shook her head. "You should have brought this to the appropriate authorities. Any of them. Earth or Oriceran. It's obvious this is dangerous."

"But it doesn't have to be." Gareth gestured around the chamber. "I spent months creating a containment area to ensure it wouldn't be easily detected. The heavy involvement of hypomagic techniques in its design made it practical, but covering up the chamber's background magic was necessary. I needed an excuse." He pointed at the ceiling. "So I tried to drown it out with other spells above."

"Your lab did feel a little over-enchanted," Izzie agreed.

Rafe put on his sunglasses. "You should see this if you're not already."

Izzie squinted and cast a spell to visualize the flows directly. Magic poured out and back into the amulet in two overlapping, shrinking and growing Möbius strips of braided light and dark magical flows. During the shrinking cycle, the flows vanished completely, matching what Izzie felt.

"What do you mean by this is power, Professor?" Rafe's attention stayed locked on the amulet, although his tech-nomagic glasses hid his eyes. He snapped pictures.

"The Glorious Foundation referred to it as a grand soul amplifier," Gareth explained. "In short, it can massively enhance an individual's magical abilities in potency and endurance. I prefer to call it a hypermagic amplifier."

"How much stronger could it make somebody?" Rafe asked.

"That's unclear. I was still doing research, but considerably stronger. Baseline amplification of at least ten- to twenty-fold wouldn't be unusual."

"You didn't slap it on and try casting spells?" Izzie asked.

Gareth scoffed. "This is a sophisticated and ancient device calibrated by a lost society at the peak of their use of techniques we're only beginning to understand. Attempting to wield the artifact without fully understanding it would be incredibly dangerous and foolish."

Izzie circled the rod and amulet. The cramped quarters forced her to scoot past Gareth. "You do have a sense of danger and responsibility, after all. That's good to know."

"Using this device without appropriate calibration, at

the minimum, risks an uncontrolled magical feedback loop that could kill the user," Gareth chided. "Along with a significant risk of destroying the user's soul."

Rafe winced. "I can see why you didn't want to play around with it."

Gareth folded his arms. "That's only a mid-tier risk scenario. That presumes someone is available to channel the energy and willing to risk their life and soul. Without tuning, it's just pure magical energy coursing through the wearer. Eventually, they might be able to bleed off enough energy.

"In theory, they could combine it with a containment spell that recircles the magic. I don't see why they would bother with all those risks rather than tuning it, even with the complexity and time involved." He shrugged. "Incidentally, anyone trying what I just described would almost certainly die in the process."

"Okay, that's generally terrible." Izzie tried not to stare at the amplifier. The longer she did, the colder she felt. "What's the worst-case scenario?"

He pointed up. "That out-of-control magic feeds a massive chain reaction explosion. The increasing magical pressure makes it inevitable. Too much magical power flows out at once."

"Define massive."

Gareth put a finger to his lips and frowned. "It's arguably exaggerated now that I think of it. At most, we're only talking about the destruction of a large building, like a skyscraper."

Izzie scoffed. "That's your version of exaggerated?"

"Yes, ancient references imply it could 'level a castle

town,' but we're talking the smaller scale, more geographically limited kingdoms common on Oriceran. Here it's nothing more than a building killer." Gareth nodded. "See? Exaggerated a little."

"Again, we're very glad you haven't been playing with it," Rafe replied. "Because that could kill thousands of people."

Izzie tore her gaze away from the sinister amulet. "What would it mean for a shapeshifter to be ten to twenty times more powerful?"

"The techniques used in this could interface well with shapeshifter magic from what I understand." Gareth motioned to the amplifier. "Imagine a shapeshifter that can change form instantly, flowing constantly from one form to another with almost no limits. Their outer form would mean nothing for their strength or durability. The extra magic might even be enough to let them temporarily separate their soul into pieces, to shapeshift into multiple creatures."

Rafe frowned. "How do you know that?"

"Because it's something I've read about the Glorious Foundation doing in the past." Gareth scoffed. "It was dismissed as mere legend, the so-called one-wizard culling army. I can't speak to this Arcane Syndicate, but that might be why a shapeshifter, specifically, is seeking it. They would have an easier time utilizing such techniques."

Izzie backed away toward the ladder. The room was too cramped for the intense discomforting sensations radiating off the amplifier.

"In other words, you had a magical WMD sitting

around." She shook her head. "Do you understand how insane that is? How dangerous it was?"

Gareth glared at her. "I had every intent of sacrificing my life should an experiment go awry. I was not trying to risk anyone's life or soul but mine. I never anticipated this Arcane Syndicate and this shapeshifter would be involved. You can hardly blame me when I took measures to conceal this information from dangerous people."

Izzie leaned against the wall and glanced up the ladder. "Don't you get it? I guarantee they're connected to the Patron. They knew of your desperation and used you like a pack of tissues during a bad cold, Professor. They set you up with everything you needed to open the box and get that bracelet out. Nobody ever stopped by to check on you?"

Gareth shook his head. "I made it clear to the Patron I was making good progress in my general research, and there were certain dangers I needed to attend to. Especially before publishing the most intriguing parts of my findings."

"They were patient." Rafe nodded toward Gareth. "But something with Blackstone set them off. They got worried. They were forced into sloppy moves."

"If Xelius and the others had been forthright, we could have caught them before Blackstone was killed," Izzie concluded. "You understand, Professor, there's no way we can let this sit in your basement now that we know what's going on. We'll have to take you and the amplifier in to the PDA." She sighed. "We'll make sure our superiors know you've cooperated. As irritated as I am, I understand you were trying not to get anyone hurt."

His shoulders slumped. "Once I heard Thaddeus was dead, I suspected it would come to this." He stared at the amplifier. "To be clear, this room is partially for safety and partially to hide the amplifier. Removing it from this chamber means those who know what they're looking for will be able to track it."

"We have secure vaults at our building. There's no way they're tough enough to raid our building without getting killed." She reached toward the bracelet. "Can I pull it off here without blowing up a building?"

Gareth sighed. "Of course you can. Don't put it on unless you want to risk activating its magic. At that point, you have to wear it so the flows have a place to resonate with. That will in turn stabilize them."

"Or kill me and shred my soul."

"That is a risk, yes."

Izzie's hand stopped an inch from the amplifier. "On second thought, we're not touching this until we have backup to escort it back to the PDA, including a full tactical team."

"That's a good plan." Rafe kept his distance from the artifact. That forced him not to venture far from the walls.

"All I wanted to do was uncover the truth of the past to illuminate the future," Gareth added with a slight whimper. "None of this is fair or reasonable."

"I'm no scholar," Izzie replied. "But I will say my life has taught me that sometimes certain magic is better left forgotten." She nodded up. "Rafe, I'll keep an eye on this and the professor. You wait up there until reinforcements arrive, but you better call and make sure they know the secure vault needs to be ready for immediate receipt of a dangerous artifact and that we need anti-magic emitters."

"That won't be enough," Gareth warned.

"I'm not taking any chances." She pulled out her pair of anti-magic cuffs. "I'm sorry, Professor, but we need to make sure you don't do anything stupid."

Gareth held out his hands. "From your point of view, I imagine I already have."

CHAPTER TWENTY

I zzie stared at the meeting room's boring white wall. It had been hours. The artifact was safe in the building's secure magical artifact vault, and Gareth was in protective custody in a PDA cell, but she couldn't get the odd sensation she'd felt out of her head.

Bill snapped his fingers. "You still with us, Berens?"

She blinked and offered an apologetic look to everyone gathered around the briefing room table. "Sorry, Bill. It's been a long day."

Izzie and Rafe had already briefed Bill. He called a bigger meeting with Katya as a forensics representative and Allan to represent field support. Rounding out the meeting was the quiet Luisa, an infomancer from analysis support. She sat beside burly Jackson Taliesin, the commander of the Austin PDA's tactical support division, usually called tactical support.

Jackson grinned at Izzie. "You got to have all the fun with the shapeshifter. My teams were running around looking like idiots chasing a ghost."

"Fighting the shapeshifter wasn't that fun, Jackson," Izzie replied. "He took spells and anti-magic rounds like nothing."

He pointed at his forehead. "Put a couple of anti-magic bullets through his head and see if he can regenerate his way out of that."

Luisa shivered. "I wanted to follow up and note that analysis support has found no evidence in our research that the Glorious Foundation can be directly linked to this Arcane Syndicate, scant as the available evidence is. Also, there have been no infomancy or cyberattacks on PDA systems to suggest anyone is trying to access our networks looking for such information."

"The Syndicate and the shapeshifter want the amplifier," Izzie replied. "That's as deep as it needs to be. They just so happen to share a little ideology. That might have helped the Syndicate learn about the amplifier to begin with, and they manipulated Professor Roth by supporting his research. They stole the key from Xelius without knowing Roth had already retrieved the amplifier." She snorted. "That means they aren't all-seeing in their plans."

"They killed Blackstone because he must have caught wind of them somehow," Rafe added. "He might have realized the importance of the Xelius robbery. I'm sure we'll find eventually that all the attacks were related to this."

Bill grunted. "Luck was with us today in that nobody was killed. Everyone's all healed up thanks to magic or potions, too. That doesn't mean all the damage is undone. At least we have an idea about the motive, which means we can narrow the scope of our investigation. Good job, you two." He nodded at Izzie and Rafe.

"I've already briefed the mayor and governor. They both had the same question. They want to know what the PDA is doing to capture the shapeshifter since when they asked me if I felt he'd been fatally wounded, I told them no."

"He's still alive." Izzie folded her arms. "I wish he were dead, but everything Infinite Mask told us suggests our suspect would have reverted form if he suffered fatal damage. There's no way he would have stayed as a bird or small animal. There'd be a body showing up somewhere."

Bill nodded and looked at Allan. "Field support, what do you have for me?"

Allan shook his head. "We picked up a trail from the professor's house. It went cold a few blocks later. We suspect they went into sewer tunnels. Our robots aren't designed for that environment."

"We can see if I can follow the trail," Izzie suggested. "This is the first I heard of this."

Bill shook his head. "This shapeshifter has taken advantage of his power to mess with us. You would have gotten him at the night market if it were that easy. I'm not going to send you to chase rats in the sewer."

Izzie's jaw tightened. "I'm still ready to try. We need to capture this guy or put him down before he gets lucky with the next distraction bombing and kills innocent people."

"I understand that, Berens. I want us to work smarter at this, not harder."

"Which means we need to get this guy to come to us," Jackson insisted with a huge grin. He slapped the table so hard that Luisa yelped. "Then the IRD and tactical support can work together to take him down."

Izzie rarely heard someone refer to her division as the IRD. Technically, she belonged to the investigation and recovery division, but most people in the PDA called them the field agent division.

"We have the artifact now," Rafe interjected. "Neither the Arcane Syndicate nor the shapeshifter will risk attacking our building. It's too heavily protected. It would be suicide."

Jackson smirked at Izzie. "Assuming the shapeshifter doesn't look like Berens and stroll straight in?"

"Security does a great job of checking my ID and watermark every time I enter the building," Izzie noted. "I assume they're only checking harder with a shapeshifter on the loose."

"Security has additional measures in play," Bill confirmed. "Throughout the building, not just the vaults. They're not getting in here without an army."

"He does raise an interesting point." Katya glanced between Izzie and Jackson. "The shapeshifter already infiltrated the city's employment as part of their plot. Their earlier gambit as Izzie could be a prelude to a more nuanced and subdued gambit."

"Damned shapeshifters," Bill muttered. "I'm not worried, but I'll reiterate to security to double-check everyone, no matter who they are. Make sure people in your divisions understand it'll be obnoxious until we get this situation resolved."

Katya offered a shallow nod. "I'll reinspect the wards and reinforce them in the vault."

"We could end this quickly," Rafe commented.

"How?" Bill asked.

"We make a big show of relocating the artifact out of town to a long-term secure storage facility, which ends the immediate threat. That'll give us time to track down the local Syndicate representatives and the shapeshifter."

Bill shook his head. "We take down the shapeshifter, and we can get him to cough up what he knows about the Arcane Syndicate. Also, losing access to the amplifier could make him or the Syndicate desperate. We could be looking at more random terrorism with innocent people getting caught in the crossfire."

Rafe frowned. "I understand."

Bill nodded toward his office window framing the chair behind him. "We can't win this by punting responsibility. Bodies will pile up."

Izzie rotated her arm, remembering the earlier pain of getting stabbed. "I owe this guy. He keeps cutting and running whenever he comes to dance. That's rude, and I want to pay him back."

Allan took a deep breath before speaking. "The more we focus on the shapeshifter's magical signature with our detection network, the more resources remain unavailable for other investigations. Other agents are already complaining."

"Then forward their complaints to me." Bill's RBF turned into a full-on scowl. "The shapeshifter and the Syndicate remain our top priority until we know they're done. Right now, we have no evidence that the Arcane Syndicate has other operatives in this area. Forensics and field support verified the shapeshifter's magical residue at the terror sites, which means grabbing him is a chance to get them and stop their moves in the immediate area for now."

Katya and Allan nodded. They didn't say anything.

"If we're dealing with one magical, we can take him down," Izzie remarked. "No matter how many parks he's gobbling up."

Jackson shook a fist with an eager grin. "Now you're talking, Berens."

Rafe's expression remained uneasy. "The longer we wait, the more opportunity the shapeshifter has to infiltrate somewhere. The next time he might decide to murder a victim and replace them. I don't know if it's safe to wait for him to come to us."

"Do you have a plan to find him, Martinez?" Bill asked. "Because if you do, I'm all ears. I want him dealt with as much as you do."

Rafe looked at Izzie. She knew that expression. He was asking for permission and support for something risky. She had no idea what he was planning but nodded.

"We know the shapeshifter's true goal is to obtain the amplifier for the Arcane Syndicate," he began. "That's based on what he said at the professor's house. Based on what the professor said, we also know the amplifier is trackable since we removed it from his special room."

Jackson grunted. "We went over this. They're not coming here, as much as I wish they would."

Izzie's brow lifted. "You're not getting what he's saying. It's trackable."

Jackson frowned. "I get that, Berens. I don't have to cast spells to understand the concept of tracking."

Izzie shook her head. "The PDA building is too hard of

a target. What if we gave them another target? One that's more plausible, an out-of-the-way place with defenses yet not one as hardened as the PDA building?

"What if we give them exactly enough rope to hang themselves? A tempting target that doesn't scream obvious trap? They might have to be careful under normal circumstances, but this is a situation where they can't let us send the amplifier away. They'll never have a better chance of grabbing it than in this city."

Jackson's eyes widened. "Oh, yeah. I like the sound of that."

"I don't," Bill stated. "Are you suggesting we use the amplifier as bait?"

"That's exactly what I'm suggesting," Izzie replied. She looked at Rafe, who nodded his confirmation that she understood his idea. "We have no strong reason to believe we'll be able to track this guy down otherwise. We keep reacting to what he's doing. We need to be proactive. We need to make sure he comes to us."

She nodded firmly, liking the idea more and more as she explained it. "Professor Roth was very clear that those who knew what they were looking for would be able to track the amplifier. That means they know we have it here right now, and if we move it, they'll know *when* we move it."

"We get ready for the shapeshifter, complete with help from tactical support," Rafe added. "It won't go down the same. He shows up, and we take him down."

Bill scoffed. "Last time the shapeshifter showed up, he blew the roof off a house."

"Not the whole roof," Izzie corrected. "If I had more

time to set up wards, it wouldn't have gone down the same."

"Then all you need is a place that's warded already but not as warded and defended as the PDA building," Luisa interjected. "Also somewhere you can evacuate in case everything goes badly." She almost jumped out of her seat when everyone looked at her. "It was just an idea."

Izzie snapped her fingers. "It's a great idea. I'd suggest my apartment, but there's too great a risk of collateral damage. We need a heavily warded building where only a single person or family lives who'd be willing to cooperate."

Bill shook his head. "The Magical District has suffered enough already. The last thing we can do is call people and ask if we can use their house so their roof or walls can be blown off."

"If it's a neighborhood with single-family detached houses, it'll be easier to clear people out," Izzie countered. "We can make up a story about a gas leak, a hungry genie, or something to clear the rest of the neighborhood for a day. Then we wait until he shows up, and we close the door on the trap for our shapeshifter."

"You think there's a convenient little house for you out there that's already heavily warded and they'll agree to help the PDA at the drop of a hat?" Bill scoffed. "When there's a risk their house could be heavily damaged or destroyed?"

Izzie smiled. "Actually, there is. I can think of somebody who is in our ECD and has helped the PDA in the past." She pulled out her phone. "With your permission, sir?"

Bill stared at her in open disbelief, enough that it erased his Resting Boss Face. "I want to be completely clear about this. You're saying we should clear out a neighborhood, grab somebody's house, and bait the shapeshifter there?"

"Yes. We also put out a fake news notice that we're moving a 'recovered artifact of unknown ability' to a remote security facility tomorrow to poke the shapeshifter into making his move."

"Where's your convenient warded location with your ready-to-cooperate magical?"

"Pearl Storm's home," Izzie explained.

"You want to get a civilian involved like that? Your friend?"

"She's been involved in helping us on previous cases. Before the case threatened to get away from us because there were people in the magical community who didn't want to cooperate. Why not take advantage of the opposite?"

"As long as she agrees, I could make it work." Bill's brow lifted. "You're sure you can get her to agree?"

"Yes, I am."

Bill thought it over for a moment before nodding. "This is a little unorthodox, but that's every other day at the PDA. It's also our best plan for ending the threat. Even if we move and get this amplifier on the road, it'll be vulnerable the entire time. If the Syndicate gets their hands on their artifact, there are about a half-dozen ways we'll be screwed. Taking down their primary agent will allow us a better shot of moving it to permanent storage safely."

Izzie brought up her contacts list. "I'll make the call."

CHAPTER TWENTY-ONE

P earl twirled her black wand in her pale fingers and pointed it up. She all but shouted her incantation, her voice filled with unnecessary vibrato. Izzie snickered at the obvious showmanship.

The nearby hedges grew wider and taller until they formed a natural canopy blocking the sky. Soft gray mist floated ankle-deep above the ground. With the sun gone and light provided by dancing will o' wisp-like projections, the full spooky effect was on display despite it being summer. All Pearl needed was a bucket of candy bars for trick-or-treaters.

A nearby tactical support operator jogged past Pearl and Izzie with his rifle slung over his shoulder, grenades on his belt, and his technomagical goggles already on, providing him with night vision and magical detection. Tactical pouches filled with additional rifle magazines hung from his bulletproof vest.

Much like Rafe's vest, mild permanent enchantments strengthened it and granted additional anti-bullet and anti-magic defenses. The man had everything he needed to take on a standard magical threat.

Pearl threw up her hand to stop the jogging operator. He skidded to a halt. His magazines and grenades rattled.

"Ma'am?" the operator greeted in an uneasy tone.

"Step back," Pearl ordered.

He swallowed and stepped back. The tiny witch in her long black dress staring down the huge, rifle-toting man elicited a chuckle from Izzie.

The operator's behavior was correct. Pearl was far more dangerous than she looked, and they were on land bent to her will via years of enchantments. Anybody in the PDA with an ounce of common sense understood magicals were strongest in their chosen homes.

"Is there a problem, ma'am?" the operator asked.

Pearl squinted at him. "Where's the ring I gave you?" She pointed at his hand. "I gave every one of you soldier boys a ring when you got here."

"The ring is in my pocket, ma'am."

"Not good enough, soldier." Pearl shook her head.

"I'm not a soldier, I'm with PDA T—"

"Not good enough," Pearl repeated. "You have to wear the ring, or the defenses will react to you, including the hedge maze and anything inside. I don't have enough time to tune it to you all and keep it on high activity. The ring will also make communication easier. I can't guarantee my defenses won't interfere with your normal radios or assorted nonsense."

She poked him in the chest with the tip of her wand. "Ring on. Now. You want to kill yourself, don't do it on my property."

The operator reached into his pocket to retrieve a thin black band and slipped it on his finger. "Sorry, ma'am. I didn't understand the ring's importance."

Izzie glanced at her ring. She'd forgotten about the communications aspect. Pearl hadn't activated the spell yet. Proper coordination would save lives.

Pearl smirked as the operator jogged away. "You owe me one, Izzie. You caught me in a good mood. Otherwise, I would have a tough time agreeing to something as insane as letting an Arcane Syndicate killer attack you and allowing that evil ancient thing into my house."

She wrinkled her nose. "Even in the anti-magic containment crate, it still feels off. It's like an itch I can't scratch."

"That's because the artifact's technically partially magic and partially anti-magic," Izzie explained. "The containment crate can only do so much for it. At least according to what Professor Roth said. He's the expert." She shrugged. "The crate's keeping it under control, and that's what I care about the most."

"I hope I don't end up regretting this."

"Speaking of owing you one…" Izzie smiled at Pearl. "I owe you way more than that." Her smile dimmed. "I'm sorry if your house gets blown up. I wasn't being metaphorical when I said the shapeshifter blew off the roof of the professor's house."

Pearl laughed. "If my house gets blown up by one overzealous shapeshifter using life banking, I've been doing a lousy job preparing my defenses." She looked around with a predatory expression. "Where's Rafe? I want to mess with him a little."

"Not now, Pearl." Izzie snickered. "He's tense and watching the crate holding the amplifier." She sighed. "I'm tense." She nodded toward a hole in the hedge maze leading right to the house. "Are you sure about this?"

"If I weren't, I would have said no before all the strapping men with guns and grenades showed up. This isn't the first time I've helped you with something dangerous, even if it's the first time I volunteered my home as part of the effort."

"Helping us out might put you on the radar of the Arcane Syndicate. I'm confident we can take down this shapeshifter tonight. I'm not so confident it means we'll take down the Arcane Syndicate soon. We just learned of their existence."

"Oh, I'm on the bad girl list for a bunch of annoying groups with delusions of grandeur about conquering the world." Pearl spun her wand around her fingers before slipping it into her holster. "Where's the fun of being a witch if you can't rile up a witch hunt now and again?"

"You don't have to be here," Izzie reiterated. "Bill would strongly prefer if you weren't."

"Like I told you on the phone, you're not using my house for a fun time like shapeshifter-hunting unless I'm here. I even signed that waiver your boring boss insisted upon."

"It's for your protection. This is dangerous. He wanted you to understand that."

"Anything worth doing always is dangerous, one way or another." Pearl's face grew pensive. That vanished in an instant, with a warm smile replacing the look. "I'm not enough of a team player to join something like the PDA or that newer wannabe version of the Silver Griffins. That doesn't mean I don't want to do my part to help protect the city I call home, and your defenses wouldn't function properly without me here."

"I know, Pearl. I'm not trying to question your competence. I just..." Izzie gestured at her face. "We already got bashed around earlier, and I worry about the same thing happening to you."

"I will not suffer a single blow in my own home and lands," Pearl insisted, her expression and voice instilled with concentrated haughtiness. "The shapeshifter and Arcane Syndicate will realize they should have gone after the amplifier at the PDA building."

"That's major confidence. I like it."

"I'm nothing if not confident." Pearl winked.

Izzie nodded to another tactical support operator walking by. He was wearing his ring. "At least somebody's listening."

"Incidentally, I assure you my confidence is supported by experience." Pearl reached into one of her belt pouches and pulled out a thin vial containing a light blue liquid. She held it out for Izzie. "Take this. All my playing around with rusalka might as well help maintain the local peace. I whipped this up thinking it could help before you asked for my home."

Izzie held the potion in front of her face, a little confused. "Are these rusalka tears?"

"More specifically, it's a potion made with rusalka tears," Pearl corrected. "In this case, a limited type of truth potion. To be clear, it's less about forcing someone to tell the truth and more about forcing the true forms of things to appear. Splash a little on your friend and take a picture. In case they get away. The only other way is—"

"Hurt them badly enough their true soul-linked form comes out," Izzie offered, remembering the conversation with Infinite Mask. "Our shapeshifter already got shot up pretty badly without reverting, which makes me think he needs to be close to death for us to manage that." She tucked the potion into a pocket. "Is that what you were planning to do with the rusalka tears all the time?"

"Oh no. Certainly not." Pearl shook her head. "They're useful in a number of ways. I'm helping a wizard friend suffering from a rather unfortunate and extreme curse."

She coughed. "Depending on the type of rusalka, their tears can be useful for aphrodisiac magic and related areas." She looked away. "This friend of mine, you know, should have been more careful about who he took home for a good time. Now he needs one type of seductive magic to cancel out another." She shrugged. "Another person who'll owe me."

Izzie laughed. "I used to like them, but I never had a real knack for potions. This is why. I mean, how do we go from magical Viagra to a potion that reveals the true form of a shapeshifter?" She held up a hand. "I know, I know, sympathy in form, sympathy in feeling, sympathy in shape. All sympathies are valid sympathies. We might have missed each other in school years, but I had Professor Fowler for potions, too."

Pearl winked. "You know you're not being hunted by dark wizards anymore. You hunt them."

"Yes, that's part of my job. What about it?"

"That means you can have a life."

"I do have a life." Izzie stared at her. "I have an apartment. I have weird witch friends who do me favors."

"When was the last time you went out on a date?"

"I can't believe you're asking me about this right now." Izzie shook her head. "A killer shapeshifter is coming from an evil organization called the Arcane Syndicate to steal a powerful magical artifact, and you're worried about my dating life. Is it because of your other friend?" She grimaced. "You're not trying to set me up with the guy with the magical STI, are you?"

"He doesn't have an STI. He has a curse, and no, he's not your type." Pearl shrugged. Her playful smile never left her face.

"There's always an evil magical organization, a paranoid dragon, or a dwarf crime boss plotting something out there. If it's not them, it's an evil corporation trying to make technomagic slaves or magic-sapping viruses. Life's both the dark and the light, Izzie. It always has been. It always will be."

She patted Izzie on the shoulder. "Make sure you have a reason for what you do, not just momentum from when you were younger."

"I'll worry about my dating life on another day," Izzie insisted. "Today's about capturing a killer."

Pearl drew her wand and turned away. "If you say so. I've decided I'm going to find Rafe and mess with him after all."

"Don't overdo it, and I'm officially discouraging it."

"Your objections are duly noted."

Izzie stood there and watched her friend saunter off.

She shook her head, unsurprised. Pearl had always been like that.

It would be easy to say that Izzie had suffered more, but wicked forms of darkness had also touched Pearl. Whether Earth- or Oriceran-born, the last few decades made it difficult for most magicals to avoid the shadowy villains and organizations who would use their powers for evil.

Izzie reached into her pocket and ran a finger over the cool vial containing the potion. The shapeshifter's masters needed the power of the amplifier. One scholar's genuine desire to probe into the past for the greater good had turned into a major danger.

Izzie tried to focus on that when Pearl's explanation concerning the rusalka tears resurfaced, and she laughed. "If you didn't want me so tense, mission accomplished."

She took a deep breath and slapped her cheeks. The shapeshifter would come, and there was no reason to assume he'd be alone. Forensics and field support had found the shapeshifter's magical signature at the earlier incident sites. However, they had no way of determining if other signatures present were from accomplices or victims.

The amplifier was out in the open, bait for evil. Now that they knew where their target was, there was no reason for the Syndicate not to send along help.

"Okay." Izzie nodded firmly. "Bring it on. This time, we're ready for you, Arcane Syndicate."

CHAPTER TWENTY-TWO

A tall hedge shimmered in front of Izzie. Rafe stepped straight through the dense foliage without trouble. The hedge solidified behind him.

Pearl always refused to explain the particulars of how she'd enchanted her hedge maze, more out of playful amusement than spite or paranoia. She considered it a fun game for Izzie to puzzle out all the individual enchantments and rituals that had gone into making her front and back yards places to be avoided by anyone who wasn't her guest.

One thing Izzie had realized long ago was there were too many walls with changing densities for it to be nothing but illusions. One moment, Rafe could walk through a hedge, and the next, a hedge would be as hard and impenetrable as thick stone.

Beyond the intricacy and time that had gone into enchanting the hedge maze, Pearl's specialty in plant magic meant she could pull off spells that Izzie would have more trouble with despite having higher total magical power. It was another situation where Izzie's emphasis on easy-to-use direct combat spells might have stymied her overall magical growth.

Rafe pointed his thumb over his shoulder. "Did you tell Pearl to mess with me in there? Because I'm not in the mood. I know she doesn't mean anything by it, but I'm trying to get my head in the game."

Izzie laughed. "Of course I didn't tell her to mess with you. Why would I do that?"

"She's messing with me." Rafe shook his head in disgust. "You'd think the owner of the house would understand the situation we're in. Instead, she's acting like it's a big, fun game. I don't know how I feel about that."

"It's not Pearl's first time in a dangerous situation," Izzie reminded him as they entered the house after their final perimeter check. "Come on, you know her. That's how she processes the world. It's probably healthier than me always looking for the next dark wizard emperor pulling the strings and plotting against me if I see a puppy that doesn't wag his tail."

"I'm not convinced."

Izzie smiled. "You analyze everything. I'm paranoid about everything, and she treats everything like a big joke. Everyone has their way. Wouldn't it be boring if we were all the same?"

"I suppose."

Rafe took such a deep breath his equipment rattled. He carried as much gear as the tactical support operators, including his vest, assault rifle, pistol, and anti-magic grenades. He had on his technomagic sunglasses instead of the tactical goggles used by the operators. After consideration, Izzie lifted her hand and murmured a shield spell to provide him more protection.

He looked down at his body. "It's always nice to have less chance to die during one of these situations. This one's a little crazier than normal."

"It feels like every other case we work is crazier than normal." Izzie shrugged. "Escalation."

"Nope. It's an availability heuristic issue."

Izzie squinted at him. "What?"

"In this case it's about the human tendency to overfocus on rare, negative events and falsely attribute a greater rate of occurrence to them accordingly. A non-magical example is how people think plane crashes are far more common than they are because they're reported on so much when they do."

He shrugged. "In our line of work, we don't freak out and obsess over the normal, low-stakes cases, like gnomes with crazy fake parrots. They don't linger in our minds."

"I get what you're saying." Izzie sighed. "This is different. This Arcane Syndicate represents true escalation."

Rafe shrugged again. "The nature of our job. If they were easy cases that didn't take much risk or magic to solve, they wouldn't end up in the PDA's lap. We take the lumps so the citizens don't have to."

"You trying to make me feel better or run for mayor?" Izzie grinned. "I'll need to strengthen that shield spell once in a while depending on how long this takes."

He patted his vest. "I've got this baby. I'd feel better if you wore yours." He waved his hand. "I know, I know, you think they're too bulky and you feel your shield spell is enough protection without compromising mobility."

"Exactly. I'm glad you pay attention when I talk." She gestured at the faint glowing shell of the shield spell surrounding Rafe. "It'd be more convenient if you could spontaneously become a wizard."

Rafe laughed. "Too bad it's not that easy." His smile faded. "When I was a kid, I didn't get that for the longest time. Everybody talked about the brand-new world we lived in, how fantasy was real. Elven ambassadors gave speeches about a new millennium of peace, and famous scientists discussed a future where we needed to revisit everything we knew about the world."

Izzie smiled. "It's hard for me to imagine given the way I grew up. My whole childhood was drenched in magic, both positive and negative."

"The exotic and fantastical became reality." Rafe stared at a wall. "That fascinated me. More and more magical beings either came to Earth or revealed they'd been here all along. I figured, oh, now that magic's for real, when can I learn it? I understood I would never be an elf or gnome or anything other than a human, but I figured I could be a wizard."

"Even though it wasn't all fun spells? Even back then, the darker aspects of magic made themselves known. Arguably, that's the reason magic wasn't kept secret longer."

"Even the dark magicals and rogues fascinated me. I obsessed over the Seattle incident for a long time, thinking, 'If I could have been there with magic, I could have stopped it. I would have figured it out somehow.'"

He shrugged. "Tons of little kids want to grow up to become heroes. Except I believed I could have something people now had to admit was real. Magic. Then I got older and realized that magicals truly were special and different. That it wasn't as simple as declaring my college major as sorcery."

"You never told me any of this before," Izzie replied quietly. "I never knew it bugged you that much."

"It doesn't. Not anymore. I don't think about it that much to be honest. I spend my days helping take down rogue magicals." He smiled. "That's pretty special, and I come from a long line of cops and federal agents. I'm exactly where I'm supposed to be. Sometimes it helps to have a non-magical perspective. It's like the professor said about the hammer and nail."

"You don't have any resentment about not being able to achieve your childhood dream? Not even a little?"

Rafe shook his head. "It's no different than a kid growing up thinking he'll play pro baseball. Then he realizes he was only good in his neighborhood, and he's much better at math. Reality is what it is."

He gestured at his glasses. "Besides, the best of both worlds has come. Technomagic. It doesn't matter if I'm a wizard if I can use magical items to bring down rogue magicals. By the time I have grandchildren, I wonder if there will be that big a distinction between magicals and non-magicals."

"That's true. Everything's changed so much for magicals and non-magicals these last twenty years."

Rafe motioned toward the bathroom door around the corner of a hallway connecting to the living room. The amplifier lay inside, contained in a crate, their precious and dangerous bait to draw in their lethal suspect.

"It also makes me worry that type of problem will be more common, not less." Rafe's expression darkened. "It's like you said. It's not all fun spells."

"This *is* a risky plan. It's also the best one we have for catching this guy and finding out more about the Arcane Syndicate. I have a really bad feeling about them. Any group that can be around for centuries and avoid detection is bad news. I don't want to end up in a situation where we only hear about them because they're already making their big power play."

Rafe nodded at the bathroom. "We keep him from getting that bracelet, then they'll have a hard time pulling off any power plays anytime soon."

"That's the theory. Let's hope the execution is as easy."

"There's a good chance he'll be tougher than last time. We had time to prepare. So did he."

Izzie grunted. "I know. Trust me. I've had a hard time thinking about anything else."

"I keep hoping he'll screw up his life banking and take himself out. Infinite Mask said it was inevitable."

"Inevitable doesn't mean anytime soon or conveniently in the middle of our fight." Izzie scowled out the window. "Jackson had a good point earlier. As much as I want to take this guy alive and question him about the Arcane Syndicate, I'm prioritizing PDA and civilian lives. We hold back, and he'll kill us all."

Rafe inspected his rifle. "I'm there with you, Izzie. We can't let the Syndicate get their hands on that artifact, no matter what. As long as we can do that, we can deal with whatever else they have planned."

Pearl's voice spoke into Izzie's ear. The sound was as

loud and clear as if the witch stood next to her. "I've activated the speech link spell. I've tried my best to accommodate your equipment, but I can't guarantee anything during the incident. I can guarantee my ring system won't suffer any interference from my wards."

She paused for a couple of seconds. "Usage is straightforward. Hold the ring and say unmute, mute, quiet, or hear as necessary. Everyone wearing one of my rings should be able to use it while on or near my property. I wouldn't go too far otherwise without your own preparations."

"TacSup One online, five by five," Jackson reported.

"I have no idea what that means, but I assume it's good. Or is five the worst?"

Izzie held her ring. "Unmute." She added, "He's talking about signal quality. It's good. This is Berens."

"I hear you five by five, Berens," Jackson replied. "All TacSup operators, perform comms check. Then mute on secondary system. Focus on your primary comms during the operation. I'll provide relevant pass-through to Berens, Martinez, and Storm as necessary."

TacSup Two through Eight all sounded off. The PDA had authorized two squads of four operators to supplement Izzie and Rafe at the house. TacSup One through Four were all stationed in the front hedge maze. The remaining operators patrolled the rear hedge maze.

"I still have secondary comms established with field support, Berens," Jackson reported. "Nothing unusual from the drones yet. Your boy isn't lurking around. He better not stand us up. We're supposed to have a date."

"Don't wear yourself out pacing around," Izzie replied.

"We have no idea if and when he'll take the bait. We could be here all night."

"That would be rude."

"Remember, Bill gave a deadline. If our suspect hasn't shown up by 0600 tomorrow, we'll prep to transfer the artifact back to the secure vault and wait for the final transfer to the PDA HQ high-security vault."

Izzie hated the idea. She didn't want to leave unfinished business and worried that without capturing the shapeshifter, she wouldn't see him again until he showed up with an Arcane Syndicate army.

"I'm all dressed up in my dancing boots. I'll be upset if I don't get to dance."

"I sincerely hope this won't take that long," Pearl interjected. "It's dreary to wait an entire night for someone to come and kill you."

"It all depends on how much our shapeshifter wants the artifact." Izzie muted her ring and sighed.

A thorn-covered vine snaked out from a nearby hedge. The vine twisted and slithered along the ground like a snake near Rafe and Izzie.

Rafe eyed a vine. "I don't know if I'll ever get used to that."

"It's not here to mess with you," Izzie replied. "It's here to help stop the shapeshifter."

"All you good little PDA boys and girls out there," Pearl announced. "I'm beginning the process of activating all my main defensive spells. Assume any ambulatory or hungry plants belong to me. Don't worry. Most of my little green friends are concealed underground and will only attack the intruders at the appropriate time. Whatever happens, don't lose your rings unless you want to be fertilizer."

"She's joking, right?" Rafe asked.

Izzie shrugged. "I can't always tell with Pearl. My recommendation? Don't take off the ring."

Rafe ran his finger along the side of his sunglasses before glancing at one of his rifle magazines. "If you ask me, if we don't catch this guy tonight, there's no way we'll get that artifact transferred safely. Even if they don't steal it, they'll attack whoever's transporting it. There are too many variables in that plan."

"We'll stop him here. No matter what I...we have to do."

She reached into her pocket to slip on her sunglasses, then matched Rafe's earlier motion. A small map overlay appeared in the upper right. Dots marked the position of all the PDA members, but the display didn't show Pearl's location.

"The shapeshifter shouldn't have come to my city," Izzie declared. "And he shouldn't have dared to commit a magical crime here."

CHAPTER TWENTY-THREE

The hours passed, and deep night came for Austin. Cloudless clear skies provided views of the stars, but light pollution from the ever-growing city washed them out of the sky. Pearl's omnipresent wisps everywhere, including above the roof, added more obscuring light pushing back the darkness near the house.

The PDA patrols continued with no sign of the murderous shapeshifter. Izzie stood in the heavily warded bathroom, staring at the gray crate containing the bracelet. Her thoughts alternated between boredom and paranoia. She'd never been good at stakeouts for that reason.

Boredom presented the current greatest threat. Otherwise, Izzie's confidence in the plan didn't waver. She wasn't sure if that was self-delusion. At the same time, she no longer cared. A plan was in place, and all she could do was commit to its successful execution until the deadline.

The lack of appearance by the guest of honor didn't bother her. She suspected from the beginning the shapeshifter would wait until later in the night to strike, hoping to take advantage of their more fatigued and less focused state.

It's what she would have done if their situations were reversed. Similar considerations also guided her desire not to try clever tricks with the bait's position. The shapeshifter must have already understood it was a trap. Her plan relied on his arrogance and desperation to work. Exploiting that with a more obvious bait position would keep him coming where she wanted.

A chill ran up Izzie's spine. She'd spent too many years having to think like rogues and dark magicals. Sometimes she worried that the more she thought like them, the more she turned into them in a small part of her soul.

Izzie shook her head. She wasn't like them. They enjoyed violence, suffering, and killing. She wanted the bracelet locked up where nobody could get it. The shapeshifter wanted it for power, or at best, to offer power to his corrupt masters.

"Are you going to be more careful this time?" she murmured. "Or just as bold?"

She would have preferred more backup to defend the artifact, but the rest of the local PDA assets were keeping an eye on the Magical District and working other important cases. No matter the trouble she was dealing with, there was always more out there.

Pearl had been right about one thing. No one could escape magical trouble. Danger always threatened to upset the balance between the magical and non-magical worlds. It wasn't always clear what problem of the day would be the most important. Izzie needed to remember that the world, even the darker parts, didn't revolve around her because of an unfortunate past.

She liked to attack every case with the fervor of a true believer. Despite the artifact's danger, there was no guarantee her fellow PDA agents wouldn't find something in one of their current cases that led them to an even more dangerous plot that could threaten the entire city.

She frowned and looked down at the source of all her tension and concern. The gray crate sat on the tile floor of Pearl's bathroom with the words PROPERTY OF THE US PDA. CAUTION: MAY CONTAIN HAZARDOUS MAGICAL MATERIALS on the side. The bracelet lay inside with an active anti-magic emission matrix lining the interior. This helped keep the bracelet under control despite the occasional unsettling feeling in the pit of her stomach.

Given everything Professor Roth had told her and the occasional complaint from Pearl, Izzie couldn't be sure she wasn't imagining the discomfort. Whatever else she believed, she couldn't allow such an odd and unsettling artifact to fall into the hands of the Arcane Syndicate.

Pearl and Izzie had added extra wards to the bathroom, and rotating pairs of guards kept an eye on the crate and double-checked the batteries for the anti-magic emission matrix throughout the night.

Izzie stepped into the hallway and closed the bathroom door. She'd chosen the bathroom for the crate because of the room's centralized location. The location also kept the artifact above ground to present a more tempting target. It would encourage a dedicated assault on the house rather than a clever heist involving digging spells or any other complicated scheme she could scarcely imagine.

The balance between temptation and defense stood razor-thin. The target's location was obvious, assuming Roth was right about detecting the artifact's signature. The shapeshifter had to bypass all the outer defenses around the home to get that far. Then he'd need to get through Izzie and Rafe.

They'd faced off against him twice. He'd run away both times. That boosted her confidence.

She turned the corner and walked into the living room. The furniture included a striking coffee table Izzie didn't remember being there during her last visit. Beyond the furniture, three-dimensional images displayed locations all over Pearl's home and property floated near the front window. The magical command center offered spell-provided surveillance.

Pearl sat in a chair with her legs crossed and her wand in her lap. She occasionally snuck looks at the TacSup operators deployed in her front and back hedge mazes.

"This is stressful and invigorating at the same time," Pearl remarked.

"It'll be less so when the empowered shapeshifter shows up to kill us all and steal the artifact," Izzie replied.

Pearl shrugged. "One would presume, yes. Although if you, Rafe, and I, plus all those people outside can't stop one shapeshifter, we should be ashamed of ourselves."

"I hope it's only one shapeshifter. I worry about way more than that showing up."

Izzie leaned forward with a frown when Jackson's squads spread out and readied their weapons on the feeds.

She unmuted her ring, regretting their staggered comms for the first time that night. "This is Berens. What's going on?"

"Field support drones detected the shapeshifter's magical signature coming in fast and high," Jackson reported. "But not too fast. We're assuming another bird form. Field support also picked up three vans heading our way with noticeable internal magical signatures. All TacSup teams are in preassigned defensive positions. I think it's time for the dance to start, Berens. Our boy didn't stand us up, after all."

Izzie expected the shapeshifter to come, but she'd hoped he would be alone. Reinforcements changed everything. It was a good thing she hadn't tried to protect the artifact with only Rafe. One abandoned earlier plan had relied on greater remoteness and only the pair with the hope of better drawing out the shapeshifter.

Sometimes she tried to shoulder all the magical problems of the world herself. She didn't want anyone to suffer. Now, she was no longer alone. Tonight offered another important reminder of that fundamental truth.

"Martinez and I will hold position inside near the artifact," Izzie replied. She took the opportunity to strengthen her dwindling shield spells on Rafe and herself. "We'll handle the shapeshifter before he touches anything."

"Roger that," Jackson replied. "We'll dance with whoever shows up and leave the breakdancing circle to you and Martinez."

Izzie muted her ring.

Rafe rushed down the hallway into the living room with his gun in hand. "He took the bait. Thank God."

"I knew he would." Izzie sounded more confident than she felt. She shook her hands. "He had no choice."

"You knew he would, or you hoped he would?" Pearl asked. She stood, lifted her wand, flicked her wrist, and whispered an incantation. A pulse of energy shot from her wand and spread out in a circle.

"All my anti-pest spells are now active at full strength." Pearl grinned. "I'm glad I agreed to this."

"You're enjoying this too much," Rafe grumbled. "This guy's dangerous."

"It's not often I get to test my strength against others. I take a certain pleasure in it. This battle means I get to engage my naughty impulses yet remain firmly on the side of good."

Izzie's heart kicked up as a marker for the shapeshifter appeared on the edge of her mini-map alongside an altitude and speed indicator. The theoretical threat had become real.

"How high do your defenses extend again, Pearl?" she asked.

"A little bit above the top of the roof." Pearl pointed at the ceiling with her wand. "It becomes rather draining when I extend those enchantments too far off my property and yard. The interactions of the preexisting wards and spells, as you can imagine."

"Oh, he's going with a classic. Jackson and field support were right." Izzie pointed at one of the surveillance feeds. A huge hawk with a knife in his beak circled overhead, high enough that the light from the wisps below only revealed his outline.

"What's he waiting for?" She squinted. "He's not dive-bombing the house." She glanced toward the bathroom. "He's here rather than the front door. That means he traced the artifact."

"Of course he's not immediately attacking." Pearl smiled. "There's no way he doesn't sense all the magic in my defenses. For all his power, he's assaulting a witch's home. He must suspect you're in here waiting for him too, but he can't be sure. I've covered the maze, and the heavy level of background magic will make it impossible for him to pick you out."

"If we weren't about to face off against a murderous shapeshifter, I could hug you for being so thorough." Izzie took a deep breath. "I only hope he didn't bring three vans full of warrior shifters and battle wizards."

The three vans screeched to a halt outside the front gate to the hedge maze. Izzie's brow lifted in surprise. The enemy made a tactical mistake by not trying to take part of their forces and inserting by going through a neighbor's yard. She didn't need to be Jackson Taliesin to question their tactics.

The van doors flung open, and men in urban camouflage jackets and pants wearing skull masks poured out, all carrying rifles. Izzie frowned. The weapons' barrels had runes inscribed on them.

"That's not good," she muttered.

Pearl waved her wand again. The masks, rifles, and clothes lit up on the monitors as her spells visualized the enchantments.

Izzie touched her ring. "Unmute. TacSup, this is Berens. We have confirmed contacts outside the front entrance. Per the plan, Pearl will activate one-way transparency in the forward hedges but can't allow easy pass-through in defense mode. Keep that in mind. I count sixteen men deploying from the vans."

"Copy that," Jackson replied. "That matches our drone spotted counts."

Izzie took a deep breath. "Be careful. They have enchanted rifles, masks, and clothing of unknown magical strength and ability. Our shapeshifter is also over the house in hawk form. Keep his buddies off our asses as long as you can, and we'll handle him in here."

After more wand flourishes from Pearl, fuzzy windows appeared in the front hedges on the TacSup operators' side, allowing them clear views of their enemy. They wouldn't need Izzie or the drones as a spotter in the first section of the hedge maze.

Izzie spared a glance at Rafe. He stood rigid and stone-faced. No matter how many times they faced death together, she couldn't get used to it. There was no reason he'd be different. Worrying about someone else's life always made it that much worse.

"Roger, Berens," Jackson replied. "TacSup 5 and 6, move to the front to support the squads. TacSup 7 and 8, hold position in case these tangos have a couple of invisible sneakers who made it past the drones. Remember, we're outnumbered, so do not advance past the local defensive fortification without explicit orders. Let the plants do the hard work."

That was the first time Izzie had heard an enchanted hedge maze called a local defensive fortification. At the same time, she couldn't claim Jackson's description was inaccurate.

"Put me on speaker," Izzie told Pearl. "I need the van guys to hear me."

"I don't call it speaker." Pearl rolled her eyes.

"Come on. I'm serious. You know what I mean."

Pearl snapped twice and sighed. "You're on speaker."

"Attention unknown armed men," Izzie announced. "This is Special Agent Izzie Berens of the PDA. We are prepared for your arrival, and any hostile actions will be met with immediate and extreme force. You are to drop your weapons, get down on your knees, and put your hands on your head. If you fail to comply, you will be fired upon by conventional and magical weaponry. Your safety and lives can't and won't be guaranteed without your immediate surrender."

At Izzie's nod, Pearl took her off speaker. Izzie muted her ring.

The masked gunmen's opening response presented no subtlety, nuance, or evidence of fear. They hurled grenades at the hedge wall and opened fire.

Giant fluorescent pink flytrap-like heads tore out of the ground and swallowed the grenades. The colorful heads blew apart in subdued blasts that left the rest of the hedge wall untouched.

The enemy bullets bounced off the wards. To Izzie's relief, they didn't explode, but that suggested enchantments related to helping the bullets penetrate armor and personal defensive spells. That made them less dangerous to the hedge maze but more dangerous to the operators.

The PDA tactical support operators near the front of the maze opened fire, using their visibility advantage. Their first barrage of bullets passed through the hedge wall, leaving a visible ripple in the air and the magical one-way windows. The bullets bounced off the gunmen's jackets and fell crushed to the ground.

"Tango clothing is enchanted," Jackson reported. "All TacSup operators switch to anti-magic rounds."

Izzie wasn't surprised. The lack of bulletproof vests by the masked gunmen was too bold for a frontal assault unless they had magic.

The operators all swapped their magazines with practiced precision. They spewed bullets toward the gunmen.

Izzie glanced at Rafe. He held up his rifle with a wicked smile that was more appropriate for Pearl than him.

"I'm loaded for the shapeshifter. Anti-magic, all the way. I know what hurts him. He admitted it already."

Izzie double-checked the shapeshifter. He still circled overhead in large hawk form, holding a knife in his beak. She squinted and spotted a dark bump on top of the hawk, unsure of what it was because of the dim lighting.

"What is he waiting for?" Izzie asked. "Why isn't he doing something? He didn't have a problem attacking a warded building before. This has to be more than worrying about your wards, Pearl."

"He might think he can only win against us if he has his friends with him," Rafe replied. "Or he's depending on them to lower the defenses before he presses his attack."

Pearl clucked her tongue. "A terrible plan."

"Damn," Izzie grumbled. "He better not run if his guys get beat up."

Rafe shook his head. "There's no way this guy will give up that easily when the bracelet is sitting right here."

The skull-masked gunmen spread out as they returned

fire against the TacSup operators. The bullets flashed on contact with the hedges, tearing through the outer wards before the inner wards stopped the bullets with a flash or the occasional appearance of the glyph and sigils making up the ward.

Izzie unmuted her ring and advised, "Be careful, TacSup. They have anti-magic bullets, too. Not sure how long those front wards will last."

"Copy that, Berens," Jackson replied.

Izzie muted her ring.

Pearl folded her arms and harumphed. "I'll take small pleasure in knowing it was expensive and inconvenient for these people to raid my home." Her smile turned feline and hungry. "They don't know how prepared I am, though. It'll take more than anti-magic bullets to get in here."

Another enemy barrage weakened the surviving wards. Bullets bounced off the now steel-hard hedges, another result of Pearl's earlier anti-pest spell activation. So far, everything was going about as well as Izzie could expect and hope.

Rafe frowned. "I don't know why the Syndicate didn't bother sending these guys earlier." He gestured at the monitor. "They didn't blink at Pearl's plant monsters. They keep their discipline when they can't see their attackers and are taking fire. If they'd been with the shapeshifter at the night market, we would have been screwed."

"Who knows?" Izzie replied. "I'm not going to be impressed. I figure it gives us more people to interrogate."

The first TacSup counterattacks with anti-magic bullets landed a solid hit, ripping through an enchanted jacket and drawing blood. The masked gunmen rushed backward with most falling back to the vans for cover. A gunman fell when converging bursts tore through his enchanted uniform and into his chest.

Izzie stared at the downed man, watching the wounds, not out of any morbid fascination over their injuries but to monitor for any signs of regeneration magic. The downed man crawled to the side of a van. He yanked a small flask from a belt pouch and poured the thick contents down his throat. His wounds closed.

She unmuted her ring. "Did you see that, TacSup One? They have healing potions. No sign of active magical healers."

"Copy that, Berens. They're not making it to the house. I'll make 'em use every last damned potion they have before they set one damned foot in the maze."

Pearl squinted and pointed her wand at the feed featuring the shapeshifter. "Your real guest is on the move."

The hawk spun and flew inverted. His new flight pattern revealed the bump was a small pouch tied to his back. It was open and dropping tiny, dark shapes. Seeds. Right as Izzie grasped what was happening, the first seed struck the upper wards and blew apart in a massive, fiery explosion that shook the entire house.

Pearl whipped her wand to point straight at the ceiling and chanted another spell. A bright line shot from the tip and flowed into the ceiling. "It's not going to be that easy for you either, my shapeshifter friend."

Fiery death rained down. The explosions rattled the house, peeling away the defensive wards and spewing dark smoke everywhere.

After the first few explosions, the masked gunmen

rallied and resumed their advance on the hedge maze. They broke into smaller squads to approach the yard from the side and front. A barrage of anti-magic bullets from the TacSup operators dropped two more advancing enemies. The gunmen replied with a series of conventional fragmentation grenades that blew apart hungry plants. A small handful made it past to blast a small hole in the front hedge walls.

"You okay in there, Berens?" Jackson asked. "I'm hearing way more booms than I'd like back there. The magical signature on the drone feed is going nuts."

"He's bombing us with the same damned seeds he's been using all over town, but he hasn't made it through." Izzie frowned at the feeds as the visualized magic flows over the vans brightened. "I don't know if you see this with your goggles, but magic's also increasing around the vans. Something's happening, and I doubt it's good for you."

"Copy that, Berens."

More blasts distracted Izzie. She gritted her teeth, following the hawk shapeshifter's erratic back-and-forth flight over the house. His supply of seeds seemed endless. A less hardened location like Professor Roth's home would have been a crater already. Thus far, the shapeshifter hadn't defeated Pearl's defenses.

With no visible driver at the wheel, one of the vans squealed and accelerated toward the center of the hedge maze. Two quickly tossed PDA anti-magic grenades blew apart in a white crackling flash over the van. After jumping the curb, the vehicle fell on its side and slid toward the hedges.

Pearl twisted her wand. Thick razor-tipped vines shot

out to slow the vehicle. They tore through its sides and smashed through the window to stop it.

The other vans barreled toward the hedge maze. Another group of well-timed anti-magic grenades disabled whatever auto-driving spell was in use and sent the second van careening into and bouncing off the side of the front hedge wall, taking the wards down with it.

The third van struck the front of the hedge maze and blew apart into a swirling column of purple-blue energy that vaporized the front gate and much of the front hedges. The blast scoured a deep hole in the sidewalk and front yard.

"Oh my," Pearl commented. "They're trying harder. I'll give them that."

Izzie glared at Pearl's magical surveillance windows. Their first line of defense had fallen, and the shapeshifter continued to whittle away at their second line of defense. The siege had entered a new, deadly stage.

"I'm not letting you fly out of here with that bracelet," Izzie growled.

CHAPTER TWENTY-FOUR

Pearl fed more magic into her home defenses via a thick, bright line of energy shooting into her ceiling and spreading out in every direction. Sweat poured down her forehead. She let out a bitter laugh, the first sign the attack troubled her.

"This is becoming impressively annoying. I hope you don't think too poorly of me if I admit I'm having regrets about agreeing to this plan, Izzie."

"I hate to tell you this is going far better than I expected. I half-expected this building to have lost its roof already."

"You're such a good friend, Izzie." Pearl grinned at her own sarcasm despite the pain in her eyes. She put her other hand on her wand.

"So are you, Pearl."

"Don't worry. I'll make him work as hard to get in here as he's making me work to keep him out. I owe him a little annoyance."

The overlapping heavy gunfire outside rattled the

windows. The house team didn't have time to worry about the operators despite the enemies darting forward and using the first crashed van as a barrier to cover their advance. The shapeshifter's bombardment from above continued challenging Pearl's wards. Her breathing grew more labored with each attack.

The exterior gunmen kept up a constant stream of fire while breaking into smaller groups. The initial barrages from Jackson's team kept the gunmen back.

Rafe nodded with a satisfied look at the screen. "They depended on the shapeshifter for their heavy firepower, and he's concentrating on us. Tactical support will be able to mop these guys up."

Izzie frowned, not so sure. She didn't like how the appearance of grenade-eating plants didn't cause a lapse in firing by any of the masked gunmen. That type of discipline came from experience or with the help of magic.

Pearl groaned and wiped more sweat from her brow.

"Seriously, are you doing okay, Pearl?" Izzie asked. "If it comes down to it, just make a run for i—"

Pearl cut her off with a sharp look. "If it comes down to it, I won't abandon my friends and my home to vile, remorseless killers who are plotting against the city I live in."

She scoffed. "I understand everything's supposed to be different these days like you're constantly bemoaning. That doesn't mean those of the magical community of means and power no longer have a duty to stand up against those who'd do good people harm." She managed a wink, but it looked bizarre when accompanied by her grimace.

Izzie nodded at her friend. The balance of the magical

and non-magical worlds remained in flux. That might continue to be the case for decades. All they could do there and then was stop a murderous shapeshifter from stealing an ancient artifact that would make him an unstoppable tool of a dangerous organization.

A new series of staggered blasts shook the house, including shaking Pearl's record player off its stand. The record player smashed to pieces on the floor.

"Now he went and made this personal," Pearl declared. "I'm lucky I didn't have any of my albums on there. I'm going to enjoy seeing you take him down."

Izzie saw dark smoke out the front window. Pearl's defenses impressed her. Izzie wasn't so sure her apartment could have taken such a beating without her wards failing, and she was supposed to be the paranoid one who saw a dark wizard hiding behind every bush.

"My musical problems will have to wait." Pearl gritted her teeth. "The upper wards will fail soon. I'm sorry, Izzie, there's not much more I can do. His attacks are proving more effective than I would have believed. I pride myself on the defenses and spell integration I've set up here over the years. It won't be enough."

"He's dropping enough magical explosives on us to have blown up a tank. I couldn't ask for anything more. Your defenses are doing great. Our plan never relied on being able to stop him completely from getting inside."

Rafe's hands tightened on his rifle. "He's going to come straight for the bathroom once he gets in here. His focus on attacking the house proves he knows it's in here."

The outside feeds flashed with a series of stun grenades thrown by the gunmen. Izzie didn't worry. Unlike field agents' sunglasses, the TacSup operators' goggles featured an anti-blinding enchantment to protect them from the most commonly used forms of blinding people, technological or magical.

Izzie rolled her shoulders. "Rafe's right. Knowing where the shapeshifter's going means we'll be able to stop him. Reports have come in about other major patches of dead plants, but none report an uptick of dead animals, let alone unexplained murders. He can't be that much more powerful than before, and Pearl's spells are making him use up all his trick seeds."

"That assumes he didn't hide any other sources of life banking," Rafe cautioned. "And he blinded us one time."

Izzie lifted her hand and murmured a spell. The outside of Rafe's glasses flashed. She cast the same spell on her glasses. "I've protected us from blindness. We have to bug supply about getting us the same baseline enchantments that tactical support has in their goggles."

Dust and paint chips fell in a light cloud from the push of another bombardment. In another situation, Izzie might have admired the shapeshifter's determination. This time she wanted nothing more than for him to grow frustrated and give up on his bombing runs. The sooner he showed his face in whatever form, the sooner they could end this farce.

Thick, billowing smoke clouds joined with the darkness of night to hide the hawk's form on Pearl's security feeds. Izzie could still pick out the shapeshifter with the help of the drone feed overlay on her glasses. His increasingly erratic changes in direction baffled her.

Izzie narrowed her eyes as her worry rose. "I think he

must be concentrating on bombing overlapping points in the ward arrays. No wonder he's hitting so hard and not just keeping it constant. But how the hell would he know?"

"I hate to say it, but it's not exactly a secret that Pearl's your friend," Rafe pointed out. "We should have taken that more into account in the plan."

"The fact that Pearl's my friend was a big part of why we're here."

Pearl looked at Rafe. She kept her wand feeding more magical energy into the wards via the ceiling. "What are you saying, Rafe?"

"He might have anticipated we'd pull something like that." Rafe shook his head. "It's not like our drone dragnet can be everywhere, especially when it's looking for a specific magical signature. He might have checked this place out as a hawk before we came. If he flew high enough, would you have noticed?"

Pearl frowned. "I hate to admit to flaws in my great ward plans, but you might be onto something."

"It doesn't matter," Izzie declared. "He's still having a hard time getting in here. And he's not the only one who did homework beforehand."

The intensifying crack of gunfire made Izzie spare a glance at the magical security feeds. Giant vines shot from the edge of the hedge maze. They snagged a gunman's foot and flung him backward into the street. His friends tore through the base of the vines with concentrated automatic fire from their rifles.

The ongoing battle proved how impressive Pearl's efforts were. Beyond her wards, her other spells combined with the efforts of the TacSup operators made it all but impossible for the masked goons to reinforce their shapeshifter friend. Whatever frustration Pearl felt, the enemy must have felt twice as much.

A swaying sunflower plant popped out of one inner hedge wall and opened fire. Its high-velocity seeds passed through the outer hedges like they weren't there and produced the same ripples in the air as the PDA teams' bullets. The sunflower seeds struck the thrown gunman and a trailing gunman. The seeds ruptured and released a web of thin brown fibers to constrain the men.

"They've carved through the outer defense layers in the front yard and above us." Pearl grimaced. She didn't lower her wand, and the magical stream of energy continued unabated. "I'm putting more energy into securing the house defenses. I don't know how much longer I can maintain this."

Something heavy and loud thudded on the roof. Two heavy steps followed.

"I don't think he's a hawk anymore," Rafe commented.

"Infinite Mask talked about small creatures." Izzie eyed the ceiling. "He never did make it clear how big the shapeshifter could get."

A seed dropped in front of a living room window and exploded. Izzie flinched on reflex. Pearl's wards absorbed the bulk of the damage, leaving only cracks in the rattling window and door.

"He's not done with the stupid seeds." Rafe scanned the security feeds and shook his head. "There's too much smoke to make out anything on the roof."

"I think that was part of the plan." Izzie pointed at the

window and the security feeds. "He screwed up. We know where he's coming now."

The TacSup operators up front continued to push back the gunmen aided by dangerous plants of the hedge mazes. Half of the masked men now lay dead, wounded, or incapacitated outside Pearl's lawn or within the first section of the hedge maze.

Despite the invaders carving a hole in the front with their magical van bomb, the TacSup presence made it almost impossible for them to push in farther. Their flanking attempts had gone as poorly. A near-constant withering storm of plant and TacSup operator attacks forced the gunmen's side squad to circle back to the front and reinforce their allies.

Another series of blasts rippled across the top of the house, adding to the smoke, shaking the whole building and knocking dust into the air. More heavy footsteps sounded above.

"Pearl, I'm going to shoot through your ceiling." Rafe lifted his rifle.

"I'd rather you didn't."

Izzie shook her head. "There's no point in wasting ammo with blind shooting and weakening the wards. Let the shapeshifter wear himself down and use up all his stuff. That'll make him easier to handle if he gets in here."

Rafe frowned and nodded. "It's hard to see with all the competing flows, but are the secondary and tertiary layers of wards still holding?"

"Yes." Pearl wiped her forehead. "I can't be sure for how much longer, but they're the main reason we've merely been shaken instead of blown up."

Izzie frowned and adjusted her sunglasses. The intense magic present also disrupted any attempt to pick out the shapeshifter's signature. Fortunately, the drone overlay combined with his footsteps was doing a reasonable job of highlighting his location, even if the background interference led to a fuzzy, difficult-to-discern shape.

Izzie jerked her head to the side when a shadow over the hedge wall near the front window caught her attention. A small blue gemstone dropped from above. The gemstone stopped and floated outside the window.

"Pearl, is that yours?" Izzie desperately hoped the answer was yes.

"No. Unfortunately."

Izzie lifted her arm and spread her fingers while rattling off an incantation. Bright lines followed her thoughts and traced a pattern of arcane sigils in the air. The shapeshifter needed to learn who he was fighting and that she didn't need a bag full of magical trinkets to show off her power.

She whipped her arm to the side and shouted the last word of her chant. A translucent white dome surrounded Rafe, Izzie, and Pearl before extending past the living room to cover the bathroom. It was a stronger protective spell than the personal shields she'd cast before.

"How much could that damned shapeshifter fit in his mouth as a bird?" Izzie asked. "Or was it the stupid bag?" She grimaced. "Could he be using portal spells to ship in more trouble?"

"Birds are famous for having crops and vomiting things," Rafe noted. "No portal spells required."

"Aren't crops the thing jockeys use?"

Rafe chuckled. "In this case, for birds, think of them as extra stomachs."

"Oh, great, our guy's going to win because he ate a bag's worth of disposable exploding magical artifacts." Izzie shoved more magical energy into her protective dome.

"The real question is, what is it?"

"It's trouble." Izzie raised both arms and poured more magic into her dome.

A few seconds later, the gemstone shattered with a resounding *boom* that knocked the front door to the ground. The shockwave smashed into the dome before the gemstone's pieces and the window's shattered remnants turned into shrapnel. The cloud of death bounced off the dome.

A secondary wave of blue energy struck the dome, overwhelming the spell and knocking it down, along with Pearl, Izzie, and Rafe. The stream of magic from Pearl's wand stopped. Sizzling gemstone pieces and cracked glass clattered down in a sharp hail.

Izzie sat up and reinforced her personal shield spell. Setting up the dome and surviving the blast had taken more out of her than she expected. "Everyone okay?"

Rafe hopped to his feet. "He got me worse at the professor's place."

Pearl scowled at a tear in her dress. She tightened her grip on her wand. "This was one of my favorite dresses. This annoying visitor failed to kill me when he had a chance. That was his biggest mistake."

Heavy gunfire echoed outside and shook the building's surviving windows. On the feeds, the remaining gunmen pressed their attack. A small number of invaders penetrated the hedge maze and tried to blitz past the TacSup operators. Their victory was short-lived before vines wrapped around their bodies and bound their limbs. Despite losing over half their force, the masked gunmen didn't shrink from battle or show any sign of fear.

A huge, furry half-bear, half-man complete with a furry, muzzled face and clawlike sharp nails on his hands dropped from the roof in front of the destroyed front window. A faint glowing second energy skin, a type of shield spell, covered him. Despite his current fearsome appearance, he still held the shapeshifter's rune-covered knife, confirming his identity. He smashed into the living room through the open front entrance with a roar, baring his fangs.

"The guest of honor has finally shown himself," Izzie declared.

CHAPTER TWENTY-FIVE

Before anyone could question him, Rafe hurled an anti-magic grenade behind the shapeshifter. The grenade burst with a satisfying crackle and flash. All the magical surveillance feeds winked out of existence along with a secondary shield spell surrounding the shapeshifter. His rifle bursts forced the shapeshifter back, growling.

The shapeshifter lifted the knife and hesitated. Izzie stared at him and clung to a small hope that the mind inside the furry head understood he'd been run off twice before by Rafe and Izzie.

"The exterior gunmen are almost suppressed," Jackson reported, proving that the grenade's localized effects hadn't disrupted any of the key spells in Pearl's ring communication network spell.

"Then prepare to back us up." Izzie pelted the shapeshifter with a stun bolt that didn't earn a blink. Nor did he immediately counterattack. "We're fighting the suspect, and he's a big one. He's taken a weird werebear combat form, but don't worry until you have them all secured. I don't want you guys getting shot in the back. We can handle their pet bear boss."

"Just give us two more minutes, Berens, and we'll be there."

Izzie exchanged glances with Rafe and Pearl before frowning at the shapeshifter and pointing her palm at him, readying for rapid-fire light bolts. "This is your last chance to surrender. Don't make us kill you. Our backup has taken out almost all of your backup and will soon be here. You have no chance of winning. Surrender now, and we'll consider that the beginning of you cooperating."

The shapeshifter roared and smashed a clawed fist through a closet door. He tore the entire door off its hinges. Izzie's mind registered a slight complaint about the maneuver's inefficiency before he flung the door at Pearl with blinding speed.

The door edge slammed into Pearl's abdomen. Her shield saved her from the worst of it when the door cracked and bounced off. Her spell dissipated. She grimaced and clutched her stomach. "That wasn't very nice."

Remembering what Rafe and she discussed earlier, Izzie gave up on her standard combat spells after her light bolts tore into the shapeshifter's chest. He stomped forward and bellowed, raising his knife again. She gestured and murmured a quick chant to summon a long, ropelike strand of light magic, snagged the shapeshifter's right leg, and pulled.

While her immediate plan to take him down failed, his leg jerked hard against the strand. He tugged and tugged yet couldn't move forward.

Sensing Izzie's plan, Rafe alternated shots at the shapeshifter's legs. Blood splattered on the floor. The shapeshifter roared louder, the sound overwhelming, but didn't go down. He launched the broken front door into the air with a powerful kick, only narrowly missing Rafe, who repaid him with a burst to the chest.

The earlier light bolts and rifle attacks weren't healing but also weren't slowing the shapeshifter. The team needed a different strategy, and one was paying off more than the other.

"Pearl, help me tie him down!" Izzie shouted, pushing more of her magical power into her light rope and trying to yank the shapeshifter's leg back.

Pearl glared at the shapeshifter. She waved her wand. Huge vines poked into the living room through the broken front window to snag the shapeshifter's arms and legs. His bone-shaking roar of frustration attested to the effectiveness of their tactics.

"We got you!" Izzie shouted. "That's what you get!"

Despite her taunts, her plan wasn't complete. They'd restrained him, but they hadn't brought him down.

He twisted and strained against the restraints. One of the vines tore. Izzie shoved more magic into her light rope before conjuring a second light rope to aid Pearl in pulling the shapeshifter to the floor.

"Help me pull on three, Pearl," Izzie announced. "One, two, three!"

The vines and ropes wrenched the shapeshifter's legs out from underneath him. He plummeted and smashed into the floor with his limbs splayed. He lost hold of his knife. The blade slid until hitting a coffee table leg.

Rafe reloaded his rifle and glanced at Izzie with a questioning expression. She shook her head, and he trained his rifle on the shapeshifter's head without firing.

Izzie gritted her teeth and shoved more magic into her spells. Pain spiked through her body as she tried to overcome his life banking strength with her magical strength. The shapeshifter thrashed and tried to get loose.

"I think we finally got him." Izzie panted.

Pearl twisted her wand and summoned more thick vines from underneath the front yard. "Maintaining the wards during the earlier onslaught has drained me. This is the best I can do for now."

"You're doing great." Izzie stepped backward and reinforced the vines with more of her light ropes. Glass crunched under her shoes. The sound reminded her of the glass vial in her pocket. She pulled it out and eyed it. "TacSup One, we're good in here. We've secured our suspect. You clean up out there, and we'll finish up in here."

"Roger that, Berens. We're basically done out here."

Pearl smiled at the vial. "It's your best chance to see the truth and take your first picture of your true suspect."

Izzie smiled at the shapeshifter. "We're going to put these pictures through every government database out there. All your careful shapeshifter crap won't have helped you once we ID you. There will be nowhere you can run." She looked at Pearl. "This will revert him?"

"I'm not as familiar with shapeshifting magic," Pearl replied. "As a potion to promote truth, it should let you see what his true form is."

"Not sure how that's different, but okay."

The shapeshifter growled. He twisted his head and

strained against the ropes, which were tight enough that he couldn't move his arms or legs.

Izzie stared at the potion in her palm, took a deep breath, and flung it at the shapeshifter. Walking close to a half-bear, half-man attacker was idiotic. The potion zipped across the room in a blur and shattered with a hard impact against the shapeshifter's muzzle.

The shapeshifter let out another roar. His body contorted, twisted, and shrank. The vines and light ropes tightened more. He shook violently, but his restraints kept him in place. His body shifted until a thin, elderly man in a simple brown robe lay on the floor. His wounds were gone. He glared at Izzie with hatred-filled eyes.

Izzie disabled the magical flow visualization mode on her glasses and took a picture. "I've got you. Not that you're escaping anyway. I gave you your chance to surrender. You should have taken it."

"What have you done?" the man shouted.

"I used a little potion to see the real you," Izzie said. "You should be happy we did it that way without having to almost kill you." She nodded at Pearl. "Thank you for the potion. And thanks again for loaning us your house."

The shapeshifter glared at Pearl and pulled on his restraints. "What have you done to me, you insufferable no-talent witch? I should have known you'd be involved in all of this."

Pearl's brow lifted. "Oh. I see. Interesting."

Izzie frowned. "You know him?"

"Yes, I do." Pearl chuckled. "This is fascinating."

The man bared his teeth. The canines of an old wizard

didn't offer the same terror factor as the fangs of a were-bear's combat form.

Rafe pointed his rifle at the man's head. "Stop resisting."

"The potion will wear off soon enough, and you'll go back to your cosplaying," Pearl admonished. "I'm sure they'll have you taken care of by then."

Izzie yanked out her cuffs and headed toward the restrained suspect. "Keep him covered, Rafe."

"I have plenty of ammo left in this magazine."

"Berens." The restrained suspect spat out the name like a curse. "You're a fool to think you've won. You're a fool to think this is over."

"Yes, yes. The power of dark wizardry." Izzie rolled her eyes. "You think I haven't heard every evil guy rant before?"

The man gritted his teeth. He grimaced and let out a loud groan. Izzie prepared to blast him with a light bolt, but he set his head on the floor and sighed without changing form.

"That potion is nothing more than the truth in bottle form." Izzie knelt beside him and used the light ropes to yank his arms behind his back. She slapped the anti-magic cuffs on his wrists. "These should at least slow you down. Pearl, since you know him, who exactly is this asshole?"

"You think you've won," he interrupted. "But you haven't." He stared at the bathroom. "Shifting back has only healed my wounds. You've done me a favor."

Pearl stared at the man's face and laughed. "Do you really not recognize him?"

"No. Why should I? He's a shapeshifter."

The man snorted. "Fool."

"But you do know him." Pearl gestured at his face. "You've mentioned his name in this very house." She clucked her tongue. "You must not have bothered to look at a picture." She motioned with her wand toward the pinned man. "Agent Izzie Berens, meet your robbery victim, Xelius."

CHAPTER TWENTY-SIX

"We have all our dance partners under control outside," Jackson reported. "You still doing okay in there, Berens?"

"Yes. Bring the backpack anti-magic emitter. Adjust it to low power, minimum range. I only need to make sure this guy doesn't change shape, and I'm not convinced the cuffs will be enough even with him not having his main casting aid. The guy was taking bullets and spells like he could do it all day."

Xelius glared at her. He lay on his stomach near the broken front window as he twisted and pulled. The vines and light ropes held firm.

Izzie lifted her palm and pointed it at Xelius. "Enough. If I think you're getting free, we're ending this by taking you down, understand? I've had about as much of you as I can stomach. You've caused enough trouble."

Xelius shifted on his stomach and stared at the hallway corner. The bathroom door lay beyond with his sought-after target inside.

"Despite what you said, it would be difficult for me to use full shapeshifting with these cuffs on anyway," Xelius replied. "You would notice if I attempted anything radical. If I could have shifted quickly into a smaller form, I already would have."

Rafe frowned at him. "We took you by surprise. We're not going to let you take us off-guard."

"Don't worry, Rafe." Izzie scowled at Xelius. "Once we get the emitter here, he won't be in a position to toss any spells off, even if we have our backs turned and we're making s'mores at a campfire."

Xelius chuckled. "Then I suppose you have the advantage. For now. We'll see how long that confidence lasts, Berens."

"A guy like you will have a hard time adjusting to not being able to use your magic and being able to intimidate people." Izzie narrowed her eyes. "That's what it's going to mean to go to prison. Cutting-edge anti-magic gear in those places. You'll love it."

Xelius scoffed. "You thought you had me before in the alley and at Roth's house. Why are you so sure you have me now?"

"As I recall, you ran both of those times. That means we did have you."

"A strategic withdrawal, I can assure you." Xelius harumphed.

"Before, you didn't feel you needed to bring a small army. This makes me think that even with more life banking, you didn't believe you could win. It turns out you couldn't." Izzie nodded toward the front yard.

"What about all those guys? Enforcers from the Arcane

Syndicate?" She shook her head. "D-plus, C at best. I hope you people aren't planning to take over the world with that quality of thugs. You make the dark wizards I dealt with in the past look like the crème de la crème."

Rafe chuckled. "I don't mind fighting lower-quality criminals. It makes my job easier."

Xelius glared at them. "Do you honestly believe the Arcane Syndicate would rely on such mindless thugs?"

"You tell us," Rafe prodded. "They showed up when you did. Very soon, they'll be interrogated. Then we'll learn everything we need about the Arcane Syndicate. If your friends are so much better than those guys, why aren't they here?"

"You'll learn nothing from talking to those worthless thugs," Xelius spat.

"You seem pretty confident of that. How can you be so sure?"

"They have nothing they can tell you." Xelius sneered. "They're nothing more than hired trash. None of them are wizards or magicals of any type. When you spend enough time in the underworld, you quickly learn where to hire such disposable tools."

Izzie frowned. She'd suspected that possibility. As much as she wanted to dismiss the explanation, it rang true.

"I supplied a little money and the equipment." Hateful certainty crept back into Xelius' voice. "The masks include subtle bravery enchantments, too. That was enough for them to follow me into battle without too many unnecessary questions."

He sighed. "I'll grant you people a small acknowledgment. Your efforts made other attacks against the Magical

District untenable." He glanced at one of the vines. "I didn't realize you'd recruited that annoying, pompous witch to help you either."

Izzie shrugged. "Most people in the magical community have a vested interest in stopping sociopathic murderers like you."

Pearl sat on the edge of the couch, her face pale from her earlier exertion. "You attacked expecting a hardened location."

"I anticipated a slightly greater challenge than Roth's house," Xelius replied. "Not this level of stubborn nonsense, but you'll regret opposing me, assuming you live long enough for that."

Izzie backed away. She was no longer concerned about Xelius managing a clever escape and was more annoyed with his arrogance. "I'll pass that along to my boss. We've been lucky that you've only managed to kill one person. For that matter, you're lucky you're not dead. If we had kept up the previous battle, we would have been forced to kill you."

Jackson ran up to the front door hauling a gray backpack. Dark lettering offering quick notes about technical settings covered the back. He set the backpack emitter down beside Xelius.

"I already adjusted it, so keep away from him, and you'll be fine." Jackson nodded toward the yard. "We've stabilized the survivors with healing potions." He grunted. "They're claiming they're just hired hands and are all but falling all over themselves to cut a deal."

"That matches what our suspect told us." Izzie shook her head at Xelius. "We'll verify it all later."

She didn't like the smug look on Xelius' face. He wasn't acting like a man who'd been caught and was surrounded by dangerous and well-trained people.

Field support would warn the teams if somebody else was coming. There was no reason to worry about a second ambush, yet at the same time, Izzie couldn't shake the feeling she should be worried.

"Do you have anything else you want to tell us?" She tried to keep the concern out of her voice. "Because you'll be uncomfortable for a little while. Then we'll drag you to a nice, prepared cell down at the PDA, one that'll keep you from doing anything with your magic except think about it."

"Where is that fool Roth now?" Xelius asked. "There's no way you knew about the bracelet beforehand. That means you got to him. You convinced him to help you when he was so afraid he'd lied about having it already." He ground his teeth.

"I almost thought I'd wasted my time with the spells I set up to detect the artifact. I'd convinced myself there was no way that little worm could open his box without announcing it to the Patron, if not the rest of the world." He snickered. "Yet somehow he had the foresight to hide everything from the beginning."

Rafe frowned at Xelius. "All we did was remind him of his duty and the threat to his life, which you helped by showing up and attacking. Don't pretend you weren't going to kill him the second you got your hands on the bracelet."

"It's not as if he knew my true form. Of course, I would have taken the bracelet from him. Still, he might have lived longer. A dedicated academic like him has his uses. In his heart, he cares more about his precious research than outmoded notions of good and evil."

Rafe shook his head. "I don't think you get it. This time of you being a big deal in the Magical District doesn't mean you get to call the mayor and get out of jail free. You're going down. There's no way any of this ends without you in a prison cell. Professor Roth is the least of your worries right now."

"The professor is in protective custody," Izzie added. "You're wrong, Xelius. He's been very helpful. He has a conscience. He does understand good and evil. That's why you didn't try to recruit him directly into the Syndicate, isn't it?"

"You don't understand the Syndicate," Xelius said. "Your ignorance is laughable. It'll destroy you."

Jackson eyed Xelius with a dismissive expression. He gave a curt nod to Izzie, then jogged out the front door.

Pearl rubbed her forehead. "I'll leave you to do your questioning. It'll be less annoying for me if I reinforce certain spells now while I still have a small amount of magical power left."

"Thanks, Pearl. The PDA will pay for the damage."

Pearl walked outside with a dismissive wave. "Don't worry about that. I prefer having favors from you."

Her departure left Rafe and Izzie alone with Xelius. The man kept glaring at her, though he stayed still otherwise.

"You're going away for a long time." Izzie shook her head. "You terrorized this city and murdered a man. If you don't want to die in prison, you'll help us track down your bosses. We're taking down the Arcane Syndicate with or without your help, so you might as well try to make your life a tiny bit more comfortable by offering your help."

"My bosses." Xelius let out a dark snicker. "That's how you're interpreting this situation?"

"You're an errand boy for the Arcane Syndicate." Rafe eyed his rifle before flipping the fire selector to safety and shouldering the weapon. "Or was this a rogue operation? You wanted the amplifier to give you power, help you move up in the Syndicate? Or take out your leaders?"

Xelius sighed. "You don't know what you're talking about. It's embarrassing."

Izzie stood before him with her arms folded, wearing the most irritating smirk she could visualize. He seemed the type who'd be annoyed by gloating. They needed to get him to spill anything he knew about the Syndicate.

In her experience, a suspect was more likely to shut up by the time they were fully processed and in the system. The PDA had more leeway than the FBI and local police regarding interrogations and investigations, but that didn't mean they had no restrictions.

She picked up his knife and turned it over to examine the runes. "This isn't just a weapon for you, right? It's your main casting tool." She knelt and nodded at Rafe. "Help me get him up. He might be more cooperative if he's a little more comfortable."

Xelius didn't resist as they flipped him over as Izzie sliced a portion of the vines around his arms to help him sit up. She didn't release the vines or ropes keeping him on the floor and his arms restrained.

"Why would someone like you help scum like the

Arcane Syndicate?" Izzie asked. "You're about to lose everything. For what?"

Xelius scoffed. "Do you think I wanted to help them?"

"Oh, you're claiming you're a victim now, too? Professor Roth might have let his ego and obsession get ahead of him, but he didn't kill anyone."

"I've been forced into a dangerous role, yes. Am I a victim? No." Xelius shook his head. "I once actively associated with the Syndicate, long ago in my more foolish days when my ambitions outstripped my resources. They found me useful, given that I used to specialize in shapeshifting magic. There's wisdom in securing power, regardless of the source. You would call me a villain for that?"

"Yes." Izzie scoffed. "I'd call you a villain for murdering a man and launching multiple terrorist attacks on Austin. The only reason your body count is so low is half luck and half us chasing you around town."

"The Arcane Syndicate gets what it wants." Xelius smiled. "I wasn't going to stand in their way. Why die for no reason? All I had to do was help them get their hands on one little bracelet, and my duty would be clear. If the bracelet proved powerful to me, I could have exploited that to earn freedom a different way."

Rafe frowned and walked toward the coffee table. "You said you were forced into this role."

"I have connections in this city." Xelius rolled his shoulders. "They sought to take advantage of that to get what they needed, as did I."

"Like faking a robbery against yourself?"

Xelius shrugged. "Whatever you might believe, it's been a long time since I was active in their service. That compli-

MARTHA CARR & MICHAEL ANDERLE

cated matters, and it's not like it was when it was the other Berens running around. The PDA is a problem. Even the FBI and many local police departments have magicals now. The Griffins are back."

He snorted. "This is what the Syndicate refused to understand. This area has suffered in the past, so everyone is more prepared." He frowned. "Or maybe they did understand, and that's why they wanted me. What did you call my hirelings? I'm a disposable assassin like those men outside are disposable thugs."

Izzie ran her finger along the runes on Xelius' knife. "You stole your own amulet and refused to cooperate with the police or PDA so nobody would know what was going on. Are you the Patron?"

"You haven't won. I'm not going to tell you what you want. You think you've won, but this battle isn't over." He licked his lips and smiled. "Or do you think you've won because of your little machine over here?" He nodded toward the backpack emitter. "You don't know anything, you ignorant little child."

Rafe frowned. "Keep talking like that, and you'll end up back on your stomach."

Xelius rolled his eyes. "Who are the villains now? You'd make an old man lay on his stomach in an uncomfortable position?"

"After said old man showed up as a killer bear with a magic knife." Rafe's hand tightened on his rifle. "And bombed us."

"How do you think this will go down, Xelius?" Izzie asked. "I mean, really. Your hired lackeys are all dead or secured. You're restrained with anti-magic cuffs on top of an emitter sitting right next to you." She tossed the knife on the miraculously untouched coffee table. "Right now, it's like you said, you're an old man in handcuffs. If you're hoping for reinforcements, our drones are swarming this area. We'll pick up any significant magical source miles away. Nobody's going to surprise us."

"All these new technomagical toys are interesting." Xelius stared at the emitter and cracked his neck back and forth. "Is that what you'd reduce magic to? Devices any person could use?"

Rafe narrowed his eyes. "Does the Arcane Syndicate resent non-magical humans? Is that what all this is about?"

"The Arcane Syndicate cares for power and respects power. Everything else is secondary. Of course, possessing magical ability always means one will have more power than others." Xelius' gaze drifted to the hallway again.

"I wonder about the limits of your technomagical anti-magic emitters. The professor's papers were fascinating, but he restricted himself to the most basic and theoretical thoughts beyond his precious locks. He never considered the true power of the combinations of aggressive magic and anti-magic."

Izzie frowned at him. "We're not here for a discussion on magical theory. This is one of the few chances you'll get to come clean about the Arcane Syndicate. You give up members to us right now, and that can go a long way to knocking years off your sentence."

"Who am I supposed to betray?" Xelius asked.

"They already betrayed you." Izzie gestured at the glass and wood chunks scattered around the living room. "You told us they forced you into this. That you were out of the

Arcane Syndicate. Out of the game, right? They pulled you back in when you were nice and cozy in your position."

She squatted in front of him. "Doesn't it burn you up that somebody out there views you as an expendable pawn? Who thinks you're no better than those thugs outside you threw at us as sacrifices?"

"All those who seek power act as such." Xelius locked eyes with Izzie and rolled his shoulders. "I'll let you in on a little secret, Little Berens. I couldn't tell you who the leaders of the Syndicate were even if I wanted to." He laughed, the sound low and mocking. "Because I don't know."

Izzie's hands curled into fists. "They have a way of contacting you. They must. That means you have a way of contacting them."

"As I said, they contacted me with literal whispers on the wind." Xelius laughed harder. His entire body shook. "You really think you're going to find them because you managed to learn the name Arcane Syndicate?"

"They should have stayed out of my town if they didn't want to get taken down." Izzie glared at him. "You asked me in the night market if I thought I was special." She shook her head.

"I'm not special. I don't have to be to take down assholes like the Arcane Syndicate. It's my duty. That's what it means to be in the PDA, and that's what it means to be a Berens. We find evil magicals, and we take them out."

CHAPTER TWENTY-SEVEN

Xelius' face twisted in open hatred. His voice turned low and bitter. "Oh, how adorable and naïve. Is this what your mother and father taught you? To be a good little girl and hunt down the bad wizards? That your powers are supposed to protect the weak or other such nonsense?"

"Yes, they taught me to stand up to dark and rogue magicals," Izzie replied icily. "They taught me that good people have to make sacrifices so those who would abuse their power are stopped. That's the important thing." She narrowed her eyes. "They taught me to stand up to assholes like you."

"You're so deluded it's almost pitiable." Xelius sucked in a shuddering breath. "You took the wrong lessons away, little human-elf girl."

"What lesson should I have taken then? Make me understand."

"Magic is about power in the end. Those who are powerful push their will onto those who are powerless.

Such has it been from the beginning of time." Xelius sneered. "Do you think I'm doing the bidding of the Arcane Syndicate because I care about any great ideological crusade they're on?"

He snorted. "No. I thought I was free of them. They made it clear I wasn't." His eyes widened into a manic stare. "They had more power. I was forced to do what they wanted because I had less power. It's that simple."

His voice grew louder. "Your rules, your PDA, your precious morality, all this pretending to have order, that's not power. That's a game masquerading as power. That's why you'll lose. Because the truth can be ignored for only so long."

Izzie rolled her eyes. "That would be far more convincing if we hadn't taken you down. You can rant all you want. This time the good guys had more power."

"You thought that little witch's potion stopped me by forcing me back into this form, didn't you?" Xelius snickered.

"You're in your true form." Izzie shrugged. "Her potion worked."

Rafe yanked his rifle down. "Back on the floor on your stomach."

Xelius grinned. "Now you're getting it. Threaten me. Show power. Only power controls power."

Izzie narrowed her eyes and lifted her palm. "Even if her potion wore off, we still have the cuffs and the emitters. You're unable to shapeshift. You would have already." She shook her head. "You would have turned yourself into a snake and slithered away or back into a bear-man and charged us."

"You should have talked to a shapeshifting expert." Xelius' laugh came out as a near giggle. "You might have had a small chance of understanding if you had."

"We did. That helps us greatly. His advice helped us track you down and prepare to deal with you."

Izzie's heart rate kicked up. She didn't like the manic energy in Xelius' grin. He sounded and looked like he'd won.

Rafe flipped his fire selector to burst mode and pointed the gun at Xelius. "We don't have to take you alive. You try anything funny, we're not going to take the risk. We know how dangerous you are. If convincing us of that is what this is about, mission accomplished."

Xelius didn't look Rafe's way. "If you talked to a shapeshifting expert, he would have told you that shapeshifting magic goes beyond appearances. Life banking involves active and passive magical components, as do the modifications it makes to the body. The inherent versus the active. If you've been talking with Professor Roth, you must understand modern anti-magic is far more about disrupting the active."

His smile grew. "Your little witch's potions forced me back into my original form. It didn't rob me of all my power for more than a brief window. I knew if I waited, you'd let your guard down. I took the opportunity to adjust my joints before you cuffed me and long before your other toy was delivered."

He spun, revealing he'd freed himself of the cuffs. Rafe fired a burst into the side of Xelius' chest. The shapeshifter spun and hurled the handcuffs at Rafe. The hard metal nailed Rafe in the forehead with a loud *slap*. His head jerked back, and he hissed in pain as his rifle's muzzle lowered. Blood leaked from his forehead into his eyes, half-blinding him and hampering his ability to fire.

Izzie conjured a light bolt that dimmed and shrank as it passed through the anti-magic field near Xelius. The shapeshifter ignored the spell to snatch the backpack emitter and fling the heavy bag overhand toward the bathroom door.

The emitter crashed into the bathroom door and bounced to the floor. The wards lit up the door and stayed that way, under strain from the anti-magic field.

Xelius laughed, jumped toward the coffee table, grabbed his knife, and popped back to his feet in one fluid roll. Izzie blasted a deep hole in his side with another light bolt before he plunged the knife into her stomach.

Fiery pain ripped through Izzie's stomach. She grunted and staggered back. Xelius headbutted her hard enough for a resounding *crack*. She dropped to the floor with a groan before he launched her into the wall with a kick that left her half-embedded in the drywall.

Xelius leapt for Rafe. He grabbed Rafe by the throat and smashed his head against the floor.

Izzie's vision swam. Her pulse pounded in her ears. Every heartbeat brought more pain. She reached down to her stomach wound and whispered a healing spell. The pain faded. She touched her ring.

"Unmute. Suspect free," Izzie mumbled. "Agent down. Requesting immediate backup."

"TacSup 2 through 4 with me, now!" Jackson barked over the magical comms network. "We're coming, Berens!"

Izzie's vision cleared with the departure of the last of

her pain. Xelius alternated between smashing the backpack emitter into the door with slices from his dagger against the barrier. Ward after ward flared before disappearing.

Distracted by his work on the bathroom door, Xelius ignored the recovered Izzie. She lifted both hands and concentrated, then shouted an incantation and pulled on the flows of light magic to push them together. Strands of white light swirled in front of her, layering and bundling together to form a long spear composed of pure light.

To Izzie's relief, Rafe confirmed he lived when he groaned and managed to point his rifle at Xelius. His aim wavered, but he fired. His first and second shots missed the shapeshifter. His second burst struck the wild Xelius in the side.

The shapeshifting wizard only grunted despite the blood dripping from his bullet wounds, proving the efficacy of Rafe's anti-magic rounds. The frail-looking man continued slashing and bashing at the wards in the bathroom with the speed and strength of a rabid giant bear.

Jackson charged in through the front door with three other operators behind him. He didn't ask any questions before spraying Xelius with another rifle burst. The other operators spread out near the broken front window to line up their firing angles on the suspect.

Xelius threw his head back and screamed. Izzie didn't understand why, given the delay from when he'd been shot. He spun and barreled toward Jackson, his movement so fast he was almost a blur.

Izzie flung her light spear at Xelius. Her spell exploded in a shower of white light and severed the shapeshifter's left arm. He tumbled to the floor, ironically saving him from another burst from Jackson.

Xelius rolled onto his side and jumped to his feet with a kick that launched Jackson into a hedge. Fortunately, it had softened enough to have him entangled and crunching among branches rather than slamming into a hard wall.

The other operators opened fire on the one-armed, snarling shapeshifter. Bullets tore into Xelius' body. He didn't slow down before leaping out the window to drop-kick another operator, tear his rifle away, and break a rifle in half by smashing it into a third operator's chest, sending the man crumpled to the ground. Xelius growled and whipped his knife toward the fourth operator's throat.

Izzie shoved her hand forward and struck Xelius' hand with a fireball. The knife whiffed and missed its target. She alternated blasting small fireballs and light bolts.

"Come on, Xelius!" she shouted, desperate to pull him away from the operators. "Teach me the lesson about power, not them. Take down a Berens and prove how tough you are!"

Her attacks allowed the fourth TacSup operator to jog backward and empty his magazine of anti-magic bullets into Xelius' head.

He screamed and leapt onto the roof. Izzie ran out to the front of the house and threw another fireball and light bolt pair at him. His body was already twisted and reshaping itself. Her spells struck a younger, more muscular version of Xelius' body with his wounds all healed and his arm regrown.

Rafe staggered out of the house and lifted his rifle. Blood caked the side of his head. He appeared much more alert than he had during his last shots as he clipped the jumping Xelius in the side before the shapeshifter leapt to the ground on one side of the house.

Jackson grunted and pushed out of the hedge. Dirt, leaves, and small pieces of wood covered him. He tried to line up a shot, but Xelius jerked out of the way and darted across the lawn, leaving Jackson's bullet flying off.

Izzie gave up on her rapid-fire spells. She refocused on collecting magical energy for another higher-strength spell. Vines shot from the ground and hedge maze to lunge at Xelius. Pearl stepped through a shimmering hedge with her wand pointed at the shapeshifter.

"Nice timing, Pearl!" Izzie shouted.

"Sorry for the delay. I was trying not to blow up a ward by accident," Pearl replied.

Xelius sliced through the vines with his knife. A giant flytrap burst from behind a hedge. He cut the head off at the stem, laughing manically before taking more rounds from Jackson.

Xelius barreled toward him, following a zigzagging path. Jackson's careful aim let him put more bullets in the shapeshifter. Rafe flanked Xelius with another burst. Another vine snagged Xelius' ankle, but he tore the vine apart with the forward movement of his leg.

"You need to finish him off, Izzie." Pearl twisted her wand. "I wasn't being modest when I said I was drained."

"It's like he's getting stronger and faster," Rafe complained before reloading.

"He must be burning off that energy from life banking," Izzie suggested.

Xelius veered away from his Jackson charge and leapt

through the broken front window. Jackson, TacSup Four, Rafe, and Izzie all turned to fire on him. Bullets pierced his back, legs, and arms before he slammed into the bathroom door, screaming like a wild beast.

Pearl groaned and dropped her arm. "I can't do much else, Izzie. I've used too much magic."

"I'll handle it. You've done enough."

She sprinted forward and rapid-fired piercing light bolts from her alternating palms into Xelius' back. He jerked with each hit and continued to slice away at the bathroom wards. The last ward failed, and he smashed the entire bathroom door off its hinges with a shoulder slam. The door cracked in half over the crate.

Xelius turned his attention to the backpack and stabbed and sliced into the emitter inside. Pieces and sparks flew. He added kicks between his knife strikes, his blows accompanied by loud crunches.

He grunted and swung his knife in a wide arc. A bright sphere shot from the tip of his knife and exploded against the side of the crate, knocking it onto its side.

His kick launched the crate into the bathroom mirror, shattering it. Before the crate could hit the floor, he kicked it again, this time into the side of the tub, with enough force to crack the porcelain and the side of the crate. He stabbed his knife through the crack.

Jackson and the others kept up their fire on Xelius. Izzie shifted to striking his head and shoving more magic into her piercing light bolts. His body jerked, and he stumbled backward, coughing up blood. His back was a bleeding, bullet-riddled, scorched mess. He fell to his knees. His forms twisted and contorted, reverting to his elderly body.

The shapeshift healed his wounds again, but he swayed, hunched over. His eyes rolled up.

"Cease fire on lethals!" Izzie shouted. She shifted to stun bolts and pumped them out in a near-constant stream. The bright lights struck Xelius' head one after another. She didn't stop until he fell backward on the bloody floor with his eyes closed, drooling.

"Rafe, you good?" Izzie shouted, not liking the blood all over his face.

"I took my healing potion." Rafe laughed. "Now I'll have to fill out that entire damned justification form."

"Jackson, your people?" Izzie glanced over her shoulder.

The tactical support commander knelt beside one of the downed operators. He poured a healing potion into the wounded man's mouth. "That was close, but we didn't lose anyone."

"Pearl?" Izzie asked.

The gothic witch knelt before a hedge, so pale she approached translucent. "I'm going to be sick, but I'll survive."

Jackson scowled through the window. "What's to stop him from doing that again?"

"We forced a form reversion through damage rather than a form truth potion," Izzie replied. "According to our overpaid consultant, that means our suspect will have lost the benefits of all his life banking. Right now, he's exactly as he appears—an unconscious old man who isn't super-strong, fast, and resistant to injury."

She motioned to Xelius. "Rafe, get some more anti-magic cuffs on him before he wakes up and pulls that joint trick again." She eyed the smoking emitter. "You're worried about the justification form for the potion. That potion isn't anywhere near as expensive as the emitter."

Rafe jogged inside and whipped out his cuffs. He cuffed Xelius and eyed the half-crushed and gouged emitter with a grimace.

Izzie took a deep breath before a wave of nausea struck her along with a massive pulse of magic from the bathroom. She braced herself against the wall with one arm.

"Pearl!" she shouted. "Do you feel that?"

"Unfortunately, yes." Pearl put a hand to her mouth.

"What am I seeing on my goggles, Berens?" Jackson asked. "That wasn't you?"

"What you see is a building-killing artifact that has been destabilized thanks to a berserk shapeshifter." Izzie took a deep breath and ran to the bathroom. She glared at the two halves of the door. "That last hit combined with losing the emitter must have done it."

"No damned way," Jackson shouted. "It's not that easy."

"Not that easy when you're dealing with a conventional magical artifact. Not some weird ancient artifact based as much around magic as anti-magic." She shook her head. "We were lucky it was as contained as it is. Xelius wanted to use its power, but he was desperate and didn't care about whatever risks he took."

Another powerful wave of magic pulsed out from the crate. Izzie's knees buckled.

"Jackson, you need to get the hell out of here with your people. Rafe, you take Pearl and Xelius in our car and head straight to the PDA so they lock him up."

Rafe's eyes widened. "What are you planning to do?"

"We don't have time to workshop this in a committee!"

Izzie shouted. "You heard what Roth said about this thing. If it goes out of control, it's going to blow. We can't be sure it'll be contained enough.

"We cleared the immediate neighborhood, but he said it could take down a skyscraper. You ever think about how many single-family plots would fit the base of a skyscraper?" She shook her head. "We know how to handle it, so I'll handle it."

"He also said it could shred your soul, Izzie," Rafe replied.

Pearl's eyes widened. "What is he talking about?"

"Grab Xelius and get going with Pearl already," Izzie shouted. "Pearl, your magic is drained. You can't help. Besides, I doubt there's another magical in this city who can channel as much raw magical power as I can when it comes down to it. Now move, in case my confidence is misplaced."

Rafe shook his head. "No. You can't ask us to do that, Izzie. You're talking about a suicide mission."

Izzie scoffed. "No, the whole point is to stop anyone from getting hurt, including myself. Now go. I don't have much time, and you being here will distract me and turn it into a real suicide mission."

Pearl's hand shook as she grabbed his arm. "She's doing it for us, Rafe. She's right." She headed outside, wiping tears from her face. "We need to hurry."

"All personnel," Jackson shouted. "Grab whoever you can who can't move themselves, load up, and bug out. Emergency evacuation. This is a burning staff-class situation. Go, go, go!"

A TacSup operator ran into the house to help Rafe grab

Xelius. Rafe cast a final sad glance at Izzie before heading toward the hedge maze. Pearl motioned for Rafe and the retreating operators to step through a hedge. The hedge shimmered, and they disappeared behind the vegetation.

Izzie took slow, deep breaths, trying to fight the assault on her stomach by the dark power emanating from the crate. She walked over, entered the code, and flipped open the lid of the cracked crate. Despite all the power she felt, the bracelet didn't look any different than before. She reached into the crate and grabbed the artifact.

"I only need to last long enough for everyone to get away," she murmured. "Easy enough."

CHAPTER TWENTY-EIGHT

Izzie took a deep breath and raised her hands, trying to recall every last word Professor Roth mentioned about the bracelet's power growing out of control. A small mistake now would cost her life and her friend's home at a minimum.

She wondered if Xelius had intended to push the artifact out of control on purpose as a final strike at his PDA tormentors. She didn't have time to worry about his motives. Stopping the artifact from destroying the area came first.

"Step one, let's try to play at containing the ridiculous magical energy involved," Izzie muttered. "Step two, try not to die and leave a huge crater in South Austin. I can do this." She took a deep breath and slapped her cheeks. "I've done harder things while in way worse shape. All I need to do is trust myself."

Concentrating and pulling on the magic within her, she traced arcane sigils in the air as lines of bright white light with careful movements of her hands, and rattled off equally ancient words of power. With her incantation finished, she finished drawing the shining symbols in the air, on the walls, and on the floor while calling upon more of the magic inside her.

The inside of the crate flipped back and forth faster and faster between a blinding bright light and an empty, all-swallowing darkness around the bracelet. Izzie's stomach lurched with the shift as she continued working on her containment spell. Assuming she survived, she wanted the cursed magical amplifier far away from Austin as soon as possible. She never wanted to deal with containing an artifact like that again.

The word containment was misleading. The spell was half containment and half magical relief valve designed to drain magic and bleed it off into the area at a steady, sustainable rate.

Izzie needed to make a critical decision soon. Channeling the artifact's power by pouring her magic into the containment spell presented the least personal risk. Combining that with trying to bleed off the bracelet's power could offer the best chance of preventing an explosion if the professor's theories were right.

The problem was she was operating on a couple of stray suggestions from a conversation with a strained academic and half-remembered lectures from magic school. She couldn't be sure he was right, especially with an artifact based on ancient theories no longer used in typical magical artifacts.

Izzie took slow, even breaths, trying not to vomit. Beyond her stomach's disagreeable reaction to the artifact's power, a deep cold seeped into her body, like her soul was freezing. She added more layers and magic to the containment spell and clung to the small, desperate hope that the bracelet's power would stabilize.

A desperate thought flashed through her mind, something she rarely dared consider due to the dangers involved. The power of the Berens' birthright could help. She could draw on the magical strength of the other women in her family.

She discarded the idea. Bringing outside power into an already unstable situation only asked for more destruction, not less. They already risked losing the neighborhood. She wouldn't risk losing the town.

Izzie dropped to her knees. Her jaw tightened. The spreading cold from the artifact waves offered a distraction from her nausea.

The bracelet isn't tuned, but I only have to contain it until it's done doing whatever it's doing. Everyone else is getting away. Even in the worst-case scenario, it'll only be me.

She swallowed. Professor Roth had been right about many things. That didn't guarantee he was right about every aspect of a complicated arcane artifact based on principles lost to the centuries. She was proceeding into dangerous, unknown territory.

Izzie's risk calculus had been off from the beginning. She didn't know if this artifact would incinerate only a room or take the entire city with her.

She swallowed. She'd read that before they'd detonated the first atomic bomb, scientists had to double-check because they hadn't been sure it wouldn't cause a chain reaction that would burn off the entire atmosphere. The scientists building the bomb worked as a team. Roth worked in isolation.

There was no more chance to hesitate, not when lives were at risk. She grabbed the bracelet and slipped it on, committed to doing what she could with the power and information she had.

Now that Izzie wore the bracelet, the oscillating duality the artifact displayed the entire time offered torture. Agony shot through every inch of her body and flipped over the deepest, soul-crushing numbness where even caring to live seemed a distant concern of someone else. Izzie threw her head back and screamed.

The brief flashes of awareness allowed her to push more magic into the containment spell while also flaring the power from the bracelet in controlled bursts to feed the spell. It was like she'd seen before, a Möbius strip, an ouroboros of power feeding back on itself to contain itself.

Izzie collapsed and writhed on the floor. Every nerve ending was on fire. She screamed in pain, trying to stay conscious and focused to adjust the flow of magic from the bracelet. She realized she couldn't rely on the bracelet's power without making the situation worse.

Instead, she needed to continue bleeding the power off in more regular, slower flows into the environment. Wearing the bracelet allowed her to better modulate the release of its power.

Blood leaked from her ears and mouth. She coughed up more. She fell forward, still conscious only through sheer stubborn force of will.

She heard a groan. It was her, but it sounded like someone else. There wasn't much left she could do but continue her plan. She would die containing the artifact or die anyway after failing to contain the artifact.

Izzie wouldn't let Xelius win. She wouldn't let the Arcane Syndicate win. They had come into her city and brought rogue, evil magic with them. She would punish them. First, she would stop their desperate scheme and make them understand why they should have stayed the hell out of Austin.

Darkness grew at the edges of her vision, regardless of the cycle of pain or numbness. She managed a weak smile as power kept flowing off the bracelet. Her magic was draining as she pumped more of it into her containment spell.

It was working. She needed more time, but it was working.

"Come on, you stupid Glorious Foundation piece of old junk," she whispered. "I'm willing to die to stop you. Don't screw me over now."

Izzie groaned. Her eyelids fluttered and closed. She spent her last conscious moments draining off magic. She smiled despite the pain. At least everyone had gotten away.

———

When Izzie blinked her eyes open, she lay on a stretcher in front of the charred remnants of the front of the hedge maze. Pearl held her hand. Rafe stood on her other side with a look of relief.

A gaggle of police officers, Jackson, and TacSup operators in full gear patrolled the perimeter. The masked gunmen were gone, but the wrecks of their two non-exploding vans remained. A pair of other PDA field agents in suits chatted with a police officer near the wall of police cars blocking the street.

"Welcome back." Rafe smiled.

Pearl squeezed Izzie's hand. "That was the stupidest thing you've done in a while, and that's impressive when you consider the list."

Izzie moaned. "What happened to the bracelet?"

She checked her wrist. The artifact was gone.

"It's in the secure vault," Rafe replied. "In nested anti-magic containers, more anti-magic fields, the works. Whatever you did stabilized it enough that it wasn't doing anything when we came back here. You'd think it was the safest, most harmless artifact we'd ever found."

He shrugged. "They're going to consult with Professor Roth about how to best transfer it to a permanent vault outside a major city, but it's not going to blow up for now as far as we can tell."

"I can't see past the hedges," Izzie murmured. "But I see the other houses in the neighborhood are still here. That's promising."

"The bracelet didn't destroy anything," Pearl confirmed. "When I think about it, my bathroom is rather thrashed, but Xelius wrecked it before the bracelet started leaking magic." She chuckled.

Izzie smiled weakly. "Sorry, you can send the bill to the PDA."

Pearl squeezed her hand. "It's fine, Izzie. I was planning a remodel anyway. Now I don't have to worry as much about the teardown."

Izzie sat up and rubbed her temples. Her head throbbed. It was still hard to focus.

"You had enough time to return the bracelet to the PDA, Rafe."

He nodded. "Once the drones established a big, sustained drop in magical output, we got permission to come back. A different team took the bracelet. I wanted to stay with you until you woke up."

"How long have I been out?"

"About an hour."

Izzie looked around. "But I'm outside Pearl's place?"

"I have better access to my specialty potions here," Pearl explained. "I wanted to make sure you were stable before you left. I would hate to find you'd become a vegetable due to the aftereffects of your foolish heroics."

"Every muscle in my body is sore," Izzie admitted. "Every brain cell hurts. I feel like somebody put my brain in a shredder." She laid down. "I could sleep for a week. Right now, I doubt I could light a match with my magic." She grunted. "What about Xelius?"

Rafe patted her shoulder. "In a cell at the PDA building. We secured his knife and have extra measures in place, but he's far weaker than he was. You were right. He used up everything for that last push."

"Good. We need to interrogate him and squeeze everything we can out of him."

"He's unconscious right now. You're not the only one who went all-out. Don't worry, Izzie. Nobody will take your bad guy from you. And nobody's going to yell if you take the rest of the night off."

The air felt lighter now, but there was still an ache deep inside her—a ghost of the fear she'd carried for years.

"You did good," Rafe added.

She nodded, but her mind was elsewhere. "I thought I'd buried this part of my life," she murmured. "But I guess some things never stay buried."

Rafe glanced at her sidelong. "Maybe not. But you're not the same person you were back then."

Izzie allowed herself a small smile. "No, I'm not." She took a deep breath and let it out slowly. "Neither are they."

CHAPTER TWENTY-NINE

Izzie sat across from Xelius at a bolted-down table in the secure interrogation room and sipped Gatorade from a paper cup. Rafe sat beside her sipping his morning coffee. He drank it black with no sugar.

The caffeine and sugar in the neon yellow Gatorade only did so much to tamp down the headache afflicting Izzie. Pearl had sent her home with a rack of disgusting-tasting potions to take the edge off and help restore magical balance. It had been less than twelve hours since Izzie stopped the artifact's overload.

Izzie didn't care. This wasn't her first time dealing with over-channeling magic. She knew it would take days of rest and avoiding serious magic to return to normal. That didn't mean she couldn't do the other parts of her job. Her current location made magic all but irrelevant anyway.

In addition to the anti-magic emitters built into the secure interrogation room, which would make casting a spell difficult even for Izzie at full power and feeling great, an anti-magic vest weighed Xelius down. He lacked his knife, and cuffs forced his arms against the chair. Armed security officers stood outside the room with rifles in hand, already loaded with anti-magic rounds.

"Aren't you going to say anything?" Xelius asked. "You've done nothing but drink coffee for five minutes. It's rude and obnoxious."

Izzie smiled at him. "Why? You want coffee?"

"Your attempts to manipulate me are pathetic, Berens."

"I love how you keep the 'I'm winning' attitude after we stopped your plan and you're locked up. Keep up the optimism." She raised her cup. "Someday it might work out for you."

"They said you refused a lawyer," Rafe commented to Xelius. "We can have one appointed, but I don't get it. You can afford a lawyer. Trust me. You're going to want a lawyer. Whatever encounters you've had with the law before, you need to understand there have been significant changes in recent decades."

Rafe frowned. "I have a hard time believing you don't understand that. You're from Earth. You're not fresh through the gates from Oriceran."

"I don't care about the laws of this sad little country. Things have worsened since the magical world came out in the open." Xelius sneered.

"If you're worried, don't be. I signed your PDA forms to reject the help of your pathetic defense helpers. Question me all you want. I'll tell you what I feel like and not what I don't. I'm not afraid of you."

"Like I said, keep the optimism," Izzie replied. "You're going to need it."

"You're looking at serious time," Rafe noted. "I hope you understand that. We got you on so many charges you'd need immortality magic to survive prison. You were running around ahead of the PDA this entire time, but that's over.

"It's like Izzie said. It's not like the good old days. We're not going to turn this over to the magical community to handle internally, and we're not going to sweep this away."

"I'm not ignorant, just defiant." Xelius smiled. "I'm amused that you remain convinced you've won."

Izzie folded her arms. "Every time I try to explain it to him, he must let his bias against me get in the way. Maybe you should try explaining it to him, Rafe."

Rafe shrugged. "We are the ones holding you in a heavily guarded cell, Xelius. You've used up all your life banking power and don't have a wand or your knife. You don't have the bracelet, and nobody's come looking for you."

He sipped his coffee. "We're on high alert and have other agencies ready to back us up, so even if the Arcane Syndicate comes knocking, they'll have a bad time. Do you understand all that?"

"The Arcane Syndicate can always find tools," Xelius insisted.

"Yes, like those men you hired." Rafe looked thoughtful. "We've IDed them. The survivors are all doing their best to sell you out, which is hard considering you were smart enough to hide your identity. I want to point out they were trying to sell you out starting from yesterday."

"Those men are irrelevant."

Rafe clicked his tongue. "By the way, we've contacted

our informants to spread the word. The local underworld knows that a rogue wizard hired a bunch of non-magicals as disposable wind-up toys, and the PDA broke all those toys. I think the Arcane Syndicate will have trouble fielding an army of pop-up thugs for a while."

He gestured at Xelius. "That means they're going to rely on people like you."

"The point is you lose, Xelius." Izzie frowned. "We have the bracelet safe and secure, and we have you. Professor Roth is rapidly shaving years off anything but a suspended sentence with his extensive and willing cooperation.

"It turns out he might have thought of a way to better mask the bracelet from being detected no matter where it is. That means we'll be able to move it to a long-term secure storage vault without your Syndicate buddies having a clue we're doing so. No matter how this plays out, you lose."

Xelius frowned. "You only got lucky that I couldn't destabilize the bracelet."

Izzie glared at him. "You son of a bitch. So you did do it on purpose."

"It would have been amusing to see the PDA trying to explain away the destruction of half a neighborhood. Even better, I might have been able to rid this world of a Berens." He smiled. "It was worth the gamble."

Rafe gave him a pitying look. "Don't you get it? Your stunt worked. You did destabilize the bracelet."

For the first time during the interrogation, Xelius looked uncertain. "You're lying. You would be far more irate with me if that were true. There would have been more deaths and destruction."

Rafe shook his head. "Too bad for you, Izzie contained the magic."

"Impossible." Xelius jerked his head toward Izzie. "Trying to channel that much power would have killed anyone. I don't believe it. This is a trick. A pathetic ruse."

"Believe what you want. That doesn't change what happened." Izzie set her cup down. "But nope, whatever you were scheming beyond embarrassing the PDA by trying to get that thing to overload, I stopped it, and now you're just a sad old man in cuffs and a cell."

She shrugged. "Everything you've worked for in your life will come to nothing because you let the Arcane Syndicate use you. All the reputation and connections you built won't matter. People will only remember you as the shapeshifter who terrorized the Magical District. They'll be glad when you're in prison and curse your name."

"It's not too late," Rafe interjected.

"Not too late for what?" Xelius avoided looking at Izzie.

"To get back at the people who used you up and threw you away. To get a little revenge on the people who forced you back into a game you didn't want to play. Aren't they the real problem?"

Xelius arched his eyebrows. "Interesting. You're not going to appeal to my conscience?"

Izzie scoffed. "You were the one ranting about power. We're the ones with the power over you now. We know you don't have a conscience. You only have an ego. We'll go with the realistic play."

"Power is the only truth of this world, Berens. I'm glad my actions have imparted a small bit of education into your stubborn mind." Xelius tried to lean forward, but his cuffed position would only let him move a little. "If you're not lying about what happened, you proved yourself and your power by stopping the artifact."

He smiled. "You didn't scold it into behaving. You used your power to stop it, just as you and your friends used power to bring me down." He sighed. "Why don't you understand? You're so close to understanding."

"Not agreeing with you isn't the same as failing to understand you," Izzie answered. "Here, give us a little insight into your genius. That should make you happy. The motive for Blackstone's death is obvious. He was onto you somehow. Is that why you attacked the two other victims? They knew what you were up to?"

"Blackstone was too curious for his own good. His investigation connected me with the Patron persona I used to contact Roth. That was unacceptable, especially when he started trying to get Roth to stop his research."

Izzie nodded. The pieces fit together. She was relieved a simple appeal to ego was enough to spur Xelius to offer more details. It helped that the shapeshifter already knew it was pointless to claim any real innocence.

Xelius smiled. "As for the others, I picked random people of influence in the community, but ones I knew would not be eager to work with the conventional authorities for different, unrelated reasons." He chuckled. "That was the true brilliance of my plan. It obfuscated what I was doing.

"Faking the attack on myself made it easy to push your investigatory eye elsewhere. I intended to lay down another false trail with a series of additional attacks, but you tracked me down far quicker than anticipated." His smile twitched into a frown. "I underestimated your PDA toys."

Rafe frowned. "You attacked two people as a cover-up? You could have killed them."

"I intended to survive all this," Xelius replied without the smallest hint of remorse on his face or in his voice. "Sacrificing a handful of others to do so became a necessity. Spare me the sanctimony, Agent Martinez."

Izzie folded her arms and stared Xelius down. "I'm surprised you didn't kill someone for your life banking. With that much power, you might have won."

"Oh, your ignorance is showing again. Disappointing." Xelius rolled his eyes. "Life banking would have been difficult to use on people, especially magicals, who would sense what was happening and trace it back. I'd have to kidnap and imprison someone to use the technique. The time and difficulty involved made it far less worth it than draining plants."

He narrowed his eyes. "You still don't understand how close I was. A couple more days, and I would have had the bracelet. You're not better than I am, Berens. Only luckier."

"We were lucky, huh?" Izzie offered him a defiant glare. "We chased down leads. Those leads took us to you. Luck had nothing to do with it. You got beaten by PDA agents, and this is your chance to help us make sure somebody else pays. Or you can rot in prison while your masters laugh at you for getting caught."

"She's right," Rafe added. He gestured at Xelius. "Is it fair that you're the only one who has to suffer for all this?

There has to be something else you can tell us about the Arcane Syndicate, something more than whispers on the wind. Anything you can pass along will help you and us."

"Even if I were inclined to tell you who they were, I don't know any names," Xelius replied. "I never did. I only know the Arcane Syndicate has come to this city with long-term plans. You should be worried."

Izzie frowned. "How do you know that?"

Xelius smiled. Condescension oozed from his expression and voice. "It's as I told you, whispers on the wind. 'The leader has decided this city belongs to the Syndicate. Your operation will be the first of many. Do well, and you will be rewarded.'

"I was told that and given specific information about helping Professor Roth. 'The studious fool cares more for knowledge than power. We'll use him to open his precious treasure and take the contents inside.'"

"That's all it took to get you to do all this?" Izzie asked. "A magical whisper campaign?"

"'We are those meant to rule,'" Xelius intoned. "We are those meant to shepherd true power. Those who would stand in our way will be enslaved or destroyed. For true power defines reality. We are those who will reshape this world. We are the hand of the true reality.'"

He closed his eyes. "That message was whispered in my ear by nothing before this all started, and it is the message I heard when I was inducted into the Arcane Syndicate."

Izzie watched him, waiting for a smirk or a laugh. There was something unexpected in his eyes. Fear. His failures had left him unsure and defeated in this cell, yet he'd acted like he would pull a win from a pocket. The man across from her was finally terrified, yet not of her or Rafe sending him to prison.

"They're coming for this city," Izzie replied. "That's what you said. They think this city belongs to them. What does that mean beyond them trying more crime?"

"I don't know. The only thing I know is I'm happy I'll be in a prison far from here. You would have slept better at night if you never learned the name Arcane Syndicate."

"Why don't you tell us more about how you were inducted into the Arcane Syndicate?" Izzie pressed. "We can make a deal. There's no way you're avoiding prison, but we can help get you special accommodations. Spending decades with a handful of extra luxuries can make all the difference between a tolerable Purgatory and an everlasting Hell."

"Accommodations for betraying the Arcane Syndicate?"

Rafe polished off the last of his coffee. "Think of it this way. If you're so afraid of them that you think they'll get you in prison, the only chance you have of surviving is if someone takes them down." He gestured between Izzie and himself. "Unless there's a big underworld battle between evil magical organizations, your best bet is something like the PDA."

Izzie nodded at her partner. "Do you think the Syndicate will forgive you for failing your mission? Or do you want to live the rest of your life waiting for a Syndicate assassin?"

Xelius' nostrils flared. "I hate to admit it, but you're right. Fine. I'll tell you what I know but only with specific guarantees of accommodations and assurances of safety in prison, including having my own cell. The Syndicate will try to kill me if given a chance. You're not wrong about that, and the sooner I'm out of this city, the safer I am."

"We'll get somebody in who can start the official paperwork." Izzie motioned for him to continue. "For now, tell us more about the Arcane Syndicate."

CHAPTER THIRTY

A rare smile replaced Bill's RBF. His eyes shifted back and forth while he perused documents on his computer monitor. Izzie and Rafe sat in front of his desk, awaiting his comments.

"If I'm not deluding myself, Xelius confessed to everything," Bill noted. "In exchange for his own cell and better food and books?"

"That's accurate." Rafe sounded smug.

"We'll need the full signoff from the DOJ prosecutors, but I don't see a problem pushing this through." Bill looked at his agents. "Before I go through this statement on the Arcane Syndicate, I want to hear you give me your high-level impressions."

His request didn't surprise Izzie. Not every magical secret made it into official reports at the PDA. They sometimes had to leave a detail or two out of official reports to keep a favor from an informant or not violate the restrictions associated with a spell. Rafe always had more issues with the blurry edges of their work than she did.

In this case, there was less of an issue. There were no deep-cover magical informants or curse restrictions in need of protection.

"Xelius' information tends to support what we've already figured out," Izzie began. "The Arcane Syndicate is an Earth-based magical organization. Although they are interested in gaining control of magicals, becoming wealthy, and the like, that's a means to an end." She frowned. "They reach out to people they think will match their ideology. It's all very careful and indirect. Everything involves code names and anonymity, but there are allegedly people at the top calling the shots who know the members. Xelius claims he honestly doesn't know the true identities of any living members of the organization."

Bill looked as unimpressed as Izzie had felt when Xelius explained it to her for the first time. "He conveniently doesn't know anybody?"

"He doesn't know any living members," Izzie corrected. "He identified a handful of dead magicals he claimed belonged to the organization. Initial cross-checks found one mystery death. The others were associated with other magical underworld organizations. I wasn't about to pull him out of the secure cell and risk more shapeshifting, so I couldn't use a lie-detection spell."

Even if such magic wasn't admissible in court, the PDA had no problem using it to aid initial investigations. In Izzie's experience, it wasn't required all that often. The extreme tension and drama of typical PDA cases tended to wring the truth out of people once caught. Those with greater experience with magical criminality tended to have countermeasures that could take a while to circumvent.

"Xelius claims he never advanced much in the organization, which is why he doesn't know many people," Rafe explained. "He had proficiency with shapeshifting magic and an attitude that made them approach him, but he was too concerned with keeping his local position and opportunities.

"After a couple of out-of-state assassinations, they allegedly lost interest in this area for a couple of decades. They made it clear that they would be back, and other than making sure he had contact with the rest of the magical underworld, they hadn't contacted him in years."

Bill scoffed. "He confessed to additional murders?"

Izzie nodded. "That added credence to the rest of what he said, and we were able to confirm two unsolved murders for the victims he named. The FBI will be happy."

"What's the actual goal of the Arcane Syndicate? I don't get it from what you've told me."

Izzie looked at Rafe. She had a hard time believing what Xelius told her during the interrogation. World domination made sense, not the fairy tale she'd heard.

Rafe took a deep breath. "They want to sculpt the true reality, Bill."

"What the hell does that mean? What's the true reality?"

"The idea is the more direct control of magicals and magical power they accumulate, the more they can begin to understand the fundamentals of reality itself," Rafe explained.

Bill shook his head. "You're telling me they're a bunch of asshole magical physicists?"

"It's deeper than that," Izzie replied. "Much deeper. And more disturbing."

Rafe continued. "They argue that conventional divisions such as light and dark magic, along with order and chaos, are artificial distractions from the underlying truths of reality, magic, and the nature of the universe. To sum it up, Xelius suggested they think the best way to understand reality is to first destroy it."

"Talk about your delusions of grandeur." Bill scoffed. "I miss the days when all we had to worry about was certain wizards overly concerned with their particular bloodlines running the world."

Izzie looked down, remembering the bright, almost euphoric look in Xelius' eyes as he discussed the Arcane Syndicate. The man believed they would kill him, yet he still waxed rhapsodic about their goals.

Bill's frown deepened. He'd gone far beyond his Resting Boss Face. Rafe stopped and cleared his throat with a pleading look at Izzie.

She expanded on what Rafe had disclosed. "The bottom line is that they don't let anything constrain them, not morality, ethics, religion, or common freaking sense. The only thing keeping them in check is worry about interference from authorities. They honestly seem to believe they can master reality at a fundamental level and become new gods, that sort of thing." She shook her head as Bill's face twisted in disgust. "It's half-cult, half-underworld organization."

"Xelius gave up pretty easily," Bill countered. "For a cultist, even a lapsed one."

Izzie nodded, wondering if there was a bigger prize. If her family was that prize. She wasn't ready to point that out. "Sure. From what Xelius told us, honor isn't prized, and the lower-level tools of the Arcane Syndicate who fail are expected to kill themselves before the Syndicate does.

"The Syndicate has been good at cleaning up and burying evidence by pushing the blame for magical crimes toward other groups. Basically, their ethos is power trumps all. The weak are owed nothing." She scoffed. "The problem this time is they don't have major assets in this city. The fact they had to recruit someone who tried to distance himself in the past proves it. For whatever reason, they've targeted Austin again, and at the same time, previous clashes in this area have made them steer clear of it. He says they want this city and have a long-term plan for it, but he doesn't know the details."

Bill leaned back in his seat and processed what they had told him. After a long moment of quiet, he nodded. "At the minimum, it sounds like the only reason these people aren't constantly murdering people is because of limited numbers and caution."

"That was our impression as well," Rafe replied.

"The battle ahead will be even more dangerous," Bill continued. "I'm putting you two in charge of a special Arcane Syndicate taskforce. You'll be the clearinghouse for everything we find out about them. We'll push Xelius for more information, but I'm with you. I doubt we'll get much more out of him."

"I think they only used him because he was so disposable," Izzie suggested. "It could have been a test to see how we responded."

"That means they think us knowing about their existence doesn't mean much. It's like they think we can't stop them."

"We did this time," Izzie replied. "And we will the next time."

"Okay." Bill flicked his wrist. "Get your reports in and both of you take a day off."

"What about the Arcane Syndicate?"

"They won't show up tomorrow to blow up the city, Berens." Bill frowned out his office window. "I don't need my taskforce heads burning themselves out before we catch the Arcane Syndicate." He faced Izzie and narrowed his eyes. "We need to be smart about this. We can't be forced into taking big risks with a group of ruthless psychos like we were this time."

Izzie stood alongside Rafe and nodded. "Understood, Bill. I'll take a day off. I'll think about what you said."

She turned to leave with Rafe. Before they opened his door, Bill cleared his throat loudly to get their attention.

Bill smiled, this time with unnervingly genuine warmth. "Because I didn't say it before, good job. The only non-hired goon death we had was Blackstone, and that's because of you two. I don't know if we'll be that lucky going forward, but I'll take my wins when we get them."

"That's all any of us can do, Bill," Rafe replied. "Maybe next time the rest of the magical community will be more cooperative once they understand they were being manipulated."

"I hope so." Izzie stepped out of the office. "Otherwise, the Arcane Syndicate will have fun playing puppet master."

CHAPTER THIRTY-ONE

Izzie set a bottle of red wine in the center of the table. She grabbed a couple of cans of beer from her fridge, one for her and one for Rafe, before sitting at her dining room table.

Her cozy tenth-story apartment lacked the distinctive style of Pearl's house. She always argued that her great view of the city from her dining nook through her living room window beat staring at a hedge maze with weird killer monsters.

Rafe and Pearl sat at her small wooden table. Izzie motioned to the boxed pizzas sitting in the center of the table.

"You certainly spared no culinary expense with the takeout pizza." Pearl grabbed a slice of pepperoni. "The wine is a nice touch."

"It's Italian wine, at least." Izzie grinned. "I know you prefer wine to beer." She poured a glass for Pearl and set it beside her plate. "I thought about cooking. Then I said, 'Screw it, my head hurts, and I'm tired.'"

"You didn't have to invite us over, Izzie," Rafe commented. "I'm surprised you did."

Izzie grabbed a slice from another box. So many vegetables covered it that Pearl could have used it as a dangerous guardian. After a couple of bites, she smiled at Rafe. "This case made me think tons about my past and everything since I've joined the PDA. Alison's one of the few friends I kept from the old days. She's busy living her life, taking care of her business and all her drow political nonsense. I'm just…"

"You're just what?" Pearl asked. "Are you okay?"

"I didn't want this to come off as a pity party. The point is I spent years believing it was too dangerous to have friends, and I kind of forgot how to make friends because of that. I stumbled into making friends with you two, and I don't know what I'd do without you anchoring me."

Pearl polished off her piece of pizza and sipped her wine. "I don't know if I should be considered a good influence." She fluttered her eyelashes at Rafe.

He rolled his eyes. "Nope. Not going to take the chance. That's nothing more than bait."

"I'm worried about the Arcane Syndicate." Izzie put up a hand to preempt Rafe. "More worried about them than I normally am about evil magical organizations. All that weird talk about true reality and going to this much trouble to get their hands on an unusual artifact that functioned in such a weird way unsettles me. I think they're way more dangerous than the average group of power-hungry murderous thugs we run into."

Pearl swirled her wine. "Does it matter?"

"Why wouldn't it matter?"

"Because it's not as if you'd leave them alone if they were only slightly less murderous and ambitious than the other magical criminals." Pearl drained her glass and poured herself a new one.

Rafe chugged his beer. "Pearl's right. The way I see it, this Arcane Syndicate is afraid of us. That's why they had to do everything they could to use a half-reliable old asset and not give us a solid trail to follow. They know if we get close to them it's all over." He gave Pearl a worried look. "I hope it doesn't take long to fix your house and repair your hedge maze."

"It'll be fine," Pearl replied. "The damage was rather limited, all things considered, but I don't think I'd like to volunteer my home again anytime soon."

Izzie laughed. "I'll keep that in mind." She looked out the window. "All I want to do is protect people."

"You're doing a great job of it. You care far more than I do about protecting random people."

"We got this," Rafe added. "We'll stop the Arcane Syndicate, too."

"I'll keep an ear out in the magical community," Pearl offered. "I can't have someone coming and bombing my home or city because of strange obsessions about controlling reality." She smirked. "Unless they offer me the right to control everything."

Izzie rolled her eyes. "You wouldn't last five minutes in an evil secret organization. The second they gave you an order, you'd make a big, embarrassing scene and quit."

"Oh, it depends on how they ask me." Pearl's gaze flicked to Rafe. "Everything depends on how one asks."

He drank more beer, coughing after a few sips. He

coughed again to clear his throat and avoided looking at Pearl.

"This is our city," Izzie declared while staring out the window. "We'll protect it from whoever shows up to mess with it." She narrowed her eyes. "The Arcane Syndicate will regret ever messing with Austin."

THE STORY CONTINUES

The story continues with book two, *THE DARK ARTIFACT*, coming soon to Amazon and Kindle Unlimited.

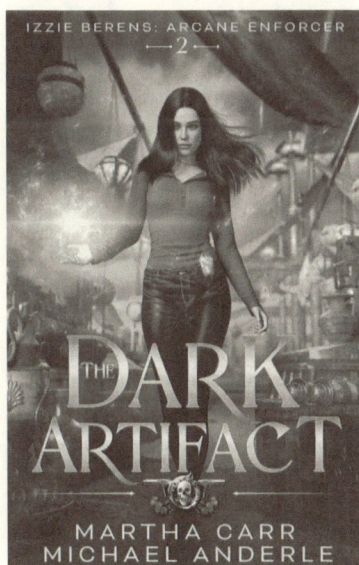

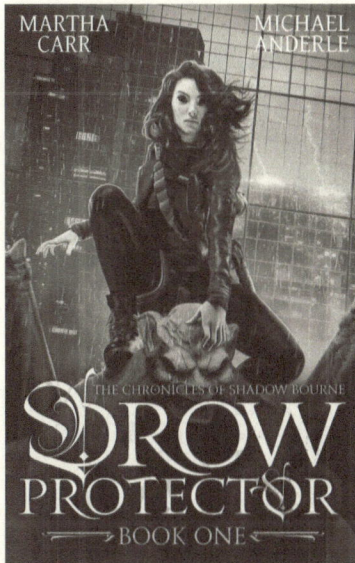

Drow Protector: Chronicles of Shadow Bourne Book 1

There is a nest of Drows living in hidden caves just outside of Los Angeles. The dark side of LaLa Land knows them well.

Young Drows come out of the shadows at nightfall, looking for trouble and it always finds them.

But then there's Ellis Burton. Half Drow, half human and searching for an identity in either world.

Her father, Connor Burton is the leader of the Drow

clan and the overseer in their underground drug traffic. It's all medicinal mushrooms. Nothing to see here.

Now her mother, that's a different story.

Mom disappeared a long time ago into the city and no one is saying anything.

Sometimes, if you want answers, you have to go in search of them for yourself.

Ellis Burton has been prowling the city at night looking for answers but instead, she's found a calling.

She is the guardian of the dwellers of LA who have to travel the streets at night. Ellis watches from her perch on the edge of buildings, keeping her part of LA safe.

Still, there's an ache and a question inside of her that will need answers.

Where is the good doctor, Claire Burton? Is she still alive? Did she find out a little too much about the Drow's magic mushrooms?

And what about the LAPD and Detective Morrissey? Does he know more than he's saying?

So many questions and one determined half Drow to find them all.

Scroll up to get the first book in the Shadow Bourne series and follow the trail through the dark streets of LA and the Drow caves with Ellis today.

Get sneak peeks, exclusive giveaways, behind the scenes content, and more. PLUS you'll be notified of special **one day only fan pricing** on new releases.

Sign up today to get free stories.

Visit: https://marthacarr.com/read-free-stories/

AUTHOR NOTES: MARTHA CARR

OCTOBER 17, 2024

I've been puttering around at this running thing for a while now. You know, dabbling in it—going for a jog here, a walk there, maybe even a light sprint if I was feeling particularly ambitious (or if there was a sale at the farmer's market). But here I am, at 65, and I've decided to get serious. Yes, *actually serious* this time. And what better way to prove it than by signing up for the Chicago Maratho 2025n?

Now, for those who don't know, the Chicago Marathon is famous for being flat. I chose it not because I'm looking for an easy ride, but because, let's be honest, at 65, I've had enough uphill battles in life—literally and figuratively. So, I figured, why not go for a marathon where I don't also have to conquer mountains?

Let's back up for a second. Running and I have had a long, somewhat rocky relationship. I've been on-again, off-again with it, like one of those sitcom couples where everyone's wondering, "Are they together or not?" Well, it's been the same with me and running. I'd buy some fancy running shoes, lace them up with the best intentions, and then promptly get distracted by…well, anything. A new plant that needed tending, a good book, the fact that it was too hot, too cold, or just the wrong day to be sweating outside. You name it, I had the excuse. But something's changed this time around.

I've got the gear. We're talking moisture-wicking fabrics, high-tech running shoes, and, most importantly, a *really good* compression sleeve. That's right, the kind that makes you look like a professional athlete or maybe someone with a very dramatic injury story (mine's not that dramatic – that whole cancer thing). The sleeve has been a game-changer, not just for keeping my knees from revolting, but for making me feel like I've finally got my act together. I mean, you don't buy a high-tech compression sleeve if you're just casually strolling through the neighborhood, right?

This time, I also have something I've never had before: a plan. Not one of those vague, "Oh, I'll just run when I feel like it" plans. No, this is a *real* training plan, with a great coach named, Violet, with schedules, rest days, long runs, and the occasional motivational mantra that pops up on my phone to remind me not to skip a day. Because, let me tell you, there have been many, many days in the past where skipping seemed like the best option. But this time, skipping isn't part of the plan.

The funny thing about getting serious about running at 65 is that people don't expect it. You get a lot of, "Good for you!" and "That's so impressive!" which, while nice, kind of feels like they're saying, "Wow, I can't believe you're still moving at all!" But what they don't realize is that I've been moving this whole time—I just wasn't moving very far.

Now, though? Now I'm all in. I'm not puttering anymore; I'm pushing.

And Chicago? Oh, it's the perfect place for someone like me. Not only is it a completely flat race, but it's also a city that knows how to throw a marathon. The crowds, the energy, the lakefront views—it's the kind of atmosphere that makes me feel like I can actually do this crazy thing called running 26.2 miles. It doesn't hurt that it's my old hometown and there will be plenty of people cheering for me – including my ride or die, Mike.

Now, I won't pretend that training has been easy. My first few serious runs felt a lot like I was being chased by invisible gremlins, and not the good kind. Every muscle in my body was suddenly very aware that I was no longer 25. But as the weeks went by, something strange happened—I got stronger. Not just physically, but mentally. There's something about sticking to a plan, putting one foot in front of the other, and realizing that, with a little grit and some compression socks, you can do a lot more than you thought.

Let's talk about the mental side of this whole adventure, because if you've ever run a long distance, you know that's half the battle. You hit a certain point—maybe around mile six, or eight, or ten—where your brain starts to suggest that perhaps a nap would be a better idea than continuing. But this time, I'm prepared for that. I've been practicing the art of self-talk. You know, the "You've got this!" and "One more mile won't kill you!" pep talks. It sounds silly, but it works. I remind myself that this is what I've been working toward. I remind myself that I'm not just running for the finish line, but for the proof that, at 65, I'm still capable of taking on big challenges.

So, as I train for Chicago, I'm embracing the fact that this isn't just about the marathon. It's about pushing myself to do something hard, to commit to it, and to see it through. It's about proving to myself that I can still surprise me. And if I can make it through this marathon, I'm pretty sure I can make it through anything life throws my way—even if it comes with hills.

And when I cross that finish line (because I *will* cross that finish line), I'll have one more thing to check off my list. Marathon runner at 65? Check. Now, pass me the Aleve and the post-run ice cream. I've earned it. More adventures to follow.

AUTHOR NOTES: MICHAEL ANDERLE

NOVEMBER 1, 2024

F irst, thank you for not only reading this story, but also for sticking around to read these author notes at the end! I truly appreciate you taking the time to let me share a little slice of my life with you.

Crockpot Chronicles: The Salisbury Steak Saga

For those who've been following my culinary adventures—yes, I'm looking at you, fellow crockpot enthusiasts —I have an update that's part triumph, part tragedy.

The other day, I decided to try my hand at a crockpot meal that should have been foolproof. You toss in some frozen hamburger patties, cream of mushroom soup, brown gravy, and a mix of spices—easy peasy, right? Well, if you know me, you know I can't resist veering off the recipe roadmap. Who follows a recipe exactly, anyway? Not me.

I'm a rebel in the kitchen.

I threw in a little of this, a sprinkle of that, and, frankly, probably too many spices. But the gravy was tasting pretty darn good, and I was feeling optimistic.

This is where it all went off the rails.

I thought I'd elevate the dish by using steakhouse burgers from Safeway. They were bigger, juicier, and seemed perfect for a Salisbury steak-style dinner. What I didn't know—and will now never forget—is that they season the **shit** out of those patties. And by "season," I mean they make them so peppery that my taste buds staged a protest.

In case you're curious about the aftermath: Out of the six patties, I managed to eat two. The other four? Sacrificed to the research and development kitchen gods. I'm getting to know them pretty well these days.

But every culinary catastrophe is a lesson in disguise. I've still got plenty of hamburger patties to give this another go. This time, I'll use fewer patties—just in case—and steer clear of the over-seasoned ones. I also experimented by adding French onion soup to the mix. It gave the dish an interesting flavor—not exactly the Salisbury steak I was aiming for, but not half bad either.

I hope those of you embracing the crockpot life during this cooler weather are enjoying savory and successful dinners!

As for me, I'm off to plan tomorrow's crockpot adventure. Maybe third time's the charm?

Until then, happy cooking, and may your meals be ever delicious!

Ad Aeternitatem,
Michael Anderle

. . .

P.S. If you've got any crockpot wisdom to share—or if you've had your own kitchen misadventures—I'd love to hear about them!

P.P.S. For more stories, updates, and perhaps a few more culinary confessions, don't forget to subscribe to the MORE STORIES with Michael newsletter here: https://michael.beehiiv.com/

BOOKS BY MARTHA CARR

THE LEIRA CHRONICLES
CASE FILES OF AN URBAN WITCH
THE EVERMORES CHRONICLES
CHRONICLES OF WINLAND UNDERWOOD
SOUL STONE MAGE
THE KACY CHRONICLES
MIDWEST MAGIC CHRONICLES
THE FAIRHAVEN CHRONICLES
DIARY OF A DARK MONSTER
I FEAR NO EVIL
THE DANIEL CODEX SERIES
SCHOOL OF NECESSARY MAGIC
SCHOOL OF NECESSARY MAGIC: RAINE CAMPBELL
ALISON BROWNSTONE
FEDERAL AGENTS OF MAGIC
SCIONS OF MAGIC
THE UNBELIEVABLE MR. BROWNSTONE
DWARF BOUNTY HUNTER
ACADEMY OF NECESSARY MAGIC
MAGIC CITY CHRONICLES
ROGUE AGENTS OF MAGIC
WITCH WARRIOR
THE AGENT OPERATIVE
BIG EASY BOUNTY HUNTER

[JOIN THE ORICERAN UNIVERSE FAN GROUP ON FACEBOOK!](#)

BOOKS BY MICHAEL ANDERLE

Sign up for the LMBPN email list to be notified of new releases and special deals!

http://lmbpn.com/email/

For a complete list of books by Michael Anderle, please visit:

www.lmbpn.com/ma-books/

CONNECT WITH THE AUTHORS

Martha Carr Social
Website:
http://www.marthacarr.com
Facebook:
https://www.facebook.com/groups/MarthaCarrFans/

Michael Anderle

Website: http://lmbpn.com

Email List: https://michael.beehiiv.com/

https://www.facebook.com/LMBPNPublishing

https://twitter.com/MichaelAnderle

https://www.instagram.com/lmbpn_publishing/

https://www.bookbub.com/authors/michael-anderle

Made in United States
Troutdale, OR
12/12/2024